SHINER

Also by Amy Jo Burns

Cinderland: A Memoir

SHINER

X X X X X

AMY JO BURNS

RIVERHEAD BOOKS
NEW YORK | 2020

RIVERHEAD BOOKS
An imprint of Penguin Random House LLC
penguinrandomhouse.com

Copyright © 2020 by Amy Jo Burns
Penguin supports copyright. Copyright fuels creativity, encourages
diverse voices, promotes free speech, and creates a vibrant culture. Thank you
for buying an authorized edition of this book and for complying with copyright
laws by not reproducing, scanning, or distributing any part of it in any form
without permission. You are supporting writers and allowing Penguin
to continue to publish books for every reader.

Riverhead and the R colophon are registered trademarks of Penguin Random House LLC.

Library of Congress Cataloging-in-Publication Data

Names: Burns, Amy Jo, 1981– author.
Title: Shiner / Amy Jo Burns.
Description: New York : Riverhead Books, 2020.
Identifiers: LCCN 2019001595 (print) | LCCN 2019002996 (ebook) |
ISBN 9780525533641 (hardcover) | ISBN 9780525533665 (ebook) |
Classification: LCC PS3602.U76486 S55 2020 (print) | LCC PS3602.U76486 (ebook) |
DDC 813/.6—dc23
LC record available at https://lccn.loc.gov/2019001595

Printed in the United States of America
3   5   7   9   10   8   6   4   2

BOOK DESIGN BY LUCIA BERNARD

This is a work of fiction. Names, characters, places, and incidents either
are the product of the author's imagination or are used fictitiously, and any
resemblance to actual persons, living or dead, businesses, companies,
events, or locales is entirely coincidental.

For my parents, who gave me everything they never had

The universe is made of stories,
not of atoms.

—MURIEL RUKEYSER, "THE SPEED OF DARKNESS"

Contents

TRUE STORY

Making good moonshine isn't that different from telling a good story, and no one tells a story like a woman. She knows that legends and liquor are best spun from the back of a pickup truck after nightfall, just as she knows to tell a story slowly, the way whiskey drips through a sieve. Moonshine earned its name from spending its life concealed in the dark, and no one understands that fate more than I do.

Beyond these hills my people are known for the kick in their liquor and the poverty in their hearts. Overdoses, opioids, unemployment. Folks prefer us this way—dumb-mouthed with yellow teeth and cigarettes, dumb-minded with carboys of whiskey and broken-backed Bibles. But that's not the real story. Here's what hides behind the beauty line along West Virginia's highways: a fear that God has forgotten us. We live in the wasteland that coal has built, where trains eat miles of track. Our men slip serpents through their fingers on Sunday mornings and pray for God to show Himself while our wives wash their husbands' underpants. Here's what hides behind my beauty line: My father wasn't just one of these men. He was the best.

Since word of his sins spilled down the mountain, folks have split from the highway, hoping to catch a glimpse of a fallen hero. They believe that this miners' outpost, shriveled since the coal barons claimed it forty years ago in the 1970s, still holds the key to my father's miracles. WELCOME TO TRAP, the new sign outside the city limits says. What it doesn't: COME HERE TO FALL IN LOVE. COME HERE TO FEAR FOR YOUR LIFE. Strangers ask what I can tell them about the snake handler and his wife. They want myths and legends. They aren't tempted by the truth.

"It's a true story," I begin, roosting in the back of an old truck. "I swear it."

Then I tell them that these woods can turn eerie or romantic, depending on the company you keep.

It's an autumn night, and the fire is lit. Moonshiners sneak in their final runs of whiskey while young women like me tell old tales. The sun sets early. Along the outskirts of Trap, you'll find me standing in a constellation of four-wheel-drive trucks in the woods behind the old Saw-Whet Motel. The mountains hover at my back.

The story of the snake handler's daughter began when I'd just turned fifteen. I knew little then of the outside world my father kept from me. *Ours is an oral civilization,* I used to hear him say, *and it's dying.* He blamed coal, he blamed heroin. He never blamed himself.

He thought he had the only tales worth telling, and he never understood what my mother had run from all her life because she'd been born a woman—

The truth turns sour if it idles too long in our mouths. Stories, like bottles of shine, are meant to be given away.

I.

SNAKE HANDLER'S DAUGHTER

BREAD AND IVY

It started with a burn, just like the stories of Moses my father used to tell. Moses, he said, was nothing more than a shepherd hiding in the hills until he scaled a mountain and found a flaming bush. Then he was never the same. My father had a tale just as magical, a story of his own origins as a man of God. He loved to tell it as much as my mother wished she hadn't ever believed it.

For as long as she was alive, she never told me her own story. I used to hear her whisper to her best friend, Ivy, that she wished she'd been known as anything other than Briar Bird's wife. I hated this about our life in the hills—mountain men steered their own stories, and women were their oars. I asked once if my mother had seen what lay beyond the bluffs, and she led me to the peak of our fields that overlooked the ra-vine behind my father's snake shed. In the distance I could see two razorback stone ridges rise from the trees. All my life these mountains had watched over me. My mother knelt beside me, put her arm around my waist.

"There are two ways to see a mountain," she said as she shielded her hazel eyes from the sun. "The view *from* the top and the view *of* the top."

Ivy came behind her, three of her boys at her back. "From the top of our mountain, the hills of West Virginia bow at your feet," she said. "But from the bottom, you bow at theirs."

My mother caught a wisp of her dark hair as it danced in the wind. Her braid fell past the waistband of her skirt, where she tucked the pearl-handled switchblade that Ivy had given her long before I was born. Ivy pressed a hand to my mother's shoulder. Their accord was unspoken, haunted by promises they'd sworn to keep.

x x x

Everything changed when Ivy caught fire. That morning, not long after my fifteenth birthday, I had spied my first summer fox from my bedroom window. The fox pranced in the morning sun as I waited for Ivy's scowl to appear on the horizon, her blond hair trembling against her shoulder.

Ivy was the only woman who knew how to reach my father's hideaway beyond the pines. We lived on the mountain's western ridge, just below the razorbacks and the highest knolls for miles, a stretch of meadow called Violet's Run. Ivy hiked the snarled hill to our cabin every day, because she and my mother could not survive without each other.

It had been that way since they were girls. Theirs was the same life lived twice over, though Ivy had four boys and a husband, Ricky—who was whiskey-sick and dope-drunk, my father liked to say. Ivy and my mother had grown up together, gone to school together, fallen in love together. This bond was the only thing my mother had that I envied. I wanted an Ivy of my own. My father envied it, too.

"Bread and Ivy," he said with his preacher's smile. "That's all your mama needs to survive."

My father buried himself in the things he loved—his snakes, his woods, his wife. Every time Ivy visited with her boys, he retreated to his snake shed by the cliff. He couldn't bear to share my mother with anyone—not with Ivy, not even with me.

X X X

Ivy came early enough the morning of the burning that she had to walk by faith to find the cabin through the fog. We lived at the top of a slick dirt path, and our gray roof faded into the dying trees above it. No outsider had ever found our road, hidden behind a swamp and a stand of balsams. My father liked it that way—being half there, half not. The cabin tilted on its beams, ready to be raptured. Even without a breeze, the house's bones moaned.

It was June, and I waited for Ivy at the window as I always did. When she and her three youngest boys crested the hill, I ran outside to greet them. Yesterday they hadn't come. My mother and I waited all morning before we ate the corn bread and molasses we'd prepared and folded up the picnic quilts we'd laid for the six of us to sit on in the tall grass. I wanted to know why they'd left us alone, but Ivy looked in no mood to be asked. Her skin glistened with sweat, and she made no sound as she headed toward the back of the house, where my mother stirred a drum of soap.

My mother liked to keep her hands busy. She made soap, made

dresses, made waves in the creek water. Those hands calmed only at dawn, when she'd stand in our field and stare at the horizon as if she expected Jesus himself to cross it. My mother was restless, and Ivy was the only person who could still her.

At the front of the cabin, Ivy's boys stared at me.

"Where did you go yesterday?" I asked. "We waited till noon."

Henry, Ivy's second-oldest, shrugged.

"Nowhere," he answered as he looked past the house toward the lean-to my father had built at the edge of the ravine. "Can we go in the snake shed today?"

"They ain't playthings," I said. "You know that."

"You've taken one up, haven't you?"

I shook my head. "Not once."

Ivy's third son, Job, turned toward me. "You scared?"

"I don't get scared."

"Liar." Henry touched the rattail at the back of his neck. "You're scared of gettin' bit."

"Henry." I straightened his collar as Pony, Ivy's youngest, toyed with the end of my braid. "If you're so brave, go knock on that snake shed and look my father in the eye."

Folks hated looking at my father. A bad storm during his boyhood had blighted one of his blue irises. He'd gone legally blind in his left eye, but folks still believed he could see. He didn't care what other people thought. He kept his serpents in boxes. They stank and needed to eat the living in order to survive. We had five of them.

"People at school down the mountain say you're strange," Job said. "That your daddy keeps you locked up with the snakes."

"I ain't so strange," I said, even though I was.

On the first Monday of the month, my mother and I went to town for groceries with the tithe money my father earned from preaching. Our shopping list never changed—flour and cornmeal for bread, beans, milk, and canned oranges and peaches. Chicken legs and sugar when we could afford it.

Every trip into Trap was a catapult through time. My father obeyed the rituals of snake-handling law, which meant he pretended we still lived in the 1940s instead of the age of the internet and all the things people did on their cell phones that I couldn't understand. Back then, George Went Hensley had convinced mountain folk that taking up serpents was the one true way to worship God. Daily, my father lifted his serpents to the sky and uttered a prayer in tongues that no one could interpret. His face looked euphoric and eerie as he babbled. He did it at Sunday gatherings with twenty people watching, and he did it alone in his shed, where I spied him from the scant window. He didn't need an audience with money to worship his God, but we did need that money to live. More than a half century had passed since snake-handling fever had swept through our hills, and now fewer than a hundred snake handlers remained across the country. No one believed in the power of taking up serpents anymore. Bitterly, my father claimed they believed in the power of prescription pills instead. The offering he collected on Sundays amounted to a fistful of quarters and a bare spread of dollar bills. It was never enough.

Once a month Ivy drove us to Trap in her old Pontiac. I sat in the back with Pony on my lap for forty minutes of twists and turns.

The stares began as soon as we spilled out of the car into the Shop 'n Save parking lot. Mothers, children, loggers, cashiers. They squinted at the pleats in the skirts my mother had hand-sewn for me from her old dresses. Their eyes tripped over the length of the French braid running down my back.

"It's sad, keeping her locked away on that mountain," I once heard a woman whisper to her grown son as he stifled a laugh and took a picture of me with his phone. I didn't even know that a cell phone could take a photograph until I flinched at the flash.

Now, in front of our cabin, we heard Ivy scream. Pony let the tail of my braid slip through his fingers, and I sprinted toward the sound. Until then the groans I knew were spirit-filled and Sunday-strong as men and women called out to God. But this was the sound of real affliction. It was pure, and there was no God in it.

When I rounded the house, I saw my mother's best friend kneeling at the fire. Smoke twirled above her as the flames caught her dress and hair. My mother's soap pot had spilled hot lye and grease down the front of her. Ivy swayed in the still air. Her braid transformed from blond to flaring orange to black.

"Briar!" my mother called out for my father.

I ran to the spigot. I filled a pail of water and doused Ivy's back. Her whole body hissed. Her scream limped to a sob as the flame surged. My mother tore her skirt and pressed it against Ivy's front. Her face contorted, but she made no sound. Ivy fell backward, and my mother looked up. Her brown hair fell from her bun as Ivy writhed beneath her.

My mother's head snapped toward me. "Wren!" she yelled. "The boys!"

It was too late to shield their eyes. Pony hung on my skirt, and I felt Job's hand on my back. His chest whistled as he tried to catch his breath.

Ivy started to convulse.

"Run as fast as you can to the snake shed," I told Henry. "Knock, but don't open the door. Tell my daddy to come quick."

He stood, petrified. He was just as afraid of the shed as anyone else was.

"Take your brothers inside the house and wait for me." I touched his arm. "Stay away from the window."

I took off for the shed, about fifty paces from the cabin. On its far side, a patch of rocks guarded the ground before it pitched off the cliff. The shed presided like a dark lighthouse over the rippled hills beneath it.

"Daddy!" I screamed.

When I reached the lean-to, I kicked the door with my foot.

"Daddy!"

I hefted the latch and flung open the door before stooping to get inside. My father was fast asleep against the far wall, his legs sticking straight out in front of him. A patch of golden hair had fallen in his eyes, and it sparkled in a shaft of sunlight.

I crouched and clapped my hands in front of his face. Startled, he came to. His bad eye was a disk of white in the dark.

"What is it?"

"It's Ivy," I said. "She's burning."

He stumbled to his feet, and I saw a slash of red across his cheek where it had been pressed to his shoulder. He bolted from the shed, and I meant to follow him. My eyes narrowed on the five snake boxes instead. I hadn't entered my father's sanctuary since I was five years old and wanted to touch a copperhead's smooth skin. That day was the first and last time my mother whipped me. Dust particles now floated in the light, and the air was rank with musk. I leaned toward the pine snake boxes, the most lavish items my father owned. Something stirred behind me. In another cage by the door, a gaggle of field mice twittered. They were waiting to be eaten.

I secured the latch after me and ran back toward the fire. Sweat trickled down my legs. My parents and Ivy sat in a lopsided circle, my father bent over Ivy's body and my mother beside her. I searched the ground for a root that could have caused her to trip, but I saw nothing. Just the thick stripes her feet had left in the dirt, as if she'd been dragging them behind her. Ivy was never clumsy or careless. I couldn't understand what had made her fall.

My father hovered his hands over Ivy's head and blew on her three times—*whoo whoo whoo*. With each breath he flicked his arms outward. Then he bent closer and whispered something in Ivy's ear before he repeated the ritual along the trail of her body.

By the time I reached them, my mother had slumped, her dress torn and lacquered with spoiled soap. My father gave Ivy a final whisper, and she exhaled and opened her eyes.

Beside her my mother held out her own hands as an offering.

"Ruby," my father said. "Your arms."

My mother's arms were pocked and inflamed, burned from fingertip to elbow. My father reached for them, and she drew them away.

"Let me," he said.

She shook her head and rose to her feet.

"I'm getting the salve," she said.

My father leaned back and sat cross-legged on the ground. "Don't bother," he said. "She don't need it."

The creases in my mother's forehead deepened.

"Wren," she said. "Take the boys home." She held her hands at her sides.

"We should stay," I said.

The boys would be better left alone by the railroad tracks than under the care of their father.

"Go," she said. "And be gone for a bit."

Her face said what her mouth did not. *Run. There's danger here.* My mother's best friend lay still at her feet. I backed into the house, called for the boys, and as we fled, the summer fox sprang from the reeds. The white of its tail flashed as it sprinted toward the ravine, and none of us looked back to see it disappear.

STRANGER

Before she'd burned, Ivy had always said that my father should have made solitude his bride instead of my mother. He loved to be alone. No one in Trap would ever hear me if I screamed, thanks to him. When my parents married sixteen years earlier, he grieved the whole mountain by choosing a secluded marshland as the home he'd offer his new wife—Ruby, who'd always been the dawn of everyone's morning.

"It wasn't right," Ivy had told me. "Closing Ruby off that way."

So Ivy convinced her husband, Ricky, to settle nearby. Back then he'd still been eager to please her. He'd wanted to live in town, closer to the seam of Randolph County coal mines and the motel where he and Ivy had met, but that was forty minutes down the mountain from my mother, and Ivy wouldn't yield.

"Ain't nobody up in those woods," Ricky had reasoned with his new wife.

"Ruby ain't nobody," Ivy said, and Ricky didn't dare cross her.

Their rusted trailer, two miles down the road, looked like it had fallen from the sky. Sun-scorched toys littered the lawn, and a ring of garbage moated the house. They outgrew the trailer in three years with their first pair of boys, but Ivy would not be moved. Her devotion to my mother was matched only by my father's.

He'd never been unkind to Ivy. He only loved my mother so recklessly that he wanted to claim all of her for himself. Other summers Ivy used to slip my mother's wedding band onto her finger when Ruby took the ring off to scour the soap pot in our backyard. My mother didn't want to lose it in the cattails, so she gave it to the one person she kept near. It never failed to roil my father's nerves. I watched his white eye twitch as Ivy slipped on the ring. She stood by until the pot gleamed— my mother close enough to be Ivy's shadow, her dark eyes and hair the opposite of Ivy's fair skin and pale topknot. Ivy hadn't made a show of the ring to rouse my father's jealousy. She'd done it because she and my mother survived their silent lives by taking care of each other, and Ivy cared for my mother better than she cared for herself.

These two women had taught me to fear what you'd find in a man once he became a father. *I went to bed with a man,* Ivy said to the empty hillside, *and woke up with a boy.* Ivy—mother of five, including her husband—didn't bear it as well as my mother did. Her green eyes shuddered like wind skimming water.

"I wish I could have been good at something besides making babies," she'd said more than once as my mother hemmed and rehemmed Ivy's skirts when they started to unravel.

My mother wasn't the kind of woman to make something out of nothing. Instead she made the most of what she had. This was what Ivy liked best about her. My mother, who could fix anything, never thought of Ivy as someone who needed fixing.

Folks said Ivy and Ricky's four sons held all the promise of the Confederate Army at Appomattox. I hardly saw her oldest boy, Bobby, who was fifteen like me. He wasted warm afternoons pinning squirrel tails to chestnut oaks in the woods. Bobby wanted to enjoy what freedom he could before he'd have to start fixing broke-down Chevrolets for cash like his father.

Now the narrow road before the boys and me curled around a cluster of white pines. We'd run away, but we couldn't escape. The images of Ivy on fire had seared the hearts of her three youngest sons. Only my mother's hands and arms had burned, and I'd never strike a match again without remembering the way she'd used her own body to dampen the flames.

The day had grown hot. The woods rustled with the sound of Job's wheezing. I turned and saw him bent at the knees. He had asthma, and the hike had worn him out.

"Come on." I turned off the path into the hillside that dipped down to the creek. "I want to show you something."

I heard the drawl of the water before I saw it. The sound hummed, native as a heartbeat. My mother and I liked to take this path in the early-summer mornings, and together we'd hold our breath, slip underwater, and disappear.

"Stretch your arms out like Jesus on the cross," she'd told me when she first taught me to float. She'd taught me everything—how to swim, how to read, how to hide.

I led the boys through the brush to the swimming hole where the creek pooled beneath a stone overhang. It was silent but for the skittering water. Thirty miles away miners were hanging their headlamps for their lunch break as the waitress at Teddy's Tavern in town polished window-side tables for the young men who came through to hike in the caves. They were lively and tan and muscled, never without a friend. I watched them on my monthly visits to town so I could replay the memory in my mind at night once the mountain went dark.

The creek shushed around me as the sun cast the rock with a pewter sheen.

"Ain't this where we do the baptisms?" Henry asked.

"It is."

Every August my father called his flock to the creek and asked who wanted to be baptized into a new life as a Christian. *Confess your sins*, he'd say. *Then go forth and be healed*. It had been years since anyone came forward. The old men had done it in their youth, and the children here grew scarce. It wasn't the kind of thing you did twice. Still, the faithful gathered, and my father prayed.

I knelt by a knobbed rock and dug through the dirt with my fingers. When I scratched metal, I lifted a tin of butterscotch candies and the silver flask I'd buried beneath it. I'd found the flask empty underneath a torn hemlock root after church let out one day last April. I filled it now with creek water and hung it with a cord around my neck.

"Shirts off," I said to the boys. "And turn your backs."

The three obeyed, and I hitched up my skirt and tied it in a knot at my waist. Pony climbed onto my back, and we entered the water. I rattled the candy in the air.

"Come and get it," I said.

Job and Henry crept as deep as they dared.

"Let me tell you a story," I said, taking Job into my arms. Water trickled over the rocks in the distance. "Violet's Run is the gorge near

the top of the mountain. That grassy stretch of meadow even farther
north than my cabin. You know it?"

Henry nodded as a crow crossed the sky.

"It's named for a young woman who lived a hundred years ago." I
took the flask and dumped water over Job's head. "She was a daredevil
like your mama." I paused.

Job closed his eyes, and I poured another round of water. His dark
hair went silky, and his body relaxed against mine.

"Violet wanted to jump off the gorge into the falls below. Everyone
swore it was no feat for a woman. Many men had attempted that same
jump, and none of them survived. But Violet knew that the secret was
being light on her feet."

Job opened an eye. "Did she die?"

"Lie back," I said, coaxing his body into a straight line. "Men love
a woman in trouble. The moment Violet jumped, a string of five lovesick young men jumped after her, each convinced he'd be the one to
save her life."

Henry wiped away a tear.

"Folks despaired, thinking they'd lost six young people to the falls.
They climbed down the ravine to fish out the corpses, and you know
what they found?" I took Job's arms and straightened them out at his
sides, leaving my hand beneath his shoulder blades.

"They found Violet carrying them out one by one, cradling each of
them like a baby boy."

"She must have been strong," Pony said.

"Like our mama," Job whispered.

"Like your mama." I nodded. "And look, Job. You're about as close
to floating as I ever saw."

As soon as I said it, a rustle in the white pines pricked my ear. My mother had taught me how to listen for a threat. The grass grew tall around our house, and we kept vigil for snakes. Ten years earlier my father had lost his prized rattler in our fields after he thrust it into the air and it squirmed out of his grasp. A snake could live fifteen to twenty years, and my mother and I readied for the day that rattlesnake would return.

I scanned the trees and found nothing. Still, the feeling hooked me. We were being watched. I'd never felt watched this deep into the woods before. Ivy was the only visitor we ever got. I undid the knot at my waist, and my skirt bloomed in the water.

"Let's go, boys," I said, giving the forest a futile glance. "Time to get you home."

x x x

Ivy's boys didn't want to return to their trailer for the same reason I didn't want to take them. Home was not home without Ivy there to make it so.

"If I have any more boys," she liked to say from her trailer's cockeyed screen door when my mother and I visited, "I'll open a reform school."

I knew that my mother wouldn't ask Ivy where she'd gone yesterday. She didn't like calling attention to the differences between them. Ivy's whole life came with proof of her existence. She had birth certificates for her babies and a deed for her house and a driver's license—the kinds of things my mother abandoned when she married my father. With a car and a docile husband, Ivy could leave the mountain when she wanted. My mother couldn't.

I arrived at her trailer with each of the boys nursing a butterscotch. Ricky's Impala sat idle in the gravel, coated in dust. The lawn was a graveyard of boyhood. A rusted trike lay on its side next to a beach ball impaled with an arrow, and a nest of squirt guns leaked water onto the dirt. Ivy called it poverty, but I called it riches. My cabin remained bare enough so I could spot the four gray corners of any room I stood in. Cracks traveled every wall. Mason jars and Bibles were our only decorations. I owned no bracelets, no diary, no pictures, no letters, no mirror on my bedroom wall. All I had were books, and most of those I hid beneath my bed so my father wouldn't see.

Ricky ought to have been alone in the trailer, since he liked to feel lonely when he drank, but when we cut across the road's sharp curve, a silver Tacoma was pulling out of their gravel drive.

The man at the wheel tucked a lock of black hair behind his ear. His face was long and solemn, with a sharp jaw. He pressed the brakes and gave us a good gawk, the kind my father's congregation of sheep gave a serpent as they wondered if they had the courage to touch it. His dark eyes settled on me, and I swore somehow he knew about Ivy. He looked at me a little too long, like he understood I'd never be out walking the mountain road without my mother unless something terrible had happened.

In the bed of the truck, a kid with no shirt and a blond cowlick crouched to embrace the carboys of whiskey at his feet. The loose clasp of his overalls smacked against the jars as he bent, and the gray mutt beside him yelped into the still air.

I'd seen the boy before, in Trap's pocket-size library during our grocery trips. While my mother paid the bill, I'd slip into the library to check out as many books as I could carry with the card I kept secret from my father. It was the only item I had with my own name on it. The boy—no more than thirteen—often sat at a desktop computer with his hand quivering over the mouse. His fingers flew across the keys. I watched him, hoping to learn. Younger than me, he'd mastered a machine I could barely use for a simple internet search. He'd never looked at me until now. His chin hung down as he watched us.

"Close your mouth," I said once we reached the gravel.

The kid snapped his mouth shut, and the man in the front seat let out a gutted laugh before pressing the gas. The truck lurched, and the jugs in the back clattered as he spun out.

"Who was that, Henry?" I asked.

Henry shrugged.

When I stepped inside the house, the stench of hot licorice whipped me in the face, and I opened the kitchen window.

"What's that smell?" I asked.

"Pipes are rusted through, and Daddy ain't fixed them yet." Henry fanned his face with his hand.

"You're not drinking out of the faucet, are you?" I asked.

He shook his head. "Been getting our water from a spigot in town." He pointed to a slew of jugs covering the linoleum.

"It would help if you let some air in." I looked past him and squinted into the gloom.

On the coffee table, Ricky had parsed out two stacks of quarters and dimes for his next pack of Marlboros. The coins' shadows towered over the empty bottles of pills scattered across the glass top.

"What's your daddy got against the sun?" I asked.

"It ain't the sun," Job answered. "He don't want to see the work he ain't finished in the backyard."

I watched Ricky from the tile by the doorway. A busted lawn mower sat in the center of the carpet with Ricky's jeans hanging from the handle. He lounged, sweating through his underwear, in the next room in front of the dim TV.

He and I rarely spoke when I came by, but we both had a crush on his cable television. On any other day, I'd have been hungry for the signs of life it promised. The news program flashed a series of lead stories in the outside world: the spiking unemployment rate after another mine shut-down, a dead body found in a far-off creek, a chemical spill at the coal treatment plant nearby. Their TV had taught me that you could buy anything in the world with a flat piece of plastic called a credit card, and that there were people charging money for the kind of healing my father claimed to do for free.

A toothpaste commercial broke the spell of dispatches from beyond our mountain, and I looked back at Ricky.

"Ricky," I called. "There's been an accident."

Silence.

"Ricky," I said again, and he tilted his head.

He didn't answer, so I tried a third time.

"Who was that man?" I asked.

His face released a wave of sweat. "A compatriot," he said. Ricky flicked his eyes at the bottles. He meant that man was a moonshiner—or a shiner, as my father would say.

At the base of his recliner sat a cluster of glass growlers like the ones in the back of the shiner's Tacoma. They'd each been painted milkman white across the middle. The television's glare cast a diamond shimmer onto the liquor. I wanted a jar for myself.

I'd seen these bottles before. My mother had lined the tops of her kitchen cabinets with them. But hers stood empty because my father thought whiskey was a sin.

"You want the remote?"

Ricky pitied me, and on any other day I would have let him. He knew I loved the swirls of chocolate frosting on the cooking channel and the tick of the spinning circle on *Wheel of Fortune*, the swell of an orchestra when a hero in one of Ricky's westerns kissed a girl. We didn't have a TV because my father feared it would infect us with the world's wisdom. *The television gives you thoughts instead of you having your own,* he'd told me.

I went to the trailer's closest window and slid back the curtain.

"Ivy's hurt," I said to Ricky. In the backyard a broke-down school bus faced off against a refrigerator. The cap of an old Ford sat upturned in the dirt, and Ricky's tools moldered inside it. "She got burned at our fire pit."

The boys huddled together, hoping their father would spring to life.

Ricky sat up, as if he'd finally heard me. "She all right?"

"I ain't sure." We stared at each other. This was the first time I'd had to deliver bad news, another act Ivy swore a woman did best. People here were primed for it. A mine collapse, an overdose, another merciless snowfall blocking our way off the mountain for a month.

"Ivy seemed all right when I left," I lied. Ricky didn't seem sober enough for the truth. "My mama is taking care of her."

He sat there, stiff and bent at the waist. He'd once been handsome, Ivy liked to recall. Now he was bloated and crow-eyed. He lit a cigarette.

"First the baby," he said as smoke unfurled from his nose. "And now this. Living on this mountain ain't nothing but cursed us."

Ricky had left his family behind near Elkins when he'd followed Ivy into the mousetrap she and my mother were born into. He'd wanted to leave ever since.

He shut off the television. "Did you know we had a dead baby? Right after Bobby?" His voice cracked. "I never even got to see him."

Pony crawled into his lap, and Ricky clutched him around his middle.

I sat in the wicker chair across from him. "I'm real sorry, Ricky," I said. "Let me fix you something to eat."

"Ain't nothing to fix," he said.

His eyes flitted to the bare window before he turned the television on again, and I searched through a kitchen drawer until I found a jar of peanut butter under a swarm of Bobby's absence-ridden report cards and a reading list for next fall's courses at the county high school. I slipped the piece of paper beneath the belt of my skirt. During the school year, Bobby never paid me or his homework any mind. Whenever I had the chance to visit Ivy, I took his books and did the work so I could learn it myself. My father had a strict curriculum of Bible learning I followed, but my mother submitted a wider study plan based on Bobby's lessons to the county so I could get real credit. My father didn't know.

As I handed each boy a plastic spoon for the peanut butter, I heard the strike of a match. The end of Ricky's second Marlboro glowed, and Job coughed.

"You can't smoke in the house," I said. "Job is sick."

He closed his eyes for the next pull. If Ivy had been there, she'd have ordered me to fight.

Ricky won't fend for our boys, she'd have said. *So you have to.*

I crept behind Ricky and lifted the cigarettes from the edge of the armchair. Then I took Henry aside by the door and handed him the pack.

"Hide these outside," I said. "Near the engine of the school bus. Tell him if he wants to smoke, he has to lift the hood."

Henry nodded, but his mind was elsewhere. "Do you remember the dead baby?" he asked. "The one Daddy always talks about?"

I shook my head. "I was too young. Why?"

Henry slipped the cigarettes into his back pocket. "If that baby lived, do you think I would have been born?"

"Shhh," I said. "Now go."

Once the boys left the trailer, I lifted a jug from behind Ricky's chair while he dozed. I stole into the kitchen to dump it down the drain, but I filled the flask at my neck instead. *Ivy might need it*, I reasoned. *For the pain.* But I had lied to myself. I wanted it because my mother had these empty carboys in her kitchen, and that meant someone had drunk them, once upon a time.

X X X

By the time I reached the creek path, the sun had grown fat in the sky. When I met the riverbed, I buried the flask in its hiding spot and forgot about the feeling of being watched. The water called out to me. At the creek's edge, I thought of Ivy, burning. My mother had told me to stay away, and I wanted to. All my life my chances for escape were so few.

I shed my dress and fell into the water. As I floated on my back, I prayed for Ivy. I never felt closer to God than when the shock of a cold stream hit me, and it never happened on a Sunday. Diving deep, I prayed that every shiver would take the heat from Ivy's body. I prayed for my own way of getting burned. When I resurfaced and opened my eyes, I saw someone sitting on the rock above me at the edge of the overhang.

I could only see the diamond of his back, and he was holding the flask I'd buried. He looked a year or two older than me, and he hummed a tune I didn't know. The rasp of his voice rippled in the well of my chest.

The boy stretched, and his muscles sang. His shoulders spread wide like a crucifix, the white of his shirt like a soul washed clean. He knocked back the bottle and sighed as the whiskey clawed his throat.

"Hey," I called, and he turned to me.

His skin was black, his eyes like copper. I'd never seen a stranger look at me without pity before. I waited for him to laugh at me the way folks in Trap did, but he didn't. I'd stripped myself of my mountain-girl costume, my homespun dress left on the bank and my thick braid undone. I was naked with creek water rushing over me, and I felt afraid.

I pointed to the bottle. "That—" My voice buckled. "That ain't yours."

"It isn't yours either, is it?" His head cocked toward mine, and my breath stopped. I wanted to answer; I wanted to hide.

"Who are you?" I asked.

Music lifted from the cell phone that flashed next to his sneakers. Clean and white, it buzzed. I wanted to hold it to my ear, just to see what it felt like. We didn't even have a landline at our cabin.

Ricky was the only person I knew with a cell phone, even though it rarely worked. The signals from Trap's cell towers weakened up the mountain like dying men. This boy, in a white shirt and faded jeans, must have come from a city—maybe Morgantown or Pittsburgh. Places farther off to me than heaven itself.

"That thing." I pointed to his phone. "Does it take pictures?"

He nodded.

"Don't take one of me."

"Okay." He hesitated. "Are you scared of getting your picture taken?"

"No," I lied. "I just ain't a joke."

He paused again. "I understand."

I treaded water as he watched the clouds pass.

"Where did you come from?" I asked.

"Let's trade," he said. "A drink for a question." He turned his back and stared into the forest. "I'll wait for you to put on your dress."

I swam to the bank, threw on my dress, and met him at the overhang. He handed me the bottle, and I brought it to my lips. It tasted warm and fiery.

"My name is Caleb," he answered. "I'm staying at Aunt Bette's in Trap."

"The home," I said.

Aunt Bette only attended my father's church when one of her foster kids could drive her fifteen-passenger van up the mountain. They'd have to wait for the train to cross the tracks as long as snow hadn't blocked them, then scale the corkscrew road up the hill for the better part of an hour, longer in the rain. Then they'd have to hike the remaining half mile, leaving the van by the downed trees. Everyone called her Aunt Bette, just like everyone called her house "the home." She'd been taking in kids since her husband died in a coal-mining accident fifteen years back. My father forbade me to speak to Aunt Bette's wards, even when I sat next to them in church. His word was law: No outsider would ever talk to his wife or his daughter.

"So that's what you call it?" Caleb drank. "The home?"

"It is." It shamed me to say it. Even I knew that no one felt at home there. "What are you doing up here?"

He passed the flask. "I wanted to disappear."

"No one will find you here."

His fingers skimmed mine as he took back the bottle. He swallowed the shine, and the sky spun above me. My body swayed.

"I'm Wren," I said. "I live up the hill."

"I liked that story you told those boys today." Caleb set the flask next to the sketchbook and charcoal beside him.

"You were watching me."

"I was." He paused. "I wasn't sure if it was safe to show myself."

"Why?" I asked.

"Why do you think?" he said.

My father preached that all were welcome inside his church, but his church was white. It was easy to think the snakes scared off anyone not born in these hills. It was even easier to think that was how God wanted it.

"You don't have to be scared of me," I said. "I won't hurt you."

"Your people might."

"Why did you change your mind?" I asked.

"You won't tell anyone you saw me," he answered. "Any girl hiding whiskey has enough secrets of her own."

Secrets. I'd never had one of my own before Ivy caught fire. Now I had Caleb and the whiskey, both. A catbird called out as it dove into the trees.

"What are you drawing?" I pointed to his book, and he handed it to me.

Each page of Caleb's sketchbook featured a different portrait. On the first page, he'd drawn a mirror image of two boys.

"My brothers," he said.

They sat back-to-back on top of a mountain, each casting out a fishing pole toward the stars. I touched the delicate branches of their arms. The paper stubbled against my fingers.

"I've never seen anything like this," I said. "How did you make the gray background with such bright stars?"

"Like this."

He pulled out a piece of soft charcoal from his pocket along with a white cloth. After turning to a fresh page, he drew three lines across it. Then he passed his cloth over the lines until they blended into each other, and he used a pointed white eraser to etch the stars in the midnight sky.

"It's beautiful," I said.

The next picture he'd drawn was a replica of the hanging wooden footbridge that was suspended between the two razorback stone ridges, the same ones I saw every morning as I looked out across the ravine toward West Virginia's highest peak. We lived in the foothills of the razorbacks, tucked between them and the only road that led to town. In the fog the ridges looked like two giant daggers. Caleb captured their shattered profiles in a charcoal maze of angles and curves. On the bottom of the page, he'd drawn a hand reaching out from the bridge into the dead drop.

"You went to the razorbacks?" I asked.

Anyone not born in our hills needed a guide to find their way to the base of those mountains. The razorbacks were as beautiful as they were fatal. Folks had died trying to cross the cavern.

Caleb shook his head. "A picture I found at Aunt Bette's."

I pointed to the final portrait in his book.

"What about this one?" I asked.

It was a rough sketch of a young woman holding a little boy in a pool of water. The corner of her shoulder cut like a cliff's edge, her face sheathed by her long hair as it spilled into waves made from teardrops.

"It's you," he said.

I pictured the crest of his finger softening the charcoal edges of the young woman's curves. My curves. My breath caught, and I clutched the edges of his book.

"You said you wouldn't take a picture of me," I said.

"I didn't."

"You can't keep this."

I tore the page from the book and rose to my feet.

"The flask," I said. "I need it."

Caleb surrendered it, and I ran up the hill without looking back. I thought of Ivy and my mother on the ground next to the fire, so close there wasn't a breath between them. I remembered Ivy's skin. The flames. My mother's arms. My father's wayward eye settling on the nook in Ivy's collarbone as his hands traveled her wounds. Soon he'd realize how long I'd been gone.

x x x

I stalked the cattails when I returned home, right in the spot where I'd seen the fox from my bedroom earlier that morning. I'd been a different girl then, hidden and untouched. Now I'd collided with the world my father feared—the nip of cold whiskey, a stranger to share it with. All because Ivy had been so badly burned.

I crept to the window and looked through it. Ivy sat upright in my bed. She looked like the fire had never touched her, but here was the curse: She also looked like nothing else had, either. Her skin beamed. Ivy's hair had been wiped clean from her head.

She slept, and her head sank to the side. Along the back of her skull ran a thin seam of red, like a rash. It started at the crown and slipped down her spine.

I backed away. Ivy was better, Ivy was new. I'd never seen my father work this kind of magic before. I'd only heard stories from mountain folks about the powers God had given him, but today I witnessed them for myself. The miracle saddled me with dread. My father had healed Ivy without so much as touching her. He'd brought himself into the holy temple of my mother's friendship with Ivy, and I knew it couldn't withstand the three of them. After hiding the flask in the reeds, I halted at the cabin's corner when I heard my parents trading whispers on the back steps. They cast their glances into the shadows.

My mother still hadn't changed her dress, and it hung in tatters at her knees. She dropped her chin into her hands, then grimaced. Her skin was swollen and stippled red from the flames, even though Ivy's was pristine. The bandages she wore reached up to her elbows as she looked out over our land. The only sign of life beyond us was a thin cord of smoke from a mine slicing through the horizon. The fire still smoldered at their feet as the soap hardened in a mound on the grass.

Slowly, she leaned back and stretched out her legs. My father sat beside her, skating a pointer finger along his jaw.

"How'd you do it, Briar?" she asked. Her voice was weary. "I've seen you perform plenty of signs and wonders, but nothing like that."

He leaned back next to her, and my mother was too tired to pull herself away. I couldn't remember the last time I'd seen them sit side by side. The step bowed beneath their weight.

"It was done to me once, a long time ago," he said.

"After the storm?"

He gave a gentle nod.

"I thought you didn't remember it."

His eyes dug into hers, wanting to give love, wanting to take it away. "I don't."

And there my father went, spiraling into his own mysteries just as he'd done ever since the day lightning had come hunting for him.

SIGNS AND WONDERS

The mountain folks living along our lonesome road had always called my father by his real name, but anyone beyond Trap's borders who'd heard the stories of the young man and his lovesick snakes knew him as White Eye. I knew because my father traveled to Jolo a few times a year for his snake handlers' circle, which was full of men twice his age who knew how to keep his secrets. As soon as he left for the day, we'd sneak into town. Ivy and my mother would watch old movies at the dollar theater while I went to the library. I had two hours to myself— a gift in those days before Ivy caught fire—and I'd determined to spend them teaching myself to use a computer. My mother couldn't teach me, and I wanted to learn. I opened up an internet browser, and the cursor blinked like the glassy pupil of a copperhead.

Every time I typed the same words with my index fingers:

P-R-E-A-C-H-E-R

W-H-I-T-E E-Y-E

S-N-A-K-E-S

I scanned the results slowly, unsure at first how to coax the mouse into clicking on each link. Local papers wrote of a lightning-struck man with a white eye, a mountaineer who served strychnine for breakfast and slept with his snakes. Folklore sites listed his whereabouts for the last fifteen years as anywhere from the Appalachian Trail to the Smoky Mountains, and none of the information was true. My father had never traveled farther than the four-hour trip to Jolo in his entire life. I found no pictures, no mention of a wife or child, even though rumors swirled around Trap that he kept us chained with the snakes. My father had no first name or last, only a title. *White Eye.* Even his own mother, legend insisted, had called him that before she died.

There's a self-generating power born from a fitting name, the same way a clenched fist shoots blood through a vein. My father had been baptized as Briar W. Bird, but his mother started calling him White Eye the day he got hit by lightning.

The night of the storm, my father was asleep on the lofted floor above the kitchen in the cabin he shared with his mother. His father: a committed logger and an absent husband. They hadn't seen him in over a year. A lightning bolt busted through the window, shattering the glass pane and scorching a cedar plank in the floor. A beam from the loft's ceiling had fallen and knocked him unconscious. My father hadn't yet seen his eighteenth birthday.

By the time he opened his eyes, a gang of flies had infiltrated the open window and all the glass had been swept. My grandmother, who died in her sleep less than a year later, never bothered to send for the doctor. In our hills folks drank poison in the name of God and handled snakes when the Holy Spirit led. For us sickness never rested in the body. It rested in the spirit. If illness came for one of the faithful, we prayed and waited for God to move. Evidence of God's favor relied on how many times death was cheated when you called it by name.

The first miracle in my father's life: He was fine. His body betrayed no sign of the electricity that had shot through him—until he opened his eyes. One eye held its blue color, and the other strayed toward silver-white. Ever since I'd known him, my father's eyes straddled his two lifetimes, the moments before lightning struck and every moment that came after.

Though he'd told me this story countless times, the memory itself never belonged to my father. He couldn't recall any of it. But his mother told anyone who would listen, and the tale grew a life of its own. Soon everyone from peak to crag owned the story of the day White Eye wrangled with the lightning bolt and won. Almost two decades later, long after my grandmother's death, the shared memory had collected itself into an undisputed truth.

"That father of yours," folks would say to me on Sundays, "is gonna save this mountain."

I'd learned a long time ago to smile and wait.

"I still remember the day he got struck." The stories always started this way. "It was like the lightning was hunting him. Your gran went running at the sound of prickling glass. Sliced her feet up good."

My father's version didn't feature a lightning bolt, but I never tired of hearing it. While he slept through the storm, an angel came to him in a dream and touched a hot coal to his lips. He couldn't see her face. He only felt the burn. He also felt himself opening, like he was breathing for the first time. Then a frost set in that sent a shiver through his body. Sometime after that he opened his eyes. That was the first story he ever told me.

Before I was old enough to shake a tambourine at a Sunday service, my father entrusted these secrets to me for a simple reason. I was easily impressed, and my mother no longer was.

"It takes no bravery to work a miracle," she'd say, digging potatoes from her garden's brittle earth. "What takes bravery is when there's no miracle at all."

My father couldn't fathom a life without miracles, not when he saw evidence of them every day in the mirror. He told me God wanted him to see the world in two separate realms. The dark eye, as he called it, saw the fallen earth as it was, and the blighted eye saw the spirit world.

I knew enough not to ask about the spirit world. It was a treasure I should have been able to follow his map toward, being his daughter. It was the same map my mother once followed, and she had turned back. My father sank so deep into himself when he spoke of holy things that there was no way for either of us to follow. The more I tried to understand him and his religion, the further he drifted away from me.

X X X

The day Briar Bird got struck turned out to be the first day of the rest of his life. He'd been wooing serpents for a long time before then, but that was the day he transformed from just another boy from the hills into a man. To be called a man at his age was to be granted an imaginary scepter and sword. It fostered mettle in his fresh heart, but not kindness. That was the day he became a snake handler.

Snake handler. My father's temper would flare if he heard me call him that. He loathed the term. *Taking up serpents*, he always said. Taking up serpents was biblical. Snake handling was a sideshow. Most churches who practice the art of taking up serpents don't allow anyone under the age of eighteen to partake. My father did it more than twenty years ago when he was twelve. This was another story he liked to tell.

During a Sunday service at the abandoned gas station, the local kids played in the gravel lot next to the open maws that Texaco had left in the earth. Before that day the ramshackle building had closed when a crowd of hardwoods toppled after a blizzard and blocked the main road to the station. The faithful started to squat there every Sunday morning until it felt like home. They'd been looking for a place to gather, and God had provided one. The only way to reach it was to double back down a mule path and circle the rear of the building by following the creek line. The seclusion lent to the excitement. Whenever an outsider in Trap asked for directions to the snake-handling church, they got the same response: *You can't get there from here.* My father had groomed a congregation of secret keepers, and the only directions they offered were how to get off the mountain.

My father claimed to remember that day he first took up a serpent without error: autumn, unseasonably sunny, the aging leaves bloodred against a periwinkle sky. A group of boys huddled around the old preacher's truck, where some snake boxes had been left. They dared one another to open the lids that kept them safe from copperheads, cottonmouths, and rattlesnakes. Boys five years older than my father refused.

"Briar?" one of them finally said. "You game?"

He was game, all right. My father hopped into the back of the truck and lifted the lid from one of the boxes. Inside it lay a serpent, spun up like a whip. It had the colors of a burned field. The serpent raised its head and reached out for him, the way my father told the story. Not to strike, but to be embraced. The crowd of boys peered over the lip of the truck, not a blink among them.

My father took the snake in both hands, one close to its head and the other near the tail. The snake wavered. The boys shrieked. Young Briar fell under the serpent's spell by looking into its elliptical eyes.

The screams had drawn a crowd. Behind him a man spoke in a steady voice.

"Briar, do you know what that is?"

"It's a snake, sir."

"It's a canebrake."

"The unicorn of the South," my father whispered as the snake held him in its thrall.

The man nodded. "That's it. As rare as it is venomous. If your daddy was here, he'd tell you one nip from that serpent will send you to the grave. Do you understand?"

"Yes, sir."

"You scared?"

"No, sir."

"You ought to be. Put it back in the box, son."

My father obeyed, but the canebrake had charmed him. He had an itch only a venomous snake could scratch, and no church in our hills would let him. If he wanted to take up serpents, he'd have to capture them first. He made his own catcher from an old broom handle and a wire hanger. At twelve years old, he forged up the mountain, armed only with his tool and a pillowcase. There wasn't a companion in sight who dared go with him.

My father played the lone hero in all his stories. He had no faithful friend, a trait that followed him into adulthood, as far as I could tell. As he grew from a young boy into a man, he first caught a water snake, then a queen snake, and finally a copperhead and a yellow rattler. He kept them boxed in the fireplace until he married my mother, who demanded he keep them in the shed.

Surviving a lightning strike gave Briar Bird the kind of power folks longed to follow. My father was leading the church that had first denied him his serpents by the time he was twenty. I was just shy of a year old. In a community that feared its way of life was dying, word of the young snake handler should have traveled fast. Briar was proof of God's favor on our hills. People should have come from all over to see my father and his snakes, but White Eye didn't want them to.

Trap was an exit off an exit from the highway, a town caught in the mountains between Interstates 79 and 81. It was a hard place to get to and an even harder one to leave. We were a stone's throw from Judy Gap and the thrilling heights of the gorges and straight-backed stone spires West Virginia is known for. Trap wasn't even a town, even though we called it one. "Unincorporated" is how outsiders referred to us, as if we'd been disassembled from the inside out. There just weren't enough people in Trap with the mining industry dwindling, the coal treatment plant laying off workers, and folks taking any escape route they had. It puzzled my mother most of all, who used to believe that our mountain didn't need anyone as long as we had Briar Bird.

My father swore he first noticed her with his white eye, even though I knew he couldn't see much out of it. *Ruby was the prettiest girl on the mountain, sparkling like the stars,* he used to tell me. They grew up down the creek from each other, but it took a lightning strike to spark the attraction between them. My parents fell in love when they were seventeen, and for my father it was simple. He saw her, he wanted her.

But knowing my mother's heart was more like searching for the sun on an overcast day.

"Was there ever anyone else?" I'd asked my mother, as hungry for her stories as I was for my father's. "Besides Daddy?"

Her answer was flat. "No."

All my father had to do was set a trap and wait. It took time for my mother to fall in love with the man behind the snakes. The man who whistled in his mother's garden. The man who cried when he laughed. The man who could bag a snake and fry an egg but couldn't hang a porch swing to save his life. The man who would never stop loving my mother. His love for her was bare-hearted and deep, and he didn't care who saw it. But he did care that it made him weak.

My father thought people ought to be as easy to maneuver as his serpents. For all the gifts he had, he could never rule my mother's heart. It made him love her in a selfish way. This was the truest lesson my father taught me: Love that hopes to conquer only twists itself into hate.

x x x

As a child I came to know every mountain-snake myth by heart, because my parents told them to me once they could no longer find a way to speak to each other. My favorite was the story about the black serpent who wove itself among the branches of an elm shade tree and sang out an aria. When my father told the tale, the snake had the bellow of an angry god. When my mother told it, the snake was a lonely mountain siren. My father's stories strutted with prowess, and my mother's wept with sorrow.

I listened to these stories long after I outgrew them, because they kept me from having to share any of my own. There were things I couldn't speak of, too.

I trusted my father's God, but not his religion.

I believed in the kind of evolution I read about in Bobby's textbooks.

I thought about sex.

"Sex is best when it's wrong," Ivy had once whispered in my ear on one of our swims at the creek.

My mother swatted her hand as Ivy laughed, though I'd never seen her look so sad. She and my father never had any more children, and I wondered if it was because my mother flinched every time he touched her.

"Sex ain't so great," my mother whispered, and it was the most heartless thing she'd ever said to me. "You'll see."

Those words were the only ones I'd heard about sex, because my mother was the only teacher I'd ever had. There was a small school for the kids in our hills if you took the creek road all the way down to the south end of Trap, but I'd never set foot inside it. My school days were spent at the kitchen table, reading books assigned by my mother and doing my own research on the growing patterns of wild ginger in the fields surrounding the cabin. In the mornings I recited lengthy passages from the Old Testament for my father. In the afternoons I drew reproductions of the photosynthetic process on a handheld chalkboard. I grasped what mathematics I could from a book and an old calculator. My mother taught me geometry with the plastic protractor she'd once used in Trap's high school classrooms twenty years before. Every spring my mother took my father on a daylong hike to lay flowers on his mother's grave deep in Logger's Nook on the other side of the mountain while Ivy drove me to the county seat for testing. Somehow I always managed to pass, thanks to Bobby's abandoned schoolwork.

His textbooks called it Darwinism, but I taught myself about evolution as I witnessed its opposite in my parents' marriage. I charted its demise in my school notebook alongside the calls of barred owls in winter and the bashful violets in spring. *Viola rotundifolia. Viola canadensis.*

Viola pedata. Sometimes love doesn't die. It reverses itself like a watch ticking backward.

There's no one lonelier than the wife of a preacher. My mother loved her husband but didn't trust him. She used to tell me she fell in love with him on the day he got struck by lightning.

"Briar had experienced something real," my mother said, soft enough to make it feel like we were finally sharing secrets. "Something that exists on the other side of this life. Something that came from our land. That's what Briar brought here. And I wanted to be part of it."

I understood. As a girl, I'd adored my mystical father. Even as my mother's reverence for him waned, I couldn't help but fall in love with him when he held a serpent. He looked regal and bold. Venomous snakes turned to silk in his hands, and he treated them the way I wanted him to treat me—with tenderness and wonder. Folks said he was born to take up serpents, and I'd never doubted it. I once asked my mother if she thought my father would handle snakes in heaven.

She laughed. "If he does, I won't be watching."

She'd meant it as a joke, but I couldn't stop thinking about her words: *I won't be watching.* I knew that her fiercest longing had just slipped out of her mouth.

I caught glimpses of her lost freedom on those long afternoons my father spent in Jolo every year until I turned fifteen, when my mother and Ivy laughed in the back of the movie theater like they were girls again. That's when I felt my loneliest, and the lurch in my stomach drove me to the library's computers to find out what we were to the rest of the world.

I got my answer a week before Ivy caught fire. At the back exit of the library, I'd dropped my pile of books when I pushed through the door. Bobby's spring reading list included *East of Eden* and Shakespeare's tragedies, and I'd tucked *Tiger Eyes* in between the stack so my mother wouldn't see it. The books fell from my hands when I stumbled into a clump of kids who were smoking a shared Virginia Slim after school had let out. I held my breath and looked at the cement. I waited to hear their laughter. When I bent to collect the books, a boy kicked *Tiger Eyes* away from me and left me on my hands and knees.

"Don't let Mommy see the smut you're reading," he said.

The others snickered, and a red heat crawled up my neck. I bit the inside of my cheek and pressed my palms to the ground until a girl with dirty-blond hair shushed the laughter.

The cigarette dangled from her lips as she knelt and handed me the book. Her fingernails shimmered bright pink, and they matched the muddy, glittered tips of her cowboy boots. I stood and smoothed my skirt before looking at the boy.

"Don't you think I want to live, also?" I asked, too quietly.

He looked away, and I knew that no one had heard me, the same way I felt when I stood at the ravine behind my father's snake shed and screamed into the abyss. The girl stamped out the cigarette with her boot as I walked away.

SPEAKING IN TONGUES

The Sunday service following Ivy's miracle began as nothing special. A faithful band of two dozen had gathered from the farthest pockets of the mountain in the gutted gas station. The air filled with heads nodding like breeze-blown rocking chairs as Hawley Boggess, a farmer with a beard as long as his suspenders, lazily beat a snare drum. My mother sat in the corner and shook her tambourine. Light struggled to break in through the whitewashed windows, but I could still see something new. Aunt Bette brought her clan to church, and Caleb had driven them.

I sat across a makeshift aisle from him with Ivy's boys, who were as antsy as ever. I felt Caleb watching me as I slipped butterscotch into the boys' palms. During the sermon Caleb's eyes slid toward me. An animal warmth curled its way from my stomach into my chest.

This was a dangerous game. My father didn't fool around with outsiders. He waited until the gas station emptied each Sunday before locking it and scaling the back ridges through the holler with his snakes in tow. It was five miles home to our cabin, and Ivy always gave my mother and me a ride. It took my father most of the afternoon to dodge through the overgrown paths and make sure he wasn't followed. He loved his solitude, and he'd forfeit anything to protect it. If my father took notice of Caleb's stares, he'd tell Aunt Bette not to return, and I'd never see him again.

I wasn't the only one watching Caleb. Old Lady Frye sat in front of me and squinted at him while stroking her gray braid. She was no friend to strangers.

Beside him sat the girl with the dirty-blond hair and glittered nails who had handed me my book outside the library. When she noticed Frye's leer, she touched Caleb's shoulder. Together they stared Frye down, but she would not relent.

Ivy's boys nodded off beside me. At the pulpit my father lifted his favorite serpent—a yellow timber rattlesnake—toward heaven. His heart got overcome, and his breath whittled to a gasp. Before us he preached on. He spoke of God's word being made manifest in our hearts. Then he went to his pine box, lifted out a copperhead, and held it aloft next to the rattlesnake. He closed his eyes and squinted, like he was listening for an oncoming storm. Soon he began to speak in tongues, and his eyelashes fluttered. He babbled: *Na-shadada-dannah*. It was a sound I'd grown up hearing, a sound I couldn't repeat. Only God could grant it.

My father never looked more like his serpents than when he spoke in tongues. It sounded like a lullaby. Everything here echoed the snake's delicate anatomy. The chattering tambourine, the quivering tongues, the outstretched hands gliding toward the sky.

For the first time in her life, Ivy joined him. Her mouth shuddered with words no one could understand.

My father laid the copperhead back in its wooden lair and looked toward the crowd. "I witnessed a miracle this week," he said.

The room stilled. These were the words the faithful had waited for since the day my father had been struck by lightning. Finally White Eye's legend continued. He gestured toward Ivy, who rose from her seat like a fog. My mother looked up at her friend. The bonnet she'd sewn for Ivy's bare head lay deflated in her lap. Ivy looked otherworldly. Her eyes bored into the waiting crowd. I closed my own eyes and saw her burning.

As Ivy recounted the fire, I started to feel like I couldn't breathe. I stood and bowed my head as I backed out of the room.

Once I left the building, I fled to the rear of the church, where I'd found the empty flask last April. The trees shivered. I closed my eyes again, slumped against the building's wall. I heard no footsteps, only a voice.

"Wren."

I opened my eyes.

"I scared you," Caleb said.

"No." I straightened myself. "I don't scare easy."

He held his post. "Meet me later at sundown," he said. "At the swimming hole."

"Why?"

He fastened his eyes to the ground. I waited.

"I want you to teach me to swim," he said.

"Swim?"

He nodded.

"In the dark?" I asked.

His eyebrows lifted, and his thick lashes shielded his eyes. "You think daytime is better?"

I considered it, and he was right. "Why me?" I asked.

"Because I don't know anyone here, and neither do you."

"That ain't true." I almost laughed. "I know everyone here."

"But you don't trust them." He stared at me for a moment. "And that's the same as being alone."

He waited. I could feel the ghosts of Ivy's and my mother's younger selves when they'd been my age, urging me forward, coaxing me back.

"What good is falling in love," Ivy had asked one afternoon when she thought I was dozing, "if it feels like jumping off a cliff?"

"Love doesn't always feel like that," my mother answered as she tore out the stitches of an old dress. "But the best kind does."

Ivy had laughed, and I knew then there were stories they'd never tell me. The kind of stories that hurt to remember. The kind I wanted for myself.

"Come," Caleb said. "And bring the whiskey."

He slipped back into the church, and I followed a few minutes later so no one would know we'd spoken. Inside the gas station, my father pronounced that the time had come to pray over Ivy, to thank God for healing her. She had turned magnetic, drawing most of the crowd to a cluster at the front of the room. She stood in the center of them, looking reborn. The hands of the faithful covered her bald head, and a chill coiled up my back. This was what folks had been waiting for. A sign that God hadn't forgotten us, even if the rest of the world had.

My mother stood off from the crowd, eyes wide open. She stared at my father as he prayed for Ivy with foreign utterings, her best friend falling to the floor as a soft sigh escaped his mouth. After a life of predictable magic, my father had finally surprised his wife.

I asked her once why she never took up a serpent, and she paused for a long time before answering. "I always had you," she said. "I saw no point in the risk."

The hive of prayers hushed when Ivy finally opened her mouth.

"When White Eye put his hands over me," she said, "I felt a chill like I've never known."

All eyes were on Ivy, but I watched my mother from the back. I saw her skepticism melt away and then return twofold as Ivy's words dripped from her mouth. Ivy was Ivy, and then she wasn't. She'd never called my father White Eye before, and she'd never lifted her hands to the sky and moaned as her body shook. My mother watched her best friend disappear and glared at my father, who had taken her away.

Ivy had been healed. No one could refute it. My father had performed a miracle, and yet something was wrong.

NIGHT SWIM

Our cabin sat quiet after Ivy's testimony. The sun disappeared into the horizon, each she-balsam a black stroke against its warmth. My mother hid in her bedroom, and my father did not follow her. I cooked canned beans and Swiss chard from the garden for dinner, and my father and I ate like escaped convicts on the back porch—in the dark and in a hurry.

We sat side by side, just as I'd found him and my mother on the steps after Ivy had burned two days before. It was safer this way. I could keep watch with my father without having to look him in the eye. If that white eye got hold of mine, he'd know about Caleb and the whiskey.

"What do you think," he finally said, "about Ivy's miracle?"

My father never asked a question he sought an answer to. He didn't care what I thought. He cared only about my mother.

"Nobody can make sense of what happened to Ivy," I said.

His head sagged to the side. "I see. And your mama?" His blond hair looked silver in the night. "What does she think?"

Before us the snake shed crowned the ravine. The shadows doubled it in size.

"She's thinking Ivy ain't herself," I said. "Like she escaped but left her body behind."

I watched him from the corner of my eye as he arched his back. "You think Ivy needed to escape?"

Everything inside me warned against answering him.

"It's just . . ." I tried to find the words. "That she's new now, in body and mind."

"There is no sickness in the flesh. Only sickness in the spirit."

"I know, Daddy." I'd heard him say those words so often I recited them in my sleep. "But Ivy's different now. You saw how she was at church."

"And it's my doing?" he said. "And not hers?"

"It seems so."

"And your mother doesn't like it."

"I think she liked the old Ivy just fine."

Ivy had never been afraid to tell my father she thought he didn't amount to much without his copperheads and rattlers. *Just because a snake don't bite you don't make you a god,* she'd said, making him mad enough for his skin to purple. And now that my father's miracle had transformed Ivy's body, it seemed he'd changed her mind, too.

He scowled as he leaned toward the earth, plucked a blade of grass, and stuck it in his mouth. "I should have let her burn, then."

"Watch, Briar. That mean spirit will be the death of you."

My mother's voice flooded toward us. I turned and saw her face aglow through the screen door. She looked worn, her thick hair grazing her waist, her palms flush against the sides of her patched skirt. I waited for my father to spout an apology, but my mother did instead.

"I'm sorry I doubted you after Ivy caught fire," she said as she stared him down with her dark eyes. "But Wren is right. Ivy ain't herself. She's never liked showy religion. You shouldn't have called her up front today. You know that's not her way."

My father's lips formed a heartless smile, just like they always did when he figured he'd backed her into a corner. "God's ways are not our own," he said.

My mother exhaled and pulled her brown hair into a bun. "I offered you my apology, Briar. You can take it or let it lie."

She slipped into the shadows and headed for their bedroom. My father rose to his feet, placed our dishes in the sink, and tailed her. I heard the hush of their bedroom door as my father closed it behind him. His voice whispered to her, and my mother's voice echoed his. I came to my feet and stretched my arms out into the stillness. Those murmurs would fool anyone into believing they were still in love.

It had taken my mother all day to apologize for doubting my father's gifts. Maybe she'd been yearning all this time for her own miracle, and it had gone to Ivy instead.

This kind of longing my father would never understand. He could drop God's blessings like pennies in a fountain and never miss them. Ivy had experienced something real and holy and not of this world, and he wanted to fan it to a flame. After years of bucking against his wife's best friend, he had finally found something he liked about Ivy—a glimmer of himself.

x x x

The trek to the creek was dreamy and hazed. I couldn't stop myself from running to the water. I felt scared of what was happening to Ivy—of what was happening to me. Her accident had cracked open my deserted world. It made me reckless. Alive.

The creek called me onward. Even at night the water never stilled. It always ran cold, the way old moonshiners liked it. My mother taught me this about our mountain's fierce waters: If I wanted to conquer them, I had to give myself over to them first.

Caleb sat cross-legged at the bank in a hooded sweatshirt. He'd taken Aunt Bette's van in the night and parked it on a patch of dirt about thirty yards away at the top of the creek's path. The engine ticked as I passed it. At the water he'd left his sketchbook and pencil by his shoes. It was cool out. I'd come barefoot, flask around my neck. I gripped it tight so Caleb wouldn't see my hands shake. Then I walked past him and sank my feet into the water.

"You ready?" I asked, hooking my eyes over my shoulder.

He stood and pulled his hoodie over his head. I caught sight of his shoulders again, bare and muscled and tight. I'd never wanted to touch someone like I wanted to touch Caleb then. My dress slipped off my body. Underneath I wore a faded navy swimsuit that had once belonged to my mother. Most of what I owned had first been hers.

I looked at Caleb. *Touch me,* my body begged. *Please.*

I waded into the water up to my neck and took a sip of whiskey. Caleb still waited at the water's edge.

"You scared?" I asked.

"I don't get scared unless I need to."

"Me, too," I said.

"Is it always so cold at night?" he asked. He dipped his fingers into the water and drew them to his lips. I waited for his mouth to curve, for his fingers to go back for more. The creek water was sweetest in June.

I smiled. "You'll get used to it."

"I don't want to." He took a step into the creek, and his eyes gleamed, two soft summer moons. "Coming here was like falling off a map."

Above us, atop the forest's tallest spire, someone had planted three white crosses—one for Christ and the other two for the thieves crucified with him. The crosses' silhouettes draped the creek like robes falling from the sky.

"It's easy to get lost on this mountain," I said as I lifted my eyes to his.

I offered the moonshine I'd stolen from Ricky. He stepped back, took it, and drank. I would come to know this about Caleb—he was as brave as he was cautious, never careless. I forged deeper as the water rushed past me, and Caleb followed with his arms overhead.

"First," I said, turning toward him. "Breathing underwater is just breathing out. Ready?"

I didn't wait for an answer. I took his hand and pulled him down, and he let himself be taken under. I held him there, feeling the weight of his palm on mine. I opened my eyes into the black. My dark hair swayed in the flux. Caleb's hand tightened around mine as he pulled me to the surface. Our bodies sighed into each other. I'd never admit it, but I was freezing.

"So is that it?" he asked. Drops of water glistened on his lips.

"You've got to learn to float." I stepped behind him and put one hand between his shoulder blades. "Lean back."

"You can't hold me."

"I'm not holding you. The water is." My voice softened. "Just lean."

He pressed backward, and his body folded in half. He flailed for my arm, and I took hold of him. Around us the water licked the rocks.

"Floating feels like sinking at first," I said. "Stretch your arms out and keep your body straight."

Again my hands found his back, and again he folded. His teeth chattered.

"Try again," I said. "And lock your knees."

His body straightened against my palm, and I cradled my other hand around the soft bend in his knees. I'd never guided a man's body with my own. It felt powerful and fleeting and terrifying. It was volcanic, how close our hearts were. I thought of my father and his magic palms, the fingers that soothed serpents and cooled flames. This must have been what he felt when the power left his body, a sensation so intimate he couldn't help but crave it.

x x x

Caleb walked me home in the dark. We both shivered in the empty night as he told me about the Ferris wheel he used to ride every summer in Richmond, where he'd once lived. It was the first picture he'd ever drawn, a panorama of the city buildings reflected on the water before him when the ride's alternator stalled and he got stranded with his brothers at the very top.

"Your brothers," I said. "The two boys in your sketch pad?"

He nodded. "Twins."

"Where are they now?"

He sighed. "Not far. A few towns over from Trap. My mother's job transferred nearby, and that's when the trouble started."

"Trouble?" I asked.

"This place is all kinds of trouble," he said.

I couldn't understand what Caleb meant. The only trouble I'd heard of was the kind that waited for me if I left this mountain—if I ever left my father and his serpents behind.

We reached the bottom of my hill and pushed through the wall of balsams. Across from the gang of pines, an empty mailbox stood crooked in the ground. My father had camouflaged it with fir branches. Our cabin didn't even have an address. The only mail we got was about my schooling, and it was delivered to Ivy's mailbox. Above us Royal Empress trees trimmed the sky. Caleb pulled up the hood of his sweatshirt.

"My father has a shed out back," I said. "That's where he keeps his snakes."

"He sure knows how to hide himself away from the rest of the world," Caleb answered. "There isn't another house for miles."

"He hates the thought of getting laughed at." I thought of myself on my knees outside the library as the boys around me snickered. "And so do I."

The point of Caleb's elbow touched mine. "I'm not laughing."

The softness of evening settled around us as the crickets cried out and the sound of the creek died away.

"Folks ask you about the snakes, right?" Caleb leaned against the trunk of a tree. "They ask me why I'm separated from my family. Do you want to know?"

"Yes," I said.

"The twins," he began. "They're only twelve."

I nodded. The tree branches spliced the moonlight into spindles.

"I took them out on my neighbor's four-wheeler last March," Caleb continued. "It was risky, and that's why I did it. I was so sick of sitting around this place where there's nothing on the radio but static. I thought the risk would keep me alive in such a dead town.

"I learned to drive in the city, and I knew that country roads were rougher. I'd heard stories of people losing control in the woods, and I wanted to feel it. I thought I was strong enough to steer as we spun out." He waited. "But I wasn't."

"What happened?"

"I hit a boulder I didn't see. The four-wheeler bucked, and my brother Derrick flew off the back and hurt his spine." He clutched the nape of his neck. "Been in bed ever since, and we don't know if he'll walk again. And Surley—the other twin—said he didn't blame me, but he can't talk to me anymore. Not even my mother can."

"That must be lonely," I said.

He nodded. "The separation is temporary, until my mother can adjust to caring for Derrick. But what they all need is to forget that I was the one driving. I could stand to forget it, too."

His shoulders curved in, and his face disappeared behind the fabric of the hood on his sweatshirt. I placed my hand on his back. His muscles tensed, then he sank a hand into his pocket.

"Families take me on for a few weeks, and then I get sent to a new spot," he said. "The farther we get from a city, the less people want someone like me around, and you know what?" His eyes flashed like oncoming headlights. "It's like getting punished again, every single time."

He sighed, and his breath grazed my neck.

"When I saw you with those boys in the creek," he said, "it reminded me of my brothers."

I took Caleb's hand, and his heat became mine. Our palms together: urgent, soft, dangerous.

"Hey." I could barely get the words out. "Do you want to see the snakes?"

Caleb grinned, and together we forded the swamp and hiked the steep hill. Our shadows merged in the moonlight. The entire house stood dark as we passed it.

We walked through the cattails until we reached the shed. I lifted the leather latch on the door. We stepped inside, and the door clanked shut behind us.

"There's no light in here," I said, Caleb's chest against my back. "I never realized till now."

The only flash of brightness came from a tiny window on the far wall, and the space was so small that Caleb couldn't stand straight. When I'd found my father dozing in his shed just a few days ago, he'd seemed asleep in paradise. But in the midnight air, I saw that he'd built himself a coffin. It was death-quiet inside. Not a hiss snuck out of the five boxes.

Caleb and I sat shoulder to shoulder across from them.

"So," he said. "You believe in all this?"

It was an outsider's question. I didn't have an answer.

"The snakes are real enough," I said.

"Seems like testing God to me."

"'And these signs shall follow them that believe; in my name they shall cast out devils; they shall speak with new tongues; they shall take up serpents; and if they drink any deadly thing, it shall not hurt them—'"

"'—and they shall lay hands on the sick, and they shall recover.'" Caleb finished the verse from Mark's sixteenth chapter. "I've read it."

His voice, a knell in the silence. It made my skin flush. My words might have honored my father and his religion, but my actions defied him. I'd never been a better daughter, sitting in my daddy's shed and reciting his favorite Scripture, but I'd broken his fiercest rule. I'd let an outsider in—not only into my father's sanctum but into mine.

A spool of light drifted in from the small window and cast a spare gleam on our outstretched legs. I looked over at Caleb.

"You think I'm odd," I said.

"No." He spoke with care. "But your father is."

"What if I took up a serpent?" I asked. "Would I be odd to you then?"

Our bodies were close and still not close enough. He leaned toward the cases where the snakes lay waiting.

"Do it," he said.

My hands slipped against each other. "It ain't meant to be a performance."

"Isn't it?"

"Tell me what you mean."

"Only that you can do it or you can talk about doing it. It's up to you."

I started to regret bringing Caleb here. He'd never fallen for the sick beauty of a serpent—lifting it beneath the jaw with one hand, tucking its tail behind his thumb with the other. Letting it move him, letting himself go palm to palm with his own death and defeat it. As my father's daughter, I'd been waiting for the day I'd hold a canebrake aloft, my fingers finding the pulse of its three-chambered heart, its vertebrae swaying the way waves came to shore. But I'd never found the courage.

"My father might be odd," I said, "but he's no fool."

"I never said he was a fool," Caleb countered. "I—"

I clapped my hand across his mouth when I heard a twitch outside the door.

"Hide," I said.

"No," he answered.

"*Please,*" I begged. The sound came closer, footsteps breaking through the parched earth from the fire.

"Don't make me hide," Caleb said. "Don't do that."

I saw then I had no right to invite him here. "I'm sorry," I whispered. I sprang to my feet and grabbed the latch when I heard my father's voice.

"Who's there?" he asked. He knew enough not to open the door to a room full of snakes.

"It's me, Daddy," I said.

"Wren." He hardly ever said my name. "What are you doing?"

I bit my lip as I looked at Caleb. The flask dangled from my neck. "I'm praying," I said, and my voice lost its strength.

He was silent for a moment. "The snakes," he called. "They locked up good?"

"They are."

I could picture him pursing his lips, wondering whether or not this was a day to trust his daughter.

"All right, then," he said. "I'll see you in the morning."

I waited until I heard the screen door on the porch slap behind him, and then I turned to Caleb. I'd never felt dirtier.

"I should go," he whispered.

"I'm sorry." I couldn't look at his face.

Caleb stood and closed the door quietly behind him. I sat alone in the snake shed for the first time in my life. On my knees I crawled toward the yellow timber rattlesnake my father kept in the middle. I placed my hands flat against the glass, and I could feel it fogging from sweat. This felt safe, the snakes and me both confined. It was frail and lonely and everything about myself I wanted to change.

x x x

I would come to remember the following weeks by three measures: how much I thought of Caleb, how quickly Ivy got sick, and how much Ivy's sudden illness provoked my father.

By the time July came and went, Ivy had gotten clammy and congested, and her boys stayed as needy as ever. The sickness had set in quicker than her hair had caught fire. A red rash spread like fireworks across her skin, and she vomited once an hour. The whites of her eyes went pink, and her lips turned blue. All day she quivered, coughed, and spit. Every hour she coated herself in a salve of tallow and beeswax, an old mountain remedy. Even Dr. Ed from Trap's free clinic couldn't help her, but not because he didn't try. My mother, who could always get anyone to do anything, convinced him to pay her three visits. But she couldn't convince Ivy to heed his counsel.

"It's likely bronchitis," he'd estimated from the door to Ivy's trailer. She wouldn't let him in, because she believed her sickness was spiritual, even though her veins had gone gray. "Or pneumonia. I won't know for sure until I examine you."

When my mother found a flyer for Dr. Ed's new clinic eight years ago, she'd hugged me so tight I couldn't breathe. Dr. Ed had a Ford full of supplies he was eager to deliver up the mountain: vaccines, penicillin, vitamins. Since then anytime I'd been ill, Dr. Ed paid us a visit at Ivy's. My father saw no use for modern medicine, not when divine healing was at his disposal. Not once had he tried to lay hands on me and pray, not even when I'd had a writhing fever from the chicken pox. My mother hadn't let him.

Ivy had never liked prescription drugs, because Ricky was so smitten with them. She thought they made the sick on our mountain sicker, dependent on a lie.

"You think coal killed this mountain?" she asked me once. "Try pharmaceuticals."

She didn't believe in cures, she said. She only believed in trading one kind of hurt for another. But since the burning, she had come around to a providential kind of healing, and the only advice she would take was my father's. He claimed she needed prayer and fasting. My father joined her and held her up when she was too weak to stand. He fed her chicken broth as he prayed, and it was the only thing she would stomach. He visited her every day, and he fought with my mother about it every evening.

"Send her to the hospital, Briar," my mother insisted over a dinner of lentils and tomatoes, night after night. I'd never heard her plead so much in her life. "She'll listen to you."

"It ain't me she's listening to, Ruby." My father offered up his hands to her. "It's God."

He put on an act of frustration, but I knew him better than that. He never loved my mother more than when she fought with him. They got so whipped up in their fights that I made good use of their preoccupations. I took to walking the deserted creek road, hoping to find Caleb and finding myself alone.

I saw Caleb every Sunday morning. I watched him just as he'd watched me on that first Sunday, but he didn't look back. He must have felt hurt that I'd invited him onto our land only to hide him in a shed from my father—and I didn't blame him. I'd shared just a single midnight swim and a handful of glances with Caleb, and I still felt the tiniest part of myself unravel. I wanted to see his Ferris wheel, listen to his music, touch the fingers of his right hand as he drew the rock spires that lanced the clouds. It hurt because I knew he wouldn't stay. I didn't want this heart I had, fragile and unstitched and nothing like my mother's, which beat true on its own.

Ivy didn't have the strength to scale our hill, so my mother and I visited her instead. We left early in the morning when even an earthquake couldn't rouse my father. Every day it was the same. Ivy sat bundled in bed, shivering like mad in the heat. Ricky was pale. The boys were paler. The licorice smell in their trailer mixed with the stench of sweat and filth. It didn't matter what we brought, though my mother tried onions and mintweed and gingerroot. No poultice could cure what was brewing. The whole family had come down with Ivy's illness, but she was the sickest of them all.

My mother remained faithful to her only friend. And because she and Ivy couldn't agree on the present, they talked about old times instead.

"Everybody in the churchyard wanted to marry your mama," Ivy told me on one of her better days. She pulled her friendship quilt up to her neck, her body dwarfed by the interlocking diamonds she and my mother had sewn together as girls, her head still slick.

"Stop," my mother said.

"You should tell Wren about the whiskey we drank."

My mother laughed with relief—there was the real Ivy, her old friend. She hadn't retreated yet. "That was a long time ago."

"You should have seen us on our wedding days." Ivy turned to me. Her lips had gone dry, and her mouth released a sour smell. "Almost wet ourselves, we were so scared."

"Scared of what?" I asked.

"The rest of our lives." Ivy's eyes went blank.

My mother folded back the edges of the quilt and smoothed the sheet. "It ain't as bad as all that," she said. "We'll still grow old together."

"Will we?" Ivy asked.

x x x

The sicker Ivy got, the less I slept. Even the foxes felt the air's grisly turn. I heard them screaming as I walked to the creek. I'd given up on finding Caleb there. I knew he'd heard the stories by now. Someone had surely told him how young women grew strange in these hills. The August air had eased, and the creek water slid around me like a nightgown. Some nights I hiked against the current just to see how far I could go. I walked long after my feet had gone numb.

One night I stayed out later than I should have. The catbirds had already started their chatting. The sun had yet to show, but I could see my father waiting for me when I slipped through the back door. He ruled over the kitchen table in the dark.

"Where you been?" he asked, and his spirit eye needled me.

I had no reason to lie. "I walked to the creek."

He looked wily from all the fasting he'd done. If Ivy's miracle had stripped her down, it had charged my father up. He hadn't eaten or slept, and his entire body throbbed.

"You visit my shed again?" he asked.

I trod carefully. I'd seen this tactic in his Sunday sermons, his way of asking a question he knew the answer to.

"No," I said.

"Good." He rose from the table, and we stood as near to eye to eye as we ever would. "You ain't ready."

My father had never spoken to me like an outsider before. He'd also never seen me angry. I had always been hurtling toward him and his serpents—I'd just never had the eyes to see it until now. Until Caleb, until Ivy.

He took a thick piece of paper out of his pocket and unfolded it. The slow ease of his movements made my chest clench. In his hand he held Caleb's drawing of me. My father must have found it in my dresser drawer while my mother and I were visiting Ivy. It wouldn't have been hard to find. My drawers were mostly empty. He glanced at me, then tossed the drawing into the smoldering fire we had lit for dinner. I didn't dare breathe until he shifted to his bedroom and closed the door.

BREATHING UNDERWATER

On the morning of Baptism Day in early August, I left the house at dawn and hid myself beneath the Royal Empress trees. Today my father would baptize anyone who wanted to profess their faith in God, and he planned to start with Ivy. He still didn't understand that our mountain had so few people left—and even fewer who wanted to get born again. No one had gotten baptized in the creek since I was a girl. Not even I had wanted to, until now. If my father thought I wasn't fit for his miracles, I would prove to him that he didn't get to decide.

In the shade I skated my fingers across the tips of the tall grass. Summer had reached its peak, and so had Ivy's illness. She'd been sick for two months. Even so, she planned to hike to the creek. It didn't matter how often my mother insisted that the cold water was lethal for her lungs. Ivy still wanted to be cleansed.

"I'll be the first in line to be washed clean," she'd said while my mother wiped vomit from her mouth. "And rid myself of this regret."

Her eyes bored into my mother's until she looked away. I decided to wait until we were alone to ask my mother what Ivy had meant.

Ivy's miracle had turned her weak. Even though my father felt strong, her miracle had weakened him, too. In the weeks after Ivy burned, he coddled his serpents and nursed his strychnine as his clothes hung from his body. He'd gotten so thin that my mother had to fashion a fresh hole for his belt. I watched his body dwindle.

My father had burned Caleb's drawing of me because he was afraid. I vowed to find what it would take to make him break.

I heard my mother calling my name, her voice like the rose-breasted birds feeding at her sunflowers. I ran to her. In the kitchen she was fixing an onion-and-lavender poultice for Ivy's chest once the cold set in at the creek. If she couldn't prevent my father from working his magic on Ivy, then she'd combat it with her own.

"Stir this till it cools," she said.

I nodded and took the spoon.

"Where's Daddy?" I asked.

She jutted her chin toward the back path. "Where do you think?"

My father spent most of his time in the shed since he and Ivy had started fasting as a way to arm-wrestle God into showing himself. If he'd healed Ivy once, he reckoned he could heal her again. He'd had no appetite for anything but the daily argument with his wife.

"You think he talks to those snakes when no one's around?" she asked me.

She grinned, but she was sad. This summer of miracles had emptied her out. I wound the spoon through the poultice and watched the ellipse of her back. My mother's vigilance over me had waned as Ivy grew sicker. I missed the way she used to draw me close to the things she loved—swimming, sewing, soaping. She didn't know I was wandering at night.

"Mama," I said. "What makes Ivy feel so much regret?"

Her eyebrows flinched. "She just misses the baby she lost a long time ago."

"Henry asked me about it," I said. "What happened?"

"It wasn't Ivy's fault."

"Then why does she want to be forgiven?"

She looked at me, her eyes rimmed in red from the onion.

"What does Daddy think?" I asked.

She didn't respond, and she didn't need to. The answer was plain. My father didn't know.

"I need some thistle from the garden," she said. "You'll find it along the fence."

I stepped outside, toeing the cliff of my mother's confession. There was a storm coming. I could tell by the way the birds pecked at their own tails in the white ash trees. It was a ways off, still. I turned my face toward the porch, a chill at my back. The wind chimes on the eaves clattered, and the cabin looked empty, like no one had lived there in a long time.

X X X

The creek-side water glinted in the noonday sun, and Ivy looked ready to wilt. My mother brought her marriage quilt to wrap Ivy in once the baptism ended, and she tried to coax Ivy toward it to take a rest, but Ivy would not be moved. The quilt had a patch from everyone who'd attended my mother's wedding, including a square of black corduroy from Ivy herself. She'd sliced it from the pants her dead father once wore. I used to drape that quilt around my shoulders like a cape until Ivy pulled it off me.

"Weddings are funerals," Ivy would say as she pushed the quilt beneath my mother's bed. "Don't you dare dream of them."

The air clotted as the storm drew near, and Ivy's boys hung so heavy from my father's arms that he'd already sweated through his white collared shirt. Like my father, his sheep wore white on Baptism Day. This was how we knew who had decided to give their lives over to the Lord— the folks getting baptized were the only folks dressed in dark colors.

Twenty people from the congregation waited by the water to watch the ceremony. All of them had known Briar Bird since he was a boy. Ivy looked like a puckered rose, standing in the creek in a scarlet dress. My mother lay in the shade. My father stood beside Ivy, the two of them closer than I'd ever seen.

An engine growled at the top of the hill. Aunt Bette's van heaved up the mountain and squawked to a stop, then five of her wards skulked down the hillside. The girl with the glittered nails led the way, the strap of her guitar tamping down her blond hair. Caleb followed her.

I couldn't hide how fiercely I was drawn to everything about him: his smile, his stare. He turned his face away from where I stood at the water. It stung, but not enough for me to wish I could forget the way it felt when our bodies met.

"Hi," I said, and that was the beginning of the end.

My father's eyes ricocheted between Caleb and me until he grabbed my elbow and forced me toward the soft ground by the overhang.

"You're hurting me," I whispered.

"All you've done is bring danger here," he said.

I felt twenty pairs of eyes fixed to my back as my father's breath started to pitch.

"You're the one who brings danger here," I said. "You bring it every time you pick up a snake."

I'd never spoken to my father that way. His white eye narrowed, and he looked ready to strike me when my mother called to him.

"Briar." Her voice from the shade was calm, full of purpose. "You best let go of my girl."

The crowd gagged, and my father released my arm. I turned my back to him and found my place in line behind Ivy. My father splashed cold water on his face, then stepped into the current. The girl with the shimmery nails stood on the overhang and started to strum her guitar. My father snarled his lip at the music.

"Arledge," he summoned the oldest in the crowd. "Lead us in 'Washed by the Blood.'"

The strings on the girl's guitar shrieked as her playing came to a stop. She looked at me and raised her hand in a half salute, as if she were trying to tell me it was safer to take a step toward her and move away from the water.

I lifted my hand in return as Brother Arledge stood and started a slow clap. The sound felt orphaned until he started to sing. The congregation joined him, and the chorus swelled.

The clapping quickened as my father beckoned Ivy to join him. I shivered in the heat. Ivy floated toward him, transfixed by the crescendo of the creek. His face had that euphoric gaze I'd seen too many times. Ivy covered her nose and mouth with one hand as my father wrapped an arm around her waist. He tipped her backward and doused her in creek water. Ivy bobbed up, a waterfall spilling off her gossamer skin. My father relished Ivy's luster. She lifted her hands as he clamped a palm on her shoulder. She fell to her knees, crawled toward the bank, and spread herself wide to dry out in the sun. The smile on my father's face stretched immortal.

It was my turn.

The clapping sped to a dizzying pace. Arledge's voice fizzed into static. I stepped into the water and rode the wave toward my father. His blue eye sparkled like a jewel. I wanted my father to reckon with me, and I waited for the flare of his touch. He paused for a moment and shut his eyes. I closed mine and felt the weight of his hand beneath my chin.

I baptize you in the name of the Father, the Son, and the Holy . . .

The final word vanished as he dipped me backward. All sound shushed as I sank. I'd gone under these waters a hundred times, but never by my father's hand. He'd rarely touched me, and I'd never wanted him to. The heady glug of bubbles vibrated against my lips, and I opened my eyes. Sediment floated by like specks of gold. The sun blurred above me, and I felt my gravity shift. Once my head reached the creek bed and my feet left the earth, I realized my father wasn't letting me up.

My first thought: *Wait him out. He's testing you.*

He wanted to know if I had the kind of faith that would move mountains. I went limp and let myself dangle in his grasp.

My second thought: *He knows. He knows you let an outsider into his shed of serpents.*

He knew about Caleb, about the flask. The picture had betrayed us. I'd committed my sin in private, and he wanted to sentence me in public.

My third thought: *He's drowning you.*

All air left my body as my face slammed against the earth. My mouth gasped and filled with water. I clawed at his pant leg. My feet flailed and clocked him in the side of the face. He overpowered me, even as I fought him.

Then my father fell backward. He abandoned his hold on me, and I broke through the surface. I coughed as my nose bled down the length of my dress. The small crowd lining the creek had gone mute.

They all stared at their preacher, no more than five feet from me and slung by the collar in Caleb's grasp. He'd pried my father's fingers off my neck and held him at arm's length like he was a sock puppet. My father sputtered and kicked, but Caleb's grip stayed firm.

He didn't stay above water for long. My mother charged into the creek, thrashing the waves with her fists. When she reached her husband, she yanked the front of his shirt and forced him under. My mother wasn't strong enough to keep him down, but he let her. She held him there, and no one in the crowd rose to stop her.

"Mama," I said. "Don't."

She paid me no mind. One of my father's hands pawed at her skirt. Still she held him.

"Mama," I said again. My voice had gone hoarse. "Please."

She didn't look at me, but she heard me all the same. She relented, and my father surfaced, his limbs flagging. My mother had never looked more savage.

"The next time you want to drown someone in the name of God," she spit, "drown yourself."

The congregation stayed stunned. It reminded me of the only time I'd ever seen someone die from a snake bite. It was an old-timer, whose favorite copperhead had bitten him on his thigh. The worshippers' mouths had gone dry then, too, as my father dragged the corpse down the center aisle.

My mother took my elbow, and we stumbled out of the water. My father called after her.

"I'm sorry, Ruby," he said, but she didn't turn. "I don't know what came over me."

The crowd wasted no time thinning out. My father and Caleb stood chest-deep in the creek, both rigid and dazed. I couldn't look at either one of them.

"Let's go home, Wren." My mother put her mouth next to my ear. "Don't you fuss about your clothes."

I looked down at the blood that had stained my favorite dress.

"We'll set it right," she whispered, her eyes frantic as they searched for the horizon. "You'll see."

x x x

Ivy followed us back to the cabin, even though she lacked the strength to climb the final hill. She looked like a wraith as dusk set in through the mountain. My mother wrapped one arm around her waist and one arm around mine, and the three of us hobbled homeward. Ivy, blue-lipped and gauzy-eyed, sat with me on my mother's quilt in the middle of the kitchen floor and warmed my feet in her hands. Her breath rattled. My mother combed my hair and braided it into a crown, just the way I used to like it as a girl. My father didn't show himself.

Ivy hummed an old folk song I couldn't recall the words to. I tried to sip from a bowl of bone broth that my mother had warmed in the kettle over the fire. My head pounded. I thought of my father's confused apology—*I don't know what came over me*—one he'd offered to his wife, not to me. I couldn't tell what she thought of as she threaded her fingers through my hair. We were trapped. She'd always known it, but she'd never wanted me to. No one had said anything for a long time when Ivy abruptly stopped her rasped hum.

"Speak," Ivy said, looking at her friend. A round of thunder rolled in the distance.

Speak. This was the word they offered each other.

"There's one thing troubling me more than any other." My mother took a breath. "I can't figure out if this is a man I don't know or if this is the man I've known all along."

74

Her hands quivered at her sides, and I saw that my blood had stained her white dress, too. Her arms bore the scars from the day of the fire. Ivy still had no burns, and still no one could explain it. She started to hum again, then cut herself off in mid-verse.

"Maybe Briar Bird is finally becoming everything you dreamed he would be when you were seventeen," Ivy said.

The brush my mother held in her hand clattered against the floor.

"Do you remember the girl you used to be, so fearless and bold?" Ivy snapped. "Where is she? She'd never let Briar Bird tell her what to do."

Ivy looked out the window and started to hum again. My mother rose to her feet and opened the kitchen door. Lightning split the far skies.

"Where did you go, Ivy?" my mother asked. "The day before you caught fire?"

Ivy kept her eyes on the iron sky. My mother asked her again, but Ivy would not speak.

"You should leave," my mother said, words she'd never dreamed of uttering to Ivy before the burning.

Ivy was unfazed, even in the coming storm. She gathered her skirt and left the house without looking back. My mother shut the door behind her.

x x x

I slept that night with the window open, taunting my father to come to me. I had no idea where he'd gone, or if he had the courage to return and face my mother's wrath. As I lay awake, I thought of Abraham and Isaac on the day that God told Abraham to sacrifice his only son. It was an Old Testament story that bothered me every time I recited it to my father. The tale celebrated Abraham and his faith, but in the late hours of night I thought only of Isaac. What had he thought when his father raised a knife to his throat? The faithful believed he was willing to die for his father's devotion to the Lord. But I wondered if he'd said to a God so willing to let him go, *What about me, Lord? What about me?*

Then a sheep appeared, so the story goes, and—like my mother, always my mother—it saved the day. Abraham found his worthy sacrifice, and he and his son went on to do great things and rule many places. Still, I wondered what Abraham's wife, Sarah, had said when he returned home with a frightened son. Whatever she'd done, my mother's ferocity could surpass it.

My father didn't breach my open window that night, but Caleb did. His fingers, charcoaled and callused, clung to the window ledge. He'd been a stranger on the day we met, just two months ago, and now he was the only true witness to the life I'd led.

Caleb was worried. His eyes searched my cheeks, my neck, and the bruises left by my father's grip. He sighed, and his breath came through the window with the night's cool breeze. His face was tender, the calm before the storm. The storm itself.

My nightgown rustled in the wind as I came to the window ledge, and my legs tremored.

I didn't ask Caleb to come inside. We stared at each other from either side of the window, and I couldn't find the words to speak.

"Are you all right?" he asked.

"Yes," I said.

"You are?" He looked again at my wrists and neck, the spots where my body pulsed with life. His hand reached out, and I could smell him—fresh like soap and cinnamon.

"Yes."

"You know this isn't how fathers treat their daughters." He took my hand and pressed it into his chest. "Right?"

His heartbeat thrummed against my fingertips.

"You're smart, and you're kind, and you're *good*, Wren," he said, and his lip trembled. "You don't belong here."

Wren. The way he said my name felt like the wind of a city-bound train rushing past me just fast enough for me to jump on board and let it take me away. I never thought I could belong anywhere else but the lonely cabin I'd been born in.

"You'd like the city," he said, as if reading my mind. "There are programs and housing for women just like you and your mother."

I smiled. "And no Briar Bird."

It felt impossible.

"Do you know why I like drawing with charcoal?" Caleb asked.

I shook my head.

"It's raw. Just black and white, pencil on paper. It helps me be honest about what I see. I watched your father's face when you met him in the water. You know what I saw?"

I waited.

"Misery. He's stuck here, Wren. Same as you."

It was so simple a truth that I couldn't believe I'd never seen it. Even Briar Bird couldn't escape the mountain that worshipped him.

He leaned inward. "You should have seen his face when he held you under."

I already knew the answer, but I asked anyway. "What did he look like?"

"Slain." The whites of Caleb's eyes shot through the dark.

I'd beheld that face plenty of times before. It was my father's omniscience, his caprice, his pride. Anywhere I went, he would find me.

"He knows, Caleb," I said. "He knows I took you into his shed."

Caleb shook his head. "He couldn't. It was pitch-dark out. Even if he does, Wren, we did nothing wrong."

I thought about inviting Caleb into my bedroom, what we could do beneath the covers or with my back against the dresser. I wanted to feel his lips on my neck, his heart an inch from mine, his words in my ear. I wanted him to touch me. His palms pressed into the wood of my family's house. I reached out a hand, then drew it back. Somewhere beyond us in the dark, my father lurked.

"You're not safe here," Caleb said.

My hands slipped from the ledge. This was what he'd come to say.

"I've got my mama," I said. "She needs me."

"She's not safe, either."

"We've been safe this long."

He let out a short laugh. I'd lied, and Caleb knew it. We hadn't been safe. We'd been poorly, and we'd burrowed deeper into our devastated world in order to survive it. I saw then what power Caleb had. He could end my father's reign and our crooked life just by stating the truth: My father couldn't be trusted. If folks in Trap ever heard what the famed snake handler had done to his daughter, he'd be reduced to the mortal status he deserved. As much as I'd dreamed of it, I didn't know if my mother and I would survive his fall.

"Don't tell anybody," I said. "Please."

"He'll hurt you." His voice was soft. "Or someone else."

"Don't you dare," I whispered.

My hand found his. He pulled me toward him until his mouth rested against the smooth part of my shoulder. I felt the high-voltage shock I'd been hunting for all summer as lightning skipped over the hills. Caleb opened his mouth, and I waited for him to kiss me.

"Take me to Violet's Run," he said instead.

I looked past his shoulder. The wind had picked up, and it pestered the trees.

"It's going to rain. We won't make it all the way to the top in a storm."

"Take me to the bottom, then," he said. "To the spot where Violet fished her suitors out of the rapids."

"Let's go somewhere real," I said. "Let's hike to the razorbacks."

"Isn't it dangerous in a storm?"

An electric current ran between us like a live wire. "Lethal."

He smiled and pulled me toward the window. I didn't bother to change out of my nightgown. He took my hand, and I stepped out of the window and into the dark.

x x x

I didn't realize until we'd reached the razorbacks, until we had to yell to be heard, until the wind and rain snatched our breath away, that there were places on my mountain my father would not follow me. As Caleb and I crossed the footbridge, the wooden slats shook so violently they brought us to our knees. Below us and above us, there was only black, nothing but our two pairs of eyes like pearls in the night. Together we reached our hands into the abyss, and his copper eyes held mine. They reminded me of my mother's—full of warmth, full of warning. Caleb and I were both outsiders—I in his world and he in mine.

Anytime it would storm in years to come, I'd bring myself back to the memory of the two of us running like crazy through the woods on our way to the bridge, hand in hand, tripping over rocks and falling into each other. I'd bring myself back to the time when I believed that falling in love was the best and the worst thing that could happen to me. We screamed into the pounding rain.

When I returned home, I was surprised to find my mother seated at the kitchen table, one candle lit. Her hair had fallen from its braid, and her eyes settled on my collarbones when I crept through the door. She looked at me, but she didn't see.

"Mama," I said. "What is it?"

"It's Ivy," she said, like she'd always known someday she'd have to say the words she dreaded most. "She's dead."

MADE MANIFEST

Henry had found Ivy lying prostrate in her bed—eyes wide open, her mouth sagging to the side. Ricky was passed out in his recliner with a bottle of whiskey in his hand. When Henry couldn't wake him, he scaled our hill in the rain to tell my mother her best friend had died. After that he ran home in the dark, chilled and sickly himself. There was no other way for him to reach us. We had no phone, no computer, no address. We had nothing here. The house swayed with such might in the storm that it threatened to collapse around us.

My mother's hand held steady as she walked toward the dish closet and opened the King James Bible she kept hidden beneath the teacups she'd gotten on her wedding day. From the book's middle, she lifted a scrap of paper with a string of numbers scribbled on it. Then my mother picked up Ricky's cell phone from the kitchen table. Henry had left it behind so we could call someone.

She had to dial the number three times before the phone got enough reception. Finally someone answered.

"Flynn," my mother said. "It's Ruby." Her face twitched. "Ivy is dead."

She waited, wrapped in the murmurs on the other end of the line. Then she closed the phone.

"Who's Flynn?" I asked.

She didn't answer. Her chair stuttered against the floor planks as she stood. "I have to go sit with the body."

A body. Already that was what Ivy had become.

"I'll come with you," I said, breaking the distance between us. Rainwater spilled from the edge of my nightgown. "I'll take care of the boys."

My mother's arm blocked me with such force that her pearl-handled switchblade slipped from her belt and fell to the floor.

"Stay here," she said as she bent to retrieve it.

"No."

"I won't have you catching whatever still lives in that house."

"What if you catch it?"

Her face told me she ached to catch Ivy's illness. I found comfort in the deep rose tones of my mother's skin. She was flushed and alive.

"Daddy will come home," I said. "He'll be looking for you."

Her face glowered. "Then inform him of the results of his so-called miracle." She wrapped a shawl around her shoulders and tucked the phone into her pocket.

"You can't leave me here with him," I said.

"Don't fuss, Wren," she said, slapping shut her King James on the tabletop. "He don't have the nerve to come back here."

My mother wasn't mourning yet. She was angry. She stomped

toward the door and yanked it, leaving it open and wagging behind her in the dark.

x x x

After my mother disappeared beyond the Empresses, I noticed a piece of paper on the kitchen table. Before the news she'd been writing a letter. She'd left it at the head of the table, and it had fluttered to the floor. I picked it up and found my name at the top. She'd been writing a letter to me.

Dear Wren, it read. *I have to tell you—*

All my life I'd waited for a letter like this from her, if she had only finished it. Whatever she'd wanted to say, it seemed, no longer mattered.

I kept vigil over the empty house until morning broke. My mother's words proved true—my father didn't show himself. I also kept watch at the shed. The snakes lay inside, slithering on themselves. I once feared they'd find their way into the cabin, but I'd wasted my worry. They were as trapped as I was.

By the time my mother returned, I'd fallen asleep at the table with her letter in my hand. She'd set to rocking in the chair by the front window, and I roused at the chair's creaking. My mother was wide-eyed in the morning light.

"Mama?" I asked. "Are you all right?"

She didn't answer.

I tried again. "Tell me how Ivy died."

"In her sleep." My mother knocked her fist against the crook in the armrest. "I told her that water was too cold."

"It was peaceful, then."

The fist-rattling stopped. "You saw her yesterday, Wren. Did she look peaceful to you?"

My mother never spoke to me with spite.

"How's the boys?" I tried.

"Already headed to their relatives' in Elkins, and Ricky, too. The whole lot of them needs to be nursed back to health." She touched the knife at her waist before her hand fell to her lap. "They are so sick they can't sit up straight. Vomiting, rashes, bloodshot eyes. I ain't never seen any pneumonia behave like that. Their trailer is cursed, and I'll raze it myself."

"They'll need a place to stay when they come back," I said. I wanted to remain naive, even for a minute more.

"They ain't coming back."

"What do you mean?"

"Ricky isn't fit to care for them by himself." She finally looked at me. "You know that."

I strode toward her and stopped her rocking with my hand. "You know Ivy wouldn't want that. She'd want them with us."

"We aren't fit to care for them, either."

She stood and paced into the kitchen. I followed her.

"We're more fit than Ricky's family," I said to her back.

She turned and stuck her hands on her hips. "Kin care for their own kin. That's the law."

"Ivy is our kin." My voice bit. "Closer than."

"Not anymore."

She reached for her apron on the hook by the stove, and I snatched it out of her grasp.

"You told them to leave, didn't you?"

My mother's face had a thousand cracks in it. "Ricky would have done it sooner or later," she said.

"You don't know that. We could have cared for them. I could have."

"You can't care for those children, Wren. You're a child yourself."

I sank into a chair at the table and let her apron puddle on the floor. I knew they didn't need me. I needed them.

"This letter," I said, taking it from the table. "What did you want to tell me?"

My mother looked too weary and too thin. "It don't matter anymore."

"Tell me."

She gripped her neck, as if some ghost of the truth were trying to claw out of her throat. Then she hovered over the kitchen sink, soaking her hands in dirty dishwater.

"Ivy is dead, Mama. But I'm not." I stood behind her and spoke into the back of her neck. "I ain't got to be trapped here just because you are."

I knew the words would hurt her. She spun around and slapped me. Dishwater flew into the air. We stared at each other, mirror images with dark hair and burning skin. Then I left my mother there, my deepest love, to sit alone on the kitchen floor.

x x x

My mother planned to bury Ivy later that morning, to keep her sickness from spreading. I'd never felt emptier. Ivy and her boys were my family, my friends, my fortress. They'd brought life into our sickly cabin, even when Ivy had gotten ill. Our mountain was colder now, and strange.

I'd never seen my mother open and close her King James Bible as much as she did in the hours after Ivy's death as she entombed herself in plans for her homegoing service. The book had been stuffed into a bureau full of finer things we had no use for—a chipped tea service, a single silver fork, a pair of nude stockings. The Bible had been unearthed on the kitchen table, but my mother wasn't reading it. Over the years she'd squirreled away all sorts of things between its pages—phone numbers, lists, photographs, and more twenty-dollar bills than I'd ever seen.

When she finally fell asleep, I ran to that Bible. Inside it I found my father's old telephone number, film negatives from a camera I'd never known my mother had, and a picture of her and Ivy sitting beneath a willow, looking not much older than I was. Ivy had that up-to-something expression she was known for, and my mother leaned into her shoulder like they'd always been fastened together. A waterfall of sadness poured over me.

In a house where my father hunted for proof of his wife's inner life, this secret Bible had become her diary. My mother's name—Ruby Elizabeth Day—was scrawled into the opening page, and my father's had been penciled in beneath it. My name followed in red ink. A few spots sat empty for the other children my parents never had. And between Psalms and Proverbs sat a stack of old envelopes, each filled with at least one rumpled twenty-dollar bill. The oldest letter delivered to Ivy's mailbox dated back almost twelve years. There was no return address.

My mother knew her husband so well that she could likely pinpoint where he'd gone to hide. He couldn't have gone far, maybe to the church to wait out the rain or to the old tobacco barn on Brother Arledge's land. My father had fasted longer than he'd been separated from my mother. How long could he last without seeing her? At mid-morning I snuck off toward the snake shed to see his serpents. I had a theory. If my father planned to leave, he'd fetch his snakes first.

I crept around the ravine side of the shed at dawn to peek through the tiny window. It was too dark inside for me to see. When I cracked the door, I found my father lying in front of his serpents. I couldn't tell how long he'd been wasting away inside. His body made an X as he ground his face into the plywood floor. He was dirty. The clothes he'd worn for the baptism were stained, and his hair had spiked into thorns. I tried to back away, but he lifted his head.

He looked lost. I felt the phantom sensation of his hands at my neck. *I'm sorry, Ruby,* he'd said. *I don't know what came over me.* I wondered if it was dark enough that I might be mistaken for the Ruby he used to know.

When he glanced up at me, he started to sob. He brushed my foot with his hand, and I pulled it away.

"You probably ain't heard," I said, my voice straight. "Ivy is dead."

"Dead?" He wiped his nose. "How?"

My mother blamed my father. Dr. Ed blamed Ivy herself. Church folks would blame Ricky. *Too many kids,* they'd say. *Can't nobody survive with a man like that.*

"She died in her bed. That's all I know." I couldn't stop myself. "But it ain't a mystery. She should have listened to Dr. Ed."

My father came to his knees. "So I as good as murdered her, then?"

I said nothing. He'd already forgotten that it was me he'd tried to kill. Back at the house, the kitchen light flicked on. We both turned toward it, a pair of moths searching for a way out of the night. My mother's silhouette clung to the curtains above the sink. As I opened my mouth to call to her, my father rose to his feet and fled.

My mother sang out my name into the dark.

x x x

It rained just before the burial, and we left our umbrellas behind. My mother and I each carried a basket of larkspurs for the half-hour hike north to the grassy meadows of Violet's Run, and my mother had packed her tambourine. It chimed every time her basket nuzzled her side. *Don't wear black,* she had commanded earlier that morning when I came inside from the snake shed. *Ivy would have hated it.* Instead we wore the colors of the sun: marigold and rust and amethyst. Halfway up the hill, our skirts were already soaked to our knees. Soon the high grass would be matted down. My father swore that this was how he knew when someone who died was well loved in this life—their mourners' feet left a fat trail of slain grass all the way to the cemetery in the top nook of the Run.

This would be the first homegoing my father had ever missed. *Shepherding a flock is a life-and-death sentence,* he liked to say. Funerals were fewer and fewer now as our congregation dwindled, and each loss grabbed him by the shoulders and shook.

We were the first to arrive at the plot where Ivy had been laid. The pit gaped with a mound of fresh earth gone to mud beside it. Down below, Ivy's body was already tucked neatly into its wooden slot. Whoever had hauled the casket up here had taken care to avoid the rain shower earlier in the day. It looked virgin in the dirt.

I hadn't seen Ivy's dead body for myself. I didn't think anyone had, aside from my mother. There hadn't been enough time for a viewing.

"What did Ivy look like when you last saw her?" I asked.

The fellow gravestones freckled the hillside. My mother sat at the edge of the grave and let her feet dangle.

"She looked terrified," she answered.

"Of death?"

Her shoulders cowered. "Of life, I think."

"What do you mean?"

My mother sighed. "Ivy never wanted to live on this mountain. She stayed because she knew I'd never leave it."

My mother tossed a flower onto the casket as her eyes scanned the purple hills. I sat beside her, and we cast our glances down like wishes into a well.

She took her tambourine and rapped it against the heel of her hand. Then she started to sing an old hymn written from a verse in Isaiah.

Though your sins be as scarlet, they shall be as white as snow; though they be red like crimson, they shall be as wool.

My mother's alto notes swooped through the hills, and soon the coming mourners joined in the hymn. We could hear them singing from far off, their voices few. By half past ten, not as many folks had gathered as my mother had hoped. There were fewer than a dozen. My mother counted them with her eyes. Folks had clambered toward Ivy's miracle, and now they ran away from its fall.

The sun came out, and the shade of the sugar maple above the casket slowly shifted. My mother's tambourine fell asleep at her side. She opened one of my father's old Bibles and read aloud from Psalm 23. *Thou preparest a table before me in the presence of mine enemies: thou anointest my head with oil; my cup runneth over.*

Beyond our group the hills stood stoic. A rush of violets scattered across the ridge, and a flying eagle mounted the far sky. No one wept, not even my mother. Her voice trailed off until she closed the book, took a handful of dirt, and let it fall from her fingers onto the wooden box below. Together the grievers recited the Lord's Prayer, each of us taking up a fistful of earth and releasing it over Ivy's body.

The last person to approach the grave was my father. No one had seen where he'd come from. He'd been hiding among the graves, and then he came forth, his only copperhead twined around his arms. My mother's eyes trained not on his face but on mine. Her stare tried to tell me a secret.

Tell me, Mama, my own eyes said. *Just tell me what it is.*

But she didn't. Instead she thumbed through the Bible to a new passage and started to read aloud.

In my Father's house are many mansions: if it were not so, I would have told you.

"Ruby," my father called to her. The crowd turned toward him, and my mother kept reading.

I go to prepare a place for you. And if I go and prepare a place for you . . .

"Ruby," he said again. "I'm sorry."

. . . I will come again, and receive you unto myself . . .

"Ruby, please."

. . . that where I am, there ye may be also.

My mother's voice rose above his pleas.

"I'm sorry she's dead, Ruby," he finally said, and my mother stopped.

The circle of grievers shied away, heading back the way that they had come. None of them wanted to witness their shepherd get rebuked by his wife.

"It ain't my fault," my father said. "If I had Ivy's blood on my hands, don't you think God would let this serpent of mine strike me dead? God's done what He done."

My mother's Bible slipped from her grasp and landed on top of the casket. "God's done? You think God did this?"

The copperhead writhed in my father's grip. "It ain't like I stood over her bed with a gun in my hands, Ruby. She died, and I'm sorry for it, but it wasn't my doing."

My mother laughed. "She died the day you put your hands on her, Briar."

Above us passing clouds caged the coming rain. The air was graveyard still.

The copperhead had no reason to spook. And yet it did. For the first time in his life, my father could not control his serpent. The snake whipped its tail until its whole body went rigid, and my father dropped it in the high grass beneath the sugar maple. My mother flinched and drew back.

The copperhead slithered at her feet, orange and black, a fire and its ashes. It slid lazily along the gravestone, toying with the weeds around my mother's bare ankles.

"Ruby," my father said softly. "Don't you move."

She obeyed him. My father lifted his hands, and then my mother spoke.

"How dare you." Her voice shook. "How dare you bring that thing here."

My father dropped his arms. "I'll fetch it, Ruby. I swear."

As they argued, the copperhead drew me toward itself. *Come closer,* it seemed to whisper. I crept to the edge of the plot and settled onto my knees. It was a delicate animal, this serpent. Its eyes shone, and its mouth clamped like a treasure chest. I was so close.

"Wren," my mother said. "Get on your feet."

I coiled my body around the grave, moving slower than the clouds overhead.

"I'll get it, Mama," I whispered. "I can do it."

"Step back, now," my father warned. "It's a copperhead."

"I know what it is."

"Just let it be, Wren," he said.

I came within spitting distance and hesitated. The snake hedged in the grass. I saw its tongue flit-flat-flit. It paid us no mind as it settled into the shallow shade of the gravestone. I leveled my body against the ground, bit my lip, and reached out.

Nothing could have prepared me for what I felt when that animal swirled itself around my wrist. My father had always sworn that taking up serpents was like taking a deep breath, but I choked.

I held it for only an instant before my fingers seized and its head jabbed at me. I screamed. My father didn't move. Before I could drop it, my mother leaped across the plot and unhooked it from my wrist.

The serpent charged toward her, yawned back its mouth, and fixed its teeth to the flesh right above her collarbone.

"Ruby!" my father shouted.

My mother pitched forward. The snake still clung to her neck as its body twisted into a question mark. My father lunged for her, and she took his arm. Together they fell to their knees. He cinched the serpent by the jaw. Once it released, he tossed it onto Ivy's casket. It caressed the cover of his Bible before curling itself into a spiral.

I remained on my hands and knees. My father set about sucking the poison out of the open wound. He spit into the dirt, and my mother's neck blotched and swelled. Her breathing labored, and a sheen of sweat washed across her forehead. I sprang to my feet.

"We have to get her to the doctor," I said.

"She won't make it," he answered, his hands hovering above the bite.

"You have to go get him, then," I said. "You'll run faster than me."

If he heard me, he didn't respond. His lips mouthed private incantations, but he made no sound.

"Daddy!" I shouted. "Get the doctor. *Please.*"

"God's done what He done," my father whispered, my mother's head in his lap. His tears ran rivers over her eyes.

I took off running down the mud-ridden hill, beyond the rapids where Violet had saved her lovers, through the woods to the bottom of our property. I whipped past the other mourners making their way down the mountain, shouting at them to send for help because my mother had been bit. I kept running until I reached Ivy's old Pontiac, which Ricky and the boys had left behind. After I cranked the engine with the key hidden beneath the floor mat, I slammed the gas until I reached Dr. Ed's clinic at the edge of Trap. It didn't matter that I didn't know how to drive. I wouldn't wait for God to decide.

But God had already made his choice. By the time Dr. Ed and I returned to the top of Violet's Run, my mother was dead. We found her body lying slack against a tree trunk, the snake still nestled atop Ivy's casket. My father had disappeared.

Ivy had looked terrified in her last moments, my mother had said, and I would come to say in the campfire stories I told that my mother looked impatient. *Just get on with it,* her static face seemed to plead. She and Ivy had done everything else together since they'd been young, and my mother wouldn't let her beloved die alone without her. *I can't survive here anymore.*

GONE

Ever since I was young, I'd heard my father preach that God's will was like the wind. *You can't see it,* he said, *and you can't stop it.*

My mother lay at my feet. The rain beckoned, and I couldn't shield her from it. I sidled up next to her body and put my cheek to her forehead. The air stank like mud and squirrel hides. I buried my face in my mother's hair and prayed for the truth to somehow become a lie.

Dr. Ed didn't need to examine the body to see she was dead. He didn't have to tell me, either.

"Death isn't the end," I'd heard my mother say to Ivy when she thought I couldn't hear. "It's an escape."

She never feared the end of her life as much as she feared the length of it.

The doctor rested a palm on my shoulder before heading back down the mountain to send for someone. That's what he said: *I'm sending for someone.* His business was with the living, and I needed a different kind of help now.

A drizzle had set in by the time a beat-up silver Tacoma swerved up to Ivy's plot. I knew that truck, the boy in blue-jean overalls ricocheting in the back. The pickup skidded in the mud, and the boy hopped out with an armload of quilts. He draped them over my mother's corpse like a veil. The driver, the shiner I'd seen at Ricky's the day Ivy burned, stumbled out and bowed his head.

"You're drunk," I said.

He didn't disagree. Instead he stared at the mound of quilts as he steadied himself against the grille of his truck.

"You can't tear through this land like that. Folks bury their kin here."

It's what my mother would have said had she been alive. I stood and stretched out my arms as if I needed to defend her.

He sucked his teeth. "You can if you own it."

"You own this land?" I pointed across the valley drowning in violets and headstones.

"So they tell me." He looked toward the gray sky.

"Why would you turn it into a graveyard?" I asked.

"Dead bodies got to go somewhere." He rubbed his eyes. "Now, let's get Ruby Day out of the rain."

His words stopped me. My mother had been Ruby Day before she'd met my father, before she'd become a mother and a wife. She hadn't been called that name in a long time.

The man sighed. The rain fixed his black hair to the sides of his forehead, and it curled beneath his ears.

"Listen," he said. "Where's your daddy?"

"Gone."

"Gone?" He squinted.

"Gone."

The rain fell faster. The kid in the overalls tucked the edges of the quilt around my mother as the shiner knelt down to lift her. He was taller than my father, and stronger. I remembered the phone call my mother had made three days earlier.

"You're Flynn," I said.

"I am."

He cradled my mother's body into his arms and carried her to the Tacoma. As he walked, the quilts sloughed off her like shedding skin.

"She'll sit between us," he said, sliding her in through the passenger-side door. "Get in."

I climbed in beside my mother and slipped my arm through hers. Her body fell into mine.

"Wait here," Flynn said.

I watched him from the sideview mirror. He grabbed an ax from the back of the truck, and the boy balanced a long snake pole over his head. At the grave Flynn lifted the pole and told the boy to step back. He crouched down, scooped the snake up just below the jaw, and pinned it to the earth beneath the sugar maple. Then he threw the ax down, cutting its head clean off.

Aside from my father, I'd never seen someone handle a snake with such grace. He left the snake to twitch beneath the tree, tossed the pole and the ax into the back, and climbed into the front seat. The sky thundered as a wave of rain washed the windshield.

"What about your boy?" I asked.

"It's all right," Flynn said, turning the engine. "Sonny don't mind the rain."

Sonny sat on top of the wheel well and knocked on the glass of the rear window. Flynn raised his hand in recognition. His arm brushed my mother's as he shifted gears. We took off down the hill, the tires drawing angry stripes in the grass as the rain started to pour.

x x x

Flynn and his boy lived in a dark house in the woods at the base of Violet's Run, roughly five miles up the mountain from the bottom of our hill. I'd never known that anyone lived any farther north than we did. The cabin crouched behind a congregation of balsams, and it stood as long as it was tall, with a stone chimney and a lookout perch along the top. Fresh lumber lay stacked on either side of the wooden door, a hammer left on the front steps.

When I stepped out of the Tacoma, my foot snagged a wire of strung soup cans.

"Watch your step," Flynn said as he hoisted my mother from the front seat.

"You trying to keep raccoons away?" I asked.

"Something like that."

He kicked the front door open with his boot, and the house looked like it had been expecting me. The floor was freshly swept, and a mason jar of violets graced the tabletop next to a thin line of clear glass carboys.

Sonny lifted the rug on the floor and then the wide wooden plank beneath it. He stored the bottles in the hole dug into the earth below, next to some horsehair brushes and cans of white paint. Flynn took my mother's body and laid it gently on his bed. Then he took a towel and set about blotting the water from her face.

"Here," I said. "I'll do that."

He scratched his rasp of a beard and handed me the towel.

"You got any coffee?" I asked. "You could use it."

Flynn dragged himself toward the kitchen, and I sat down on the bed with my mother. Her eyelashes drooped with water. The switchblade at her hip glinted, pearlescent in the dim light. I took it from its loop, placed it in my pocket.

Flynn returned holding twin cups of coffee.

"I don't drink it," I said.

"Start," he answered.

I sat up and took a sip.

"The boy," I said. "He yours?"

Flynn nodded.

"Where's his mother?"

"Gone," Flynn answered.

"Gone?" I asked.

"Gone," Sonny repeated from the doorway.

The boy blinked at me with a blank gaze, the blond cowlick on his head spraying upward as it dried from the rain. Flynn asked me what I planned to do with the body. The *body*.

"A plot right beside Ivy's. So neither of them will be alone." I paused. "If you could get my mother's tambourine for me—and remove that snake carcass—I'd appreciate it."

Flynn braced himself against the doorframe. He stared at me in a fraught way that made me suspect he was thinking about money.

"I'll find a way to pay your fee," I said.

He looked startled. "You ain't got any money."

"I have to pay," I said. "She'd want me to."

He took a long sip of coffee and wiped his upper lip. I waited for him to ask about my father, but he didn't.

"You got a place to stay tonight?" he asked.

"Home." Tears slithered down my face as I said it.

He frowned. "How old are you?"

"Fifteen."

He sighed. "Well, shit."

A strain of guilt reared up in me. My mother would hate being beholden to this man. I remembered the money she'd stashed in her King James Bible and wondered how much was left.

"Take us home," I said. "I'll pay you for your trouble."

"Wait."

He sauntered out of the room with his empty coffee cup dangling from his grasp to make a phone call in the next room. I looked at my mother, who still had that restless expression on her face.

"I'm sorry, Mama," I whispered. "I'm sorry, I'm sorry, I'm sorry."

I'd never sounded more like my father. Flynn reappeared just as I was wiping my face with the hem of my skirt. He sat down next to me on the bed and rubbed the holes in his jeans with his hand.

"I want you to come with me," he said. His voice was kind.

"Where?"

His eyes fastened to mine. "Aunt Bette's. You'll be cared for there."

He exhaled, and then I understood. Folks resorted to Aunt Bette's when there was no one left, no kin who wanted you. I glanced over at my mother.

"I can't leave her," I said.

"You don't have to worry about her now," he said. "She won't be alone."

Sonny slipped in and dragged a large rocking chair next to the bed, and set about tilting back and forth in it.

"You can't leave her here," I said.

"Just till I get back," he said. "Sonny knows how to keep good company."

A round of thunder boomed outside, and I clenched a fist.

"Drive me home," I said. "I can take care of myself."

He sighed. "No."

"Why?"

"Because your daddy ain't around. And I ain't sure he's fit to care for you anyhow."

I looked down at the corduroy quilt on his bed, remembering how my father had held me underwater, the luster of his damp shirt, the brooding of the current.

"You heard," I said.

"Everybody heard," Sonny answered as he rocked, never once lifting his eyes from my mother's face.

"Ain't you been lonely up there anyhow?" Flynn asked.

I didn't want him to know the truth. "I'll stay here till she's buried." I clutched my mother's hand. "You can grant me that."

"You can't." Flynn sighed again. "I got business."

"I don't care about your business."

"That's just fine." His voice rocked like a lullaby. "But I do."

I watched my mother, waiting for her to tell me what to do.

Wren, she'd written, *I have to tell you—*

I knew what would happen next. These were the stones from which mountain myths were built. Word would spread, and soon there would be stories swapped among the hills about the day the drunkard drove down Violet's Run with a dead woman buckled into the passenger seat. *She looked just like a puppet,* the raconteurs would swear, and the audience would feast on it until the story became theirs to share. But that story would be a lie, because Ruby Bird had never been the puppet, not once in her life. I only wished the same could be said of me.

HOME

The first night at the home, I sat on a top bunk in the dark and listened to the gaggle of girls below me. I thought of my mother's stories about growing up as the oldest of seven girls, how she and her sisters pushed their bunk beds together. Closest to the sky, she'd said, but she'd meant farthest away from her father, from the mice on the floor, from her own mother, who always carried a baby and the flu. Her family had scattered across the state since my parents' wedding, and the only time my mother heard from them was when her father asked for money. It was no wonder she'd married my father and hadn't looked back.

Before leaving me at Aunt Bette's, Flynn had taken me to my parents' cabin to gather my things. The sun had already set. I took all the dresses my mother had sewn for me. Each one was a story from her past. I'd heard about the sweltering afternoons she and Ivy spent in matching floral skirts, lounging on a picnic bench by the school playground while Ivy flipped through magazines and my mother studied. Before my father whisked her away, she'd lived a life apart from him. She loved math, she loved to measure and sew fabric into beautiful things. Every stitch was exact, strung and restrung until it matched all the others.

She'd fashioned my dresses out of her old ones from her sixteenth birthday, from Ivy's wedding, and from the high school graduation ceremony they both had skipped.

As I stood in the hallway, I realized I wouldn't be back for a long time. I felt the grooves in the wall with my fingers, letting them lead me to my mother's door. At her dressing table, I found the mason jar she'd used as a jewelry box. It held nothing but bobby pins and loose buttons. She had treasured only one earthly thing, besides Ivy and me—the knife that Ivy had given her.

I glanced at my dark figure in the mirror. Behind me a specter hovered in the reflection. Flynn, coming to urge me along.

"Come on, now," he said, his voice a hush. "Before it gets too late."

Aunt Bette had waited up for me, a lit candle melting into a small pond on the mantel. Flynn didn't come inside. I turned to look behind me before entering the silent house. Already the Tacoma's headlights receded as he backed out of the lot.

Aunt Bette's house smelled like old milk and older yarn. One hallway vaulted into the next. She ushered me up the stairs and through the first door into a room crowded with bunk beds.

The girl with the glittery nails appeared by candlelight from the top bunk.

"I'm Emma," she said, "Dump your bag, and I'll give you an arm up."

I left my things and gave Emma my hand. There were six beds, all but one of them filled.

"You can have the one next to me," Emma said as she settled back into bed.

She found a flashlight in the bottom of her sleeping bag and thumbed the switch. Her skin glinted against the shadows.

"Whatever happened to you must have been bad. Aunt Bette never takes anybody in the middle of the night," she said.

"It's my mama," I said. "She's dead."

We sat with the flashlight between us, the gruff breathing of the girls growling down below.

"My first night here, I did this." Emma showed me three piercings along the ridge of her right earlobe. "One to remember each brother I left behind. You won't forget tonight," she said. "But soon one day will run into the next. Then it won't hurt so bad."

"Where's your family?" I asked.

"Farmed out across the county. My mom has three other kids, and our house got condemned after the chemical spill in Elk River a few years back. State of West Virginia said we had to go." She pushed her lips together. "For a long time, I didn't know who I was without my brothers."

I thought of Ivy's boys, the mothers we'd lost.

"Emma," I said. "Pierce my ears."

My mother had never owned a pair of earrings. *A name like Ruby is jewelry enough*, my mother's mother had told her when she was thirteen and asked for a necklace. *A preacher's wife needs no decoration*, my father had assured her when she walked down the wedding aisle without a veil.

"You done it before?" I asked Emma.

She nodded. "I did my own. I got just the pair for you, too. Come on."

We slipped off the beds, and she pulled out a sock full of earrings from the top drawer in the corner bureau.

"Here." She withdrew two tiny silver birds and shone the flashlight on her palm. "Perfect for a Wren."

Their wings had deep grooves, stretching them out in flight.

Emma sat me in a folding chair by the stove in the kitchen while she boiled two safety pins. When it was time, she sank a pin through my right ear, then my left. I closed my eyes. The piercing came quick and strong and silent, like the quiet fangs of a copperhead. She smoked one of Aunt Bette's Virginia Slims as she worked. The sweet smolder nested in my nostrils as Emma clasped the back on each earring.

"Done," she said.

I opened my eyes and saw Caleb standing in front of me with a cube of ice in his palm. He held it to one ear, then the other, while Emma took pulls from the cigarette. A secret conversation passed between Caleb and me about all the things we both had lost. I was someone different now. My mother was gone, and I had no fire left.

x x x

I waited three days for my father to come for me. On the third day, I stood in the front yard in a marigold dress, looking just like my mother. Even my hair was plaited, her switchblade at my hip. Aunt Bette had promised someone would take me to my mother's grave. I had dressed like my mother in the hope that it might lure my father back to me. I waited, still as a crucifix, for him to crest the hill. *Come,* I willed him. *Come, come, come.*

Flynn came instead. Sonny ate kernels of dried corn in the bed of the truck.

"My father didn't show, did he?" I asked as I climbed in.

He scratched the back of his head. "No."

Flynn stared at me a long time. Before he pulled onto the road, Emma rushed out the front door, clutching the neck of her guitar. She hopped into the back, and we wound our way up toward Violet's Run, where Flynn parked at the bottom of the hill. The sun sat low, the grass grew tall, and I knew that my father wasn't coming. Grief hadn't kept him away. Shame had. His daughter's lack of faith had made him mortal, like that moment Adam first felt shame at his own nakedness in the Garden of Eden, even though he'd been naked all along.

"I'll wait here till it's done," Flynn said as Emma and I left the truck.

"Come on," she said. "I'll walk with you."

She hooked one arm through her guitar strap and the other through mine, and together we climbed the hill. The trail of flattened grass was wider than any serpent outstretched, and it would have given my father an empty satisfaction to see it. So many folks had gathered that I couldn't even see the plot until I reached the line of maples. Ivy's grave was covered over now.

The silence of the crowd felt sharp, wintry. I closed my eyes and remembered my mother in the morning, standing in the dewy grass and staring out beyond our fields. The silence hung. I opened my eyes and found the crowd fixed on me, not fussing to hide their stares. It took time to realize that the quiet wasn't out of respect for the dead. They were waiting for the burial rite to begin. Without my father there to lead it, folks looked to me instead. I couldn't handle my father's snakes, I couldn't perform his miracles, and I couldn't slay his audience.

Emma strummed a somber melody on her guitar as the tree limbs above us sagged in the heat.

"My mother was a seeker," I said to the crowd. "She wanted the truth, even if it hurt."

"Amen," someone said. "Your mama's gone home now."

My skin prickled. She couldn't be at home so far away from me.

"When Ivy died," I continued, "my mama knew that something was wrong here. She just didn't know how to stop it."

I looked across the field, searching for violets. They'd closed up after getting beaten down by the rain.

"So I'm stopping it," I said. "Go home. Behead your serpents. Bury your strychnine."

Brother Arledge came forward. "Briar says that—"

"Do you see any Briar here?" I shouted. "Why defend a man who can't be bothered to bury his own wife?"

He stepped back.

"There ain't nothing wrong with being a sheep," I said. "But find yourselves a better shepherd."

I turned away from my mother's body and started down the hill. I should have stayed. I should have been the last to leave. That's what my mother would have done. But I'd never been as pure as her, as noble, as strong. I was my father's daughter.

x x x

The Tacoma growled to life when Flynn spotted Emma and me in the rearview mirror.

"You went back to my cabin, right?" I asked him as he drove us toward the main road. "To look for my father?"

He nodded.

"The snakes," I said. "Were they still in the shed?"

He thought on it. "No."

"Then he ain't coming back."

One of Flynn's hands slipped from the wheel. "I suppose not."

He said it like he already knew. The pines blurred past us as we sped down the mountain.

"I'll pay you back for the headstone," I said. "The plot, too."

He sighed and tapped the gas. Neither of us spoke until he pulled back into Aunt Bette's dirt drive. It still had pocks of mud from the storm. He threw the truck into park and rested an elbow on the wheel. Then he reached across my lap and opened the glove compartment, where he'd stowed my mother's tambourine.

"Can I say something?" he asked as he handed it to me. It jittered in his grasp.

I waited.

"Let the dead bury their dead," Flynn said, quoting Jesus himself.

"I've heard that verse before," I said. "Many times."

"It's sound advice all the same." He rubbed the stubble on his jaw. "You can leave all this behind now. Get yourself away from that cabin in the marshes and don't look back."

"That's what my father did," I said. "And I hate him for it."

He twisted the ring of copper around his finger. "Your daddy is a fool."

When I didn't answer, Flynn arched his back and fiddled with the gearshift.

"Well," he said.

"You've got business."

He nodded. "But promise me—stay at Aunt Bette's, and stay off the mountain."

I didn't ask why. All my life I'd been hiding, and I didn't have the strength for anything else. I slid myself out of the car and slouched toward Aunt Bette's porch. Caleb stood on the bottom step and leaned against the railing.

"Welcome home," he said to me.

Home. It was the one place I yearned for—the place that haunted all my stories—and it had never been a place at all.

Dear Wren,

I have to tell you—

> *I've started this letter a hundred times, only to throw each of them away. I thought my silence would keep you safe, keep you happy. But I was wrong.*
> *I've been wrong about so many things.*

II.

MOONSHINER'S
LOVE SONG

PRELUDE

If there was one sadness in Flynn Sherrod's life, it was this: He'd been in love with Ruby Day long before the moment he realized she was falling for his best friend. Every girl on the mountain fell a little bit in love with Briar Bird at one time or another—his lopsided grin caught between two dimples, his bachelor-button-blue eyes, his sweet tenor voice as it belted old church hymns. Flynn had never been called handsome by anyone but his mother, even if he did have a heart stronger than the first fruits of whiskey that dripped out of his daddy's copper still. With a square jaw, gray eyes, and feet almost twice the size of his father's, Flynn was taller—and sharper—than every other seventeen-year-old boy he knew. He had a mountaineer's hands, no smoother than bark, that corralled his black hair behind his ears and shielded his eyes from the sun. Every night before he rested his head, Flynn offered his own kind of prayer to the sky, that Ruby might be a woman willing to look past appearances.

Ruby—before Briar—was rosy, eager, resolute. Flynn had studied her all through high school, ever since they'd entered ninth grade and she sat in the first row of every class. Ruby raised her hand with the correct answer at the ready, even in chemistry. She never flaunted her smarts. Ruby's mind was a pistol kept at her side, brandished only when she intended to use it. Every word she spoke held the cadence of life and death, even if Flynn's ear was the only one tuned to hear it.

He couldn't part himself from the feeling any more than he could part himself from Briar, different though the boys had always been. Flynn's daddy's whiskey had been a sore spot between them even then. Briar swore you couldn't serve both God and liquor, and Flynn swore you could. But the boys still had enough hope in the strength of their friendship to weather a perennial disagreement. Flynn had dreamed of making his own shine for as long as Briar had planned to take up his own serpents. Years before Flynn realized that those snakes would cost him the woman he wanted to make his own, he made it his business to see that his friend catch one.

X X X

They were fourteen years old, fearless, and brimming with nerve, when the pair embarked on their first fall snake hunt. They'd seen their fathers hunt venomous snakes for sport dozens of times—or at least they'd seen Flynn's father, Sherrod, hunt them, since Briar's daddy was forever riding the timber wave across Appalachia. Armed with window-washing poles and wire pincers, men set out in flanks like Civil War infantrymen, scouring the hollows and abandoned barns for snakes to spike. Flynn's mother thought it was a foolish tradition. *Mountain men get to leave home to look for danger,* he'd once heard her whisper on the phone to her sister. *But trouble always finds a woman at her doorstep.* Flynn couldn't figure what she meant.

Sherrod—who was known throughout the hills by only his last name—forbade the boys to come along for the hunt, but he'd never said they couldn't set out on their own. Casting off together felt better than drinking whiskey in church, and it was a feeling Flynn would chase for the rest of his life. Briar and Flynn scoped the creek line for rattlers with only a threadbare pillowcase and a forked oak branch between them. After a long hour of stalking the reeds, they came to a bend in the creek with a small dam. Briar turned to take a piss.

"Hey," Flynn said as Briar zipped up his fly. "Look at that."

Up the bank the boys spotted the shell of an F-86 Sabre plane nestled against a gnarled tree trunk. It was small, built to fit a pilot and little else. The plane's nose had rusted clean through its rivets, and it dipped down into the water like a basset hound lapping up the stream. They waded into the water to get a closer look.

"Looks like a fighter plane to me," Flynn said. "World War II, maybe."

"Naw," Briar said, pressing a palm against the plane.

"This part of the creek runs up against Arledge's land," Flynn said. "Arledge must be hiding it."

"From who?"

"Scrap collectors."

Flynn's thoughts settled on Ruby then, whose father liked to scavenge through Arledge's junkyard on the west end of the mountain. Her name rested on the rise of his tongue, but he couldn't bring himself to speak it. He didn't dare direct Briar's gaze toward the one thing he wanted for himself. As far back as Flynn could remember, Ruby had been a fixture of his life in the highlands, until the day he found himself bewitched by the way she knelt in the fields to gather wild violets in her lap. She lifted her eyes to the clouds, her spirit like a bird destined for far skies where Flynn could not follow. To him a snake in the holler seemed a far simpler thing to capture.

"Naw," Briar repeated as he stared at the plane. "Can't be worth much."

Flynn glanced at his friend, who wielded the branch and pillowcase overhead like a butterfly net. Briar, the naive know-it-all, knew nothing about money. "Spirit rich and body poor," Sherrod liked to call Briar, and Flynn loved his friend for it. He gave Briar a leg up onto the nose of the plane before scrambling after him. Together they peered into the gutted cockpit.

"Window's busted," Briar said. "Along with everything else."

Flynn ran a hand on the seam of bolts that edged the window before snapping it back into his chest. "Oh, shit, Briar. Look at that."

Below him a coachwhip snake sat bundled in the well of the pit where the pilot's seat should have been. Coachwhips weren't native to West Virginia, but Arledge liked to collect reptiles alongside his rusted antiques, and this one must have gotten loose. Its head held steady while the rest of its body roiled into tethers. Briar slanted into the window, his face lit like a jar of fireflies.

"Look at that," he said. "Its tail is brighter than the rest of its body." He stood on his toes. "How'd it get in there?"

"Do you want to bag it or grab it?" Flynn responded.

Briar winched his lips between his teeth. He'd already flirted with a serpent in the church parking lot, and he was determined to capture one of his own. "I'll snag it with the branch. You hold open the net."

Snatching that coachwhip was just as hard as it looked. The snake lurched. Briar screamed. It wasn't venomous, but its fangs would still leave a nasty bite. Flynn hung the pillowcase on a propeller petal and held it open with a stick. Briar courted the snake like it was a preacher's daughter until all six feet of it were wound up good and tight around the branch. Then he thrust it into the case and bound it with a rubber band from his wrist. The snake threw a fit inside it, so the friends tied the bag to the end of their snake pole. They took turns carrying it all the way home, arms straight out like they were fishing for what they'd already caught.

x x x

By the time the boys neared eighteen, they'd bagged half a dozen snakes and Briar hadn't made one mention of the luminous Ruby, despite the moon eyes Flynn gave her each time she appeared. In the summertime he saw her only on Sundays: the day nobody worked and everybody fell asleep in church. The smattering of children born on the mountain spread from the base of Trap's city limits all the way north to the razorbacks and west to Logger's Nook, and Sunday was the best excuse for a gathering when June came and school let out until September. Once the church service slacked into Brother Arledge's meandering prayers, the young slipped out the back door and fled in search of shade.

Church was Briar's refuge, but Flynn remained wary of the power it held over mountain folk. He was the brooder to Briar's butterfly, who came to spy his Ruby as she sat with Ivy beneath the downcast boughs of a willow tree behind the gas station. Flynn's mother hoped taking her son to church would atone for all those summer hours her husband spent toiling at the still. From June to October, Sherrod camped himself downstream from a mighty mountain spring, armed with a copper pot, a bubbling barrel of mash, and a Marlin .35 until he met his six-hundred-gallon goal for the season. When Flynn graduated high school, he'd start spending his summers with his father at the still, too.

"Oh, that *boy*," the church ladies used to warn Briar as they weighed him down with biscuits and gravy to take home to his mother. "Flynn Sherrod needs saving."

Before Ruby came between them—because that's how the mountain would come to see their downfall, as Ruby's fault and not their own— the two boys liked to laugh about Flynn's salvation on parched Sunday afternoons outside the empty gas station. The church's faithful had long feared that Flynn's soul would be damned just because his daddy knew how to shine, and shine good.

"They's just old church ladies," Briar said once. "Feeding on gossip."

"Come on." Flynn loosened the spare ring of copper he kept around his finger. "You know those old church-lady hearts belong to you."

"Same as their husbands' mining wages belong to your daddy." Briar's lips buckled before he spit in the dirt.

Sherrod sold his moonshine off the back of his boat to out-of-the- way bars and fish hatcheries, but his best customers were miners check- ing in at the coal treatment plant who left their hundred-dollar bills in a drainage tunnel and retrieved a gaggle of jars a few days later. They liked to buy their shine from an outlaw, duty-free, since so much of their own paychecks went to county taxes. Briar had nothing against the liquor itself. He'd done the whiskey-stomp dance more than once on soft summer nights when he tasted the heart of Sherrod's run. But he didn't like that the locals' love for moonshine kept the church offering plate dry.

Now that high school graduation neared and neither wanted to sit at a desk or fall down a mine, Flynn and Briar had plans to fish, wrestle, and scheme a way to live off the mountain's bounty. Their connection had formed itself into fact, the same as the setting of the sun, the rising of our Good Lord and Savior.

But then Briar got struck by lightning.

x x x

The night before, a cold front had barged in just in time to ruin Flynn's graduation ceremony. Rain had pummeled the pasty faces of his class-mates as lightning lit the sky. Flynn figured he'd find Ruby and Ivy clinging to each other in the thrall, splitting a laugh and daring the eye of the storm to come for them. But they'd gone absent. All at once Flynn felt what a game of child's play caps and gowns were. Graduation, for a boy, might have been youth's last call before he faced minimum wage at the diner, or years of combat, or the dark maze of the coal mines. So-bered by their own futures, those boys couldn't see that girls like Ruby and Ivy had grown up long before. They knew how to feed other mouths before their own, to lie about leaving home after dark, to avert their eyes when men stared at them too long.

Flynn and Briar still wanted a final stab at danger, so they'd planned another snake hunt for the morning once they'd gotten their diplomas. When Flynn arrived at Briar's cabin after an hour's hike in the mud, the front door sighed open. The outer spigot spit water into a teeming bucket beneath it. Someone had left it running.

Flynn turned off the spigot and brought the bucket inside.

"Briar?" he called as he stepped over the threshold.

The house, dank and mussed as usual, stank of ash. Briar's three snakes slithered in a box stuck in the fireplace. Water dripped through cracks in the roof. Up above, Briar's mother hovered over Flynn from the loft, hands pinched around her hips.

"Come quick," she said.

Flynn scaled the ladder to find his friend lying unconscious in bed, arms askew. A beam from the ceiling lay crosswise on the floor. Flynn's hand steadied above Briar's head. Heat buzzed from Briar's body the way the copper cap on Sherrod's still could scorch a finger when a run of shine was hot enough to pour. Flynn felt sick.

"How long has he been like this?" he asked.

"Since the storm last night." A blush web of perspiration swathed her face. "A big crack of lightning came through the window, just like it was hunting him. Then a beam fell from the ceiling and knocked him out."

"Did you call a doctor?"

Briar's mother stared at her son, the veins on her forehead like lightning bolts of their own.

"Who he needs ain't a doctor."

"You didn't send for anyone?" Flynn wanted to shake her.

Her voice dropped. "I prayed for someone to come, and you did."

Flynn was ready to spit. "You know I can't help him."

"You can get someone who can."

"If a doctor can't help him, then who?"

"Marcella."

Flynn pushed the breath he'd been holding out of his mouth. Marcella was the mountain healer who lived way up next to the gorge at Violet's Run, beneath the razorbacks. Briar didn't have time for this kind of folly.

"I'm going for a doctor," he said, starting for the ladder.

"I ain't as crazy as you think," she said. Her teeth crowded behind her lips. "Old Marcella knows how to heal a burn better than any doctor."

Flynn rubbed the back of his neck. He'd heard stories of faith healers, and he counted them as fables. But it would take hours to make it to Trap's medical clinic, and even then he didn't know if he could convince anyone to scale the mountainside after a storm. He had little choice.

"How do I find her?" he asked.

"She's got a crooked garden in that sunny patch of land not far from the humpback bridge. I suspect she's tending her plants."

"And if she ain't?"

Briar's mother didn't answer. She fixed her eyes on her son.

"I'll be back," Flynn said.

He left the house, and then he ran.

The garden that he found beneath an easy shaft of sunlight looked more like a jungle. Glass bottles hanging from the branches glittered in the light.

"I need help," Flynn called out into the open. "My friend got burned real bad."

"Phone the doctor." A gnarled arm parted the brush. "I ain't a magician."

Flynn grabbed her hand before it could slip back into the foliage. "Please," he said. "He got struck by lightning."

The leaves parted again, and this time a hoary face appeared. Marcella's onyx eyes latched onto Flynn's.

"Lightning?" she asked.

He nodded. "You have to come," he said.

Marcella's chin dimpled as she examined the young man before her, drenched to his knees in muck. "Did you run here?" she asked.

He nodded again.

"We'll take my truck if you can drive it through the sludge."

Flynn thrust out his hands for the keys. He'd been primed for this kind of task. Sherrod had taught him to drive his old Chevy backward down a hill in the rain in case they ever needed to abandon their still site and make a quick escape from the law. When Flynn and Marcella reached Briar's house, Flynn helped her up the ladder to the loft. She strode to Briar's bedside and hovered her hands over his body.

Marcella swiveled her neck toward Mrs. Bird. "Lightning, you said?"

Mrs. Bird nodded. "Struck his eye, I believe."

Marcella's gaze orbited from Briar's face to the scorch marks left on the floor to the open window across the room. She blew on Briar's bare skin as she flicked the air away from his body three times. Then she murmured something so low that Flynn had to lean forward to hear it.

He recalled it as a verse from the Book of Isaiah:

When you walk through the fire, you will not be burned.

After repeating the phrase three times, Marcella started for the ladder.

"You can't leave yet," Flynn said. "He ain't healed."

"I healed plenty," she spit. "He'll be right by morning."

Flynn rose to follow her, but she snatched the keys from his hand.

"Stay," Marcella said. "Keep watch over your friend."

After the sound of Marcella's truck engine faded into the holler, Flynn eyed Briar from the far corner of the room. Soft air from the open window curved itself around him. He crossed the loft and grabbed the top of the ladder.

"I'm going for a doctor," he said, and Mrs. Bird touched his back.

Flynn turned to see that Briar had opened an eye.

"Hey, there, Flynn," he said.

Flynn took a step toward him. "You all right?" he asked.

"I am."

Flynn leaned over him and felt his shoulder. It was cool. Then he looked into his friend's face.

"Briar," he said. "Your eye."

Briar rubbed a delicate film from his lashes. Then he blinked as he waited for Flynn to speak.

"What is it?"

Flynn leaned in closer. "Your iris is white. Can you see?"

"It's blurry," was all Briar said.

His mama cried out as she fell to her knees. "It's a miracle."

And Flynn supposed it was.

x x x

The first Sunday that Flynn mustered the guts to talk to Ruby was also the first Sunday that Briar didn't show. The storm had hit on a Friday night, and only a lightning strike could keep Briar from missing a church sermon. By the end of the weekend, word had spread about Briar's escapades in the storm. When Ruby and Ivy left the service during communal prayer, Flynn planted himself in the shadow of the weeper beyond the churchyard, praying for the right words to flood his mouth. Ruby spoke first.

"How's your friend?" she asked, her hands braiding Ivy's hair.

"Heard he got lit up good," Ivy said.

"He's doing better," Flynn answered. "Since he got help."

He told Ruby nothing of his role in saving his friend's life. Any moonshiner knew to conceal his actions, no matter their measure. Tall tales of that night had already begun to swell: Briar had set the house on fire, Briar's toes had curled, Briar had fought the devil himself. Always the lightning had hunted him, just as his mama said. In less than two days, Flynn had already been cut out of the story.

"Well," Ruby said. "I'm glad he's all right."

"Seems Briar should call out sick more often." Ivy pursed her lips. "You're much livelier without your friend."

Flynn wiped a dark lock from his brow. "I'm my own man, same as him."

Ivy smiled. "I'm sure you are."

"Your own man, are you?" Ruby bit her thumbnail as she gave him a grin. "Ain't you a moonshiner's son?"

Flynn shrugged. "Ain't we all?"

In this his father had taught him well. *Denials make a man reek of guilt*, Sherrod had told him. *Charm the truth like you would your favorite girl, spin her around, and take her out.*

This kind of wooing had worked mysterious wonders on Flynn's mother, but Ruby didn't bite.

She flicked her braid over her shoulder. "I don't trust men who keep secrets."

"I don't trust women who can't," Flynn shot back.

Ruby laughed. "Women are better than men, I suspect."

"That so?" Flynn felt his confidence gaining. "Then let me show you something."

"Now?" She cinched her lips. "Church'll be over soon."

"Naw," Flynn said. "Brother Arledge ain't even sung the offertory yet."

Ruby looked to Ivy.

"Y'all go ahead," Ivy said, leaning back against the willow's trunk. "I'll keep watch for Ruby's daddy. If I see him coming, I'll crow."

Flynn knew this was his chance, and he took it. He led Ruby down the hill to a clump of crowded hardwoods, their backs curving toward one another like they'd been caught in a poker game. Years earlier, when his daddy still attended church, he had buried a flask of whiskey beneath the eastern tree root. The bottle was still tucked under a hemlock root arching up out of the ground—dirty, but full. Flynn knocked it back, and the liquor scrawled its rough signature on his throat. He offered it to Ruby. She shook her head.

"I don't drink," she said.

"Why's that?"

"It ain't right." The blood in her cheeks flared. "Plain as that."

"You think the world's gonna stop turning?"

She sighed. "I ain't got to like it just because you made it."

Flynn could feel the sweat on his back leaving paw prints on his shirt. "What makes you think I made it?"

"Why else would you drag me down here?"

"Maybe I just wanted to talk," he said.

"So talk."

But Flynn could think of nothing to say. This was when Briar would have swooped in, spinning yarn and winning hearts, while Flynn stood stark as a stump. There was something unapologetic and helpless in his muteness, and Ruby must have found it funny, because she laughed.

"So you're going to spend your life making shine?" she asked.

"Looks that way."

"Guess I ought to taste it, then."

Flynn hadn't realized it, but this was his hope in bringing Ruby here. He wanted his shine to speak for him. Mountain men could get drunk anywhere—they didn't need his daddy's whiskey for that. But if they wanted a piece of the mountain, something from the ground they stood on and the water they drank, a spirit made from sweet, white West Virginia corn hulled and ground at its peak by the hands of a loving father, cured and cooked until only the stoutest part of it remained, then it was Sherrod's shine they wanted. That's why they chose it: to taste the life they lived.

Ruby took the flask, brought it to her lips. Drank. When she wiped her mouth with the back of her hand, Flynn's heart parachuted into his gut.

"Well?" he asked.

Ruby's lip ticked. "It's fine," she said.

He stepped toward her. "It's better than fine."

She looked at him—her stare a knot of feeling that Flynn wanted to spend the rest of his life untangling.

"Don't you want to earn honest money?" she asked.

His lips clenched. Folks thought shiners were rolling around in tax-free dough so deep that even their briefs were lined with it, but that hadn't been true since Prohibition ended more than sixty years ago. Sherrod chose this life because it allowed him to provide for his family through the magic of his own two hands. He didn't need anyone else but his loyal customers, and he had them by the barrelful.

"Ain't nothing more honest than this." He pointed to the bottle. "It comes from the earth. *Our* earth, Ruby."

Her mouth was so close he could have kissed it. Tasted his shine on it. He spied her tongue and dared to change her mind.

"Even our Scots-Irish ancestors lived this way, Ruby. They brought their stills across the ocean so they could make whiskey in peace. You ever heard of Robert Burns?" he asked.

Ruby shook her head.

"He's my daddy's favorite poet. Burns calls those tax collectors 'horse-leeches.' They have no right to take money that belongs on this mountain."

Ruby frowned. "Your daddy ought to make it to church for a Sunday or two. Read him something else."

Flynn shrugged. "Even Jesus turned water to wine."

She smiled. "He did."

He couldn't help himself. Flynn leaned into her, and she leaned into the hemlock.

"I've never kissed anyone before," she said.

"It don't hurt."

Her eyes: wide, honest, succumbing. "Don't it?"

Flynn kissed her soft, then hard. Ruby wrapped her hands around his neck. His palms circled her waist—a small, unconquerable circumference. His knees sank into hers. He gripped her skirt, pulled it up, and clutched her bare hips.

He'd taken it too far. Ruby pulled away and slapped him. She stared him down as she wiped his kiss from her lips just like it was shine. Then she ran up the hill and left Flynn with his heart and his daddy's flask, both open and half empty.

x x x

All week the memory of that slap tortured and elated Flynn. He was wrong to push her. He'd always been guilty of wanting too much—too much whiskey, too much Ruby. He wanted so much of her that there would be nothing left for anyone else. Thoughts of her consumed him as he stirred a boiling vat of corn and sugar water while Sherrod sprinkled yeast on top. After an hour they poured the mash into a wooden barrel with a lid and left it to bubble beneath a camouflage of netted saplings. Flynn wished he could leave behind his heart for Ruby like that, so he could return a week later to find it made new.

There's danger in letting your desires define you, Briar might have said—Briar, whose own appetite for miracles brought him back to church every Sunday. And here was the thing about Sunday—it was always coming. Their lives could be sung by an arrangement of Sundays like measures on sheet music. Flynn knew he had to apologize. He wanted to. He thought of risking the hike to Ruby's cabin on the south end of the mountain, but he'd never get her free from her father's watchful eye until church kept him inside the gas station. Flynn wouldn't be able to contain his apologies when he saw her beneath the willow. They'd spill from him like water from a pitcher. *I'm sorry, Ruby. I'm sorry, sorry, sorry.*

And that was the way of it. The next Sunday, Brother Arledge took his time making it up to the pulpit. When his knees got to jiggling and heads bowed, Flynn sprang up and out the gas station's door.

A special kind of heat: running in summer, running with regret, running with shame. Queenlike, Ruby sat beneath the willow, and Flynn fell to his knees.

"I'm sorry, Ruby," he said. "I'm so sorry."

She gazed straight ahead, so unmoved it appeared she hadn't even heard him.

"I'm sorry, Ruby," he said again. "I know you ain't that kind of girl."

Her jaw rocked to the side. "Your conduct is your own. Don't use me to excuse it."

"You're right." He was sure his throat had filled with sand. "I did wrong."

She frowned and smoothed the orange-and-red pleats of her skirt. "I don't like you being so agreeable," she said.

"Would you like to fight instead?"

She smiled. "You'd like that, wouldn't you?"

"I would." He paused. "So you forgive me?"

Her smile faded as she nodded. "Just answer me one question."

"Anything."

"You and I grew up out here every Sunday." Ruby pointed beyond the vacant gas pumps. "We went to school together, too. You never talked to me—not once—until Briar didn't show."

Flynn bristled. "What's your question?"

"Don't have one, I guess." She sighed. "You don't need to hide behind him, is all."

He'd never thought he hid behind Briar, even though everyone else did. "So you think he's saving my soul, too?" he asked.

"Your soul is fine on its own."

Flynn could have died happy if those had been her last words. But they weren't.

"Besides," she said, "Briar can't get you into heaven anyhow. Your salvation is between you and God."

Flynn sank down and leaned against the weeper beside her. He'd grown tired of church folks' love affair with heaven. People talked about the afterlife when they really meant to speak on something else: pain, death, damnation, loss. Because that was the truth of it—if you believed in heaven, there must be a hell, as much dark as there is light. There ain't no healing if you ain't sick.

Before Flynn could respond, Briar sidled up beside him and kicked him in the ribs.

"Where you been?" Flynn asked.

"Testifying to the congregation," said Briar. "About the lightning."

"Good to see you on your feet." Ruby shaded her eyes from the sun.

Flynn leaned toward her. She looked pure beneath that tree, barefoot and breezy, as if she'd sprung up out of the ground like the violets at the edges of Sherrod's land. Flynn turned his gaze on Briar, who had a grin propagating across his face. He'd never paid Ruby any mind, but how the compliment of a young woman can lasso a man's heart. His white eye glowed, and Flynn witnessed Briar notice Ruby for the first time. Flynn felt a sneeze coming on.

"What was it like?" Ruby asked. "Getting struck?"

"Can't remember a lick of it," Briar said, handing Flynn the hankie out of his pocket. "But I did have a dream while I was unconscious."

Flynn would sooner join the women's choir than use a hankie. He stuffed it in his pants and wiped his nose with his sleeve.

"Well, are you going to tell us what happened, or just leave us to wonder?" Ivy came and sat cross-legged beside her friend.

"I could see two worlds," Briar said, holding both hands outward like he'd just cracked open an egg. "This world and the spirit world, which looked blue."

Ivy took the bait. "Did you see ghosts?" she asked.

Briar thought on it. "I don't know what they were—but I can still feel them. Some of them are here right now."

"Doing what?" Flynn asked.

"Listening," Briar said, and Ivy shivered.

She sniffed, remembering herself. "Sounds like flimflam."

Briar smiled that pastoral grin that Flynn would come to loathe. "All I know is, a frost came down and I heard a voice, praying a psalm over me. Then I woke up."

Flynn let him finish the story. *I woke up and saw Flynn waiting for me, Flynn who had run to my rescue, Flynn who had fetched the healer.* But he didn't.

"Do you think the dream was a vision from God?" Ruby asked.

"I do."

Flynn turned his attention back to Ruby, and his heart curled in on itself. She'd gotten swept up in Briar as if she had seen him for the first time, too. He was no longer Briar, the long-gone logger's son, but Briar who'd heard from God.

"What else did you see?" Ruby asked.

Briar knelt and detailed all the new ways he'd seen their world—the mountains shaded with cobalt, the trails flecked with indigo, the creek shimmering in sapphire. Flynn had never seen Ruby's face lit with such wonder. Every time Briar paused in his descriptions of his epic journey to the other side, Ruby tilted forward, just a little, and grabbed the hem of her skirt. Briar was rosy-cheeked and spooky-eyed and just as fetching as ever. This was no logger or miner or shiner. Briar Bird was something fresh, all his own. To see the familiar anew was a miracle indeed.

Flynn noticed Ivy peering at him.

"Come with me, Flynn," she said.

Flynn felt relieved. The pair strolled down the hill toward the same spot he'd taken Ruby to one week earlier, the hunched hardwoods still looking like they were in on some secret. He longed to go back in time and undo the slap and all that had caused it.

He dug out his daddy's flask, took a swig, and offered it to Ivy. She took it in kind.

"I hear you're a grabber," she said, swallowing. She lifted her skirt above her knees and started to laugh.

"No secrets between you two, I see."

"None." She tipped back the flask for a second hit.

"So?" Flynn asked, pointing to the bottle. "What do you think?"

Ivy replaced the cap. "I've had better."

"Bullshit."

Ivy laughed again. "So," she said, leaning into the tree just as Ruby had done. "You believe what Briar said about his dream?"

Flynn considered it. "I don't think he'd lie."

"I didn't ask if he was lying. I asked if you believed him."

Flynn paused again. "I ain't sure."

Ivy nodded, slow. "We're alike, you and I."

"How so?"

"Skeptics." The shine brought a flush to her wintry cheeks. "Ruby and Briar, they're romantics. And every romantic needs a skeptic."

"You got things figured out pretty good," Flynn said.

She ran her fingers underneath the collar of his shirt. "Do you kiss any girl down here, or only Ruby?"

Flynn braced at her touch, caught the honesty in her eyes.

"Only Ruby," he said.

Ivy sighed and nestled the flask back into its hiding place. Flynn smiled as he took her arm. Together they trudged back up the hill toward their friends—who still talked beneath the weeper and looked very much like they were falling in love.

VERSE

It was strange for Flynn to witness his best friend transform from boy to legend, but even he couldn't deny Briar's new dimension. His blighted eye had a wizened sojourner's look to it, like he was an old man telling stories of war. Under easier circumstances Flynn would have made a joke of it—called him Pap, offered to knit him an afghan— but it had been a while since Flynn had found himself in a joking mood.

Briar was just so damn *proud* of it, was the thing. He didn't realize lightning was unkind. It ought to have sent him into a coma, like Brother Arledge's nephew, who took a fall in the gorges and never opened his eyes again. And that could have been Briar, *should* have been him, to hear folks talk about his miracle recovery. His trust in God was so cavalier, so self-satisfied, that Flynn almost wanted to remind Briar that his daddy had chosen a saw blade and a tent over him and his mother. Not to hurt him but to show him that his heart still remembered how to bleed.

Flynn had a flurry of questions for his friend—like how could Briar *see* out of that white eye, for starters—but Briar didn't feel like explaining. What Briar did feel like explaining, in copious detail, was his infatuation with Ruby. Flynn and Briar had been taught by hunters and loggers and farmers that a young woman was an uninhabited land until a man laid claim to her. Both boys saw Ruby as territory to be conquered, each of them its rightful pioneer.

Flynn came by those illusions honestly—the Sherrod boys had long been the country kings of their mountain. Sherrod set his own working hours, spent his time and his earnings as he chose. He lived by his own apothegms: *Never leave the woods, never cut your hair, never tell a lie. Speak in code, work outdoors, pay in cash.* Sherrod never referred to the still as a still. She was a woman. *She's cooking good today,* he'd say. The still was his mistress, Flynn's mother his hen. That's what he called his wife: Hen. Half of Trap had forgotten that her real name was Patricia. Sherrod loved his wife and yet never remembered her birthday. He'd worn the same pair of overalls and driven the same Chevy for so many years that the rivets on his back pockets had left a cavalry of miniature bullet holes in the driver's seat. His beard had seen more Christmases than Flynn had. Sherrod had fashioned a good life by never leaving the hills that had borne him. He worked harder than anyone Flynn had ever seen, and for the first time in his life Flynn found himself wanting to work that hard for something, too.

But as much as he hoped to emulate his father, Flynn still possessed a trait his father did not understand: hope in the face of doom. He wasn't ready to give up yet. If only he could get Ruby alone again, he thought. He'd be a better man. He'd show his heart and its canyons. He had a soul, and he had faith, too—just not the Sunday-best kind that Ruby admired in Briar. Flynn's soul gazed not upward into the clouds but down deep into the roots of the West Virginia earth. For him it was a soul-splitting miracle each and every time corn and water got each other drunk.

The next Sunday, Flynn strutted toward Ruby as church let out. He knew that his chances were ghosting quick, so he caught her before the willow tree, before Ivy, before Briar. He came close enough behind her to see the stitching of her dress locked against her spine. He whispered in her ear. He didn't care who saw.

"Meet me tonight," he said. "Whenever you can get free. At the river behind your house."

She stepped back from him, pulled her braid over her shoulder. "You know I can't."

"I know you can," he said, then started to walk away. "And I'll wait."

x x x

Just after sundown Flynn chased the river to Ruby's house. The whole of her cabin sat on staggered cinder blocks, with a row of her father's steel-toed boots by a front door held shut with nothing but a leather latch. Flynn stood in the lush ground below the steep drop-off behind her cabin, peering up at the knotty rocking chairs on the porch. He watched for their tilting as evidence of life inside the house. They might as well have been stone. *Patience,* he consoled himself. He'd brought an empty mason jar with him, holes poked in the top. He caught fireflies. And he stood by, watching their lights blink. He'd wait until morning, he said. He wouldn't sleep.

Or so he thought. Soon enough he slumped against the bank and passed out. Flynn hadn't been sleeping much since the peak of shining season had hit, and he'd spent most nights at the still with his father. The jar rolled from his hands. He dreamed of high, sweet corn. He dreamed of an even higher skirt. When he woke, Ruby stood over him, an angel apparition, her face lit by the glass jar of fireflies in her hand.

"Flynn," she said.

His name. Her mouth.

"Flynn," she said again. "You're lying in poison ivy."

"Shit," Flynn said, and clambered to his feet. "It's dark as pitch out here. How can you tell?"

"This hill is covered with it." She pointed toward the rising bank at their backs. "I took a tumble down here when I was a girl. Sickest I ever been."

Flynn could already feel the itch roaming up his arms, and he was too sleepy to ward off the panic. "What should I do?" he asked.

"Jump in the river." Ruby took a step away from him. "And quick."

He obeyed and dunked himself underwater, his body bucking against the skull-shattering cold. When he came up for air, he saw Ruby sitting at the water's edge.

"You think this'll work?" he called.

Her face turned from angel to imp. "No."

"Ruby," he groaned.

"Serves you right," she said. "What do you want, Flynn?"

He believed in honesty, always. "You."

She looked sad, even in the navy shadows of night.

"What about Briar?" she asked. Her eyes slowly met his.

Flynn stiffened. "I don't want to talk about him."

"I won't come between friends." She pulled her knees to her chest. "It ain't right."

"It's too late for that."

She tossed him a glare. "Don't put that on me."

"Don't act like you don't feel this," Flynn said. "Don't do that."

Ruby took in a breath and held it. Then she undid her braid. When she remained quiet, Flynn threw a rock into the waves.

"Women's got fickle hearts," he said, mostly to himself.

He heard Ruby splash toward him, and he turned to see her hair, long and dark, grazing the stream. The switchblade at her hip shimmered in the starlight.

"That's because we're trapped, Flynn."

The words stunned him. "You're trapped?" he asked. "How?"

"What do you think Ivy and I talk about on Sundays under that weeper?" Ruby asked. "I've seen you watching us."

Flynn reddened. "Schoolgirl secrets, I guess."

"Schoolgirl secrets?" Ruby laughed, embittered. "Ain't no such thing."

She looked Flynn square in the eye. "We're planning. Ivy watches my back, and I watch hers. That's how it's always been."

Flynn eyed the rubble of the current. He remembered how Ivy stood sentry when he brought Ruby to the hardwoods behind the gas station and kissed her. It took two young women to get just one of them the kind of thrill Flynn got for free.

"Flynn," Ruby said softly. "It ain't a fickle heart I got." Her skirt swelled in the water. "My heart's shy, but it's strong, too." She paused. "Right now I can't decide which it is."

He stepped as close as he dared, let his thumb lightly trace her collarbone. "I won't kiss you again, 'less you want me to."

She moved closer still, rested her fingers on his mouth. "Don't touch my skirt."

Flynn smiled. Their lips met. He felt a rush inside he'd never felt before, his hands swimming through Ruby's thick mane. Soon her hair was all around them and Flynn got lost in it, never wanting to find his way out.

x x x

Flynn woke up late the next day, caught in a middling haze that led him to believe it was still the night before. When the sunlight broke through the parted curtains in his bedroom, his eyes opened. He blinked and squinted, shifted and yawned. It was then he realized his skin was on fire.

He staggered to the porch in search of his mama, who took one look at him and ordered him back into bed. She went about making a poultice for him from onions and garlic and some mintweed from the back garden. The house smelled like an infirmary. Flynn languished in the hot of his room, swathed in boiled herbs. Sherrod peeked in and laughed. His mother rocked on the porch. Flynn couldn't eat his lunch. And soon enough Briar came.

"Figured you'd come by the cabin this morning," Briar said, resting against the edge of Flynn's bed. "On account of the rumors about those canebrakes spotted in Logger's Nook."

Flynn had no interest in canebrakes, let alone any other kind of venomous serpent. He hoped the compress covering his eyes would rescue him, but somehow Briar knew he wasn't asleep. Even when Flynn didn't respond, Briar kept on.

"When you didn't come, I hiked over to Ruby's instead."

So that was it. Flynn let the compress fall from his face as he opened his eyes. Briar hovered, a hazy blur at his bedpost.

"Seems she ain't feeling too good," Briar continued.

Even Flynn's throat itched. "I'm sorry to hear it," he said.

Briar took a seat at the stool Flynn's mother had placed by his headboard. "You ain't gonna guess what she's got."

Flynn frowned. "And you're dying to tell me."

"Poison ivy." Briar paused to examine the red welts screaming across Flynn's chest. "She said she didn't realize it had spread all the way to the bottom of her daddy's hill."

Flynn began to sweat, and it wasn't from the poultice. The friends stared at each other—as much of a stare as Flynn could muster—as if the two were girding for a tug-of-war. Neither wanted to be the first to pull. With a sigh Briar relented.

He stood and shut the curtains. "You best rest, Flynn."

x x x

Briar visited the next day, but Flynn wasn't conscious enough to notice. He'd taken the poison ivy hard after staying out all night. The creek water had curdled his skin, brought on a bad cold, the least manly thing Flynn could imagine—when he was lucid, at least. He went from sick to sicker. A traveling doctor came and left. Flynn's mama prayed over him while his daddy gave him whiskey.

"This'll void those lungs," Sherrod said.

It took a full month for Flynn to feel like he wasn't looking at the world sideways. He was weak and kitten-mouthed. Briar visited him almost every day, even though Flynn kept terrible company. They couldn't spar the way they used to. They could barely finish a game of cards.

"Oh, you again?" Flynn would say when his friend appeared at his bedpost, a sallow smile aquiver on his lips.

"I saw your ugly face when I came to after the lightning strike. Damn near sent me back into a coma," Briar would respond, shuffling the deck of cards Sherrod used for midnight solitaire while running a batch of shine. "So consider this your due."

And God bless Briar—he didn't mention Ruby once. Flynn figured his friend was showing him mercy. But that wasn't quite the truth. It was late summer by the time Flynn felt his feet grow strong beneath him again. His daddy's business was almost closed up for the season, and Flynn had missed most of it. Only a run or two left to go before the emptiness of winter set in.

Flynn hadn't been going to church since he'd gotten sick, but he'd heard from his mother that Briar had begun to preach from the pulpit about God's miracles, destined for their mountain. *I ain't never seen so many people swoon,* Hen said, and Flynn felt relieved he'd missed it. On a quiet Sunday afternoon, Ruby paid Flynn a visit. She brought bread and a book of Robert Burns's poetry.

"I've been reading this," she said, placing the book on his bedside table. "I got it at the library book sale in Trap. Figured you'd like to read it while you recover."

He took the book and let the pages fan between his fingers. Ruby sat down, the bread nested in her lap.

"You're looking better," she said.

"Better?"

"Ivy and I came once. While you were sleeping."

"You've been getting around," Flynn said.

"Been able to get to town once a week with Old Lady Frye. I help her with her groceries and her chickens." Ruby paused. "My daddy's been spending days at the junkyard, and my mama's still nursing baby number seven. No one notices me unless I make a fuss." Her smile had pain in it. "It's a relief."

Flynn sniffed. "How's Ivy?"

"As happy as Ivy can be." Ruby tore off a piece of bread and handed it to him. "She met a boy from Elkins." She raised her eyebrows. "You jealous?"

"You know I ain't." He reached out for her hand.

"I'm marrying Briar," she said, her voice barely a whisper. "I wanted you to hear it from me."

Flynn's temperature pitched. "You ain't," was all he could say.

"Flynn," she said, so gentle that it cut him open. "You ever known me to lie?"

He couldn't bear to look at the royal contours of her silhouette as she glanced at him over her shoulder. He turned his face away.

"You *are* fickle," he said.

Ruby didn't flinch. "I don't expect you to understand."

"Why?" he said to the wall. "Because I love you and you don't love me back?"

She touched his arm, then withdrew. "Because you ain't a woman."

Flynn grunted. "What the hell's that got to do with anything?"

"Briar's a good man," she said.

"Yeah," Flynn scoffed. "The world's just full of them."

"He's honest. He'll make an honest living."

"Honest?" Flynn stole a look at her over his shoulder. "You can make an honest life having people pay you to lead them to God?"

"That's tithe money," she said. "It's sacred, even if a preacher uses it on himself."

"And I bet that's always what you dreamed of, isn't it? Living off a tenth of someone else's scraps."

"Money has nothing to do with it." Ruby could barely manage the words.

Flynn laughed, and Ruby went red.

"Briar gives me hope," she said. "Do you know how rare that is, Flynn? And it's not just hope for myself. For all of us. He'll bring good things to this mountain. Our lives will change. You'll see."

"That don't mean you have to marry him," Flynn said, but even as the words left his mouth, he could see that Ruby had sailed away from him on the wind of Briar's promises. "He's all talk." Flynn hated himself as he said it. "And that *you'll* see."

Ruby set her jaw. "He's your friend, Flynn."

"Get," Flynn said. "Just get out."

Ruby stayed calm, even though her fingers clutched her skirt. "Do you know what my father does, Flynn? How he makes his money?"

Flynn knew. Everyone knew.

"He scavenges by the quarry," Ruby said. "He takes copper out of abandoned houses. He lifts parts off of old cars by Arledge's junkyard. That's what he does." She waited for him to say something, anything, but he didn't. "A shiner gets his paychecks left in tree stumps instead of the mailbox, and I ain't gonna live like that. Not anymore."

Flynn kept his back toward her. Here was the truth: Her disapproval of his daddy and his shine hurt. Sherrod, for all his quirks, had never let his boy or his wife go hungry.

Ruby left the room so quietly that Flynn lay there a good five minutes thinking she was still perched on the stool waiting for him. He was ready to turn and say, *An honest living? Is that all you want? Then I'll do it, Ruby. I swear I will.* But he was left alone with the stool, the book, and the bread. He'd never felt lonelier.

Flynn decided he'd never go back to a Sunday service. He saw no point in it now. How flimsy his motivation had been, never once trying to fool God but hoping to fool himself. Shiners had always been decried in the hills. People drank shine in secret, but none of the work that went into it could be condoned in daylight.

He grew stronger with every chug from the growler of whiskey his father kept stashed beneath the floorboards. His lungs cleared. By early September the weather eased. The evenings went cold. Flynn stayed up and listened to the sad hooting of the owls. He would work. Every night he would work, and he'd never have to answer to any man. Shining might have robbed him of a legitimate life, just as it had robbed his father, but goddamn it—he'd choose it every day until his death because it chose him, which was more than Ruby had done.

x x x

The night before Briar and Ruby's wedding, Flynn headed to his truck to meet his father at the still site. He didn't plan on attending the church ceremony, though Briar had asked Flynn to stand beside him as his best man. It was the first time Flynn had ever refused him.

Flynn was cracking the driver's-side door of his truck and hefting his foot when he saw a flash of scarlet barreling toward him in the twilight. It was Ruby in a red gingham dress, stomping up the hill. Flynn froze, half in the truck and half out, unable to do anything but gawk.

Ruby blustered toward him, her eyes lit and her fists pinched. Flynn barely had time to rescue his foot before she slammed the door shut with her heel.

"You look real pretty," he said.

"Don't." Her cheeks flared.

Flynn sighed.

"Tell me why you won't stand with Briar," Ruby spit.

"Because I'm in love with you."

"That's selfish, and you know it." Ruby's lip ticked. "He's your best friend."

"That don't mean I think he should marry you."

She wiped the sweat from the back of her neck with her hand. "This will end your friendship. Is that what you want?"

Flynn tried to shrug. "Briar knows I don't like falsehood."

"Falsehood?" Ruby laughed. "The shiner don't like falsehood."

"Pretense, then."

"Briar ain't got hardly any family, except for you."

Flynn gave a slow nod, thinking back to the two of them hunting for snakes in the woods when they were boys.

"I'm here for anything else," he said. "Anything but this."

Ruby looked ready to shove him. "That's not good enough."

"Would you stand with Ivy if she married that drunk from Elkins?"

She bit her lip. "I would."

"That makes you a worse friend than I."

"Tell me a better option, Flynn. Please." Ruby was mad and growing madder, still. "We women ain't so free to do as we wish. You take that so much for granted it sickens me. Can't say I'm surprised. You and Briar both—you'll do just as you please without regard for anybody else."

"Ruby, if I did as I pleased, I'd put you in this truck and drive far away from here." He stepped toward her. "And I'd kiss you until you forgot all about Briar."

"Don't talk to me like that," she said.

"You want me to talk to you like that."

"Don't you dare tell me what I want." Her hands started to shake, and Flynn knew he'd pushed too far yet again. "You both think I'm a bartered calf to be passed back and forth because you're taught the world is yours for the taking. And mine is for getting took."

Ruby smoothed her hair, ran her fingers down the length of her braid. "I just came to invite you to the wedding," she whispered. "I see that was foolish now."

She turned and headed back the way she'd come. The night was bearded in black, the moon not even a sliver. A perfect night for making shine.

"Come on now, Ruby," Flynn called. "Let me drive you. It's blacker than black out."

"I can find my way."

He watched her go, and then he laid himself flat in the bed of his truck with his hands over his face. He was losing both Briar and Ruby by his own stubbornness. Soon enough folks around Trap would blame Ruby for coming between Flynn and his best friend, but the truth was that Flynn didn't care for the man Briar was becoming—the performer, the ham. The "blessed," if you believed in such things. Flynn loathed the idea that God was some kind of cheap magician. Why worship something you could find for two dollars on the midway of a county fair? But Ruby didn't see it like that. What had she said? *You and Briar both—you'll do just as you please.* In her estimation Flynn and Briar were too alike. Perhaps that was the truth of it. Flynn didn't much care for Briar anymore because he didn't much care for himself.

By the time Flynn lifted the hands from his eyes, morning had come. Behind his truck the cabin had gone golden in the early sun. He checked his watch: a quarter past five. Sherrod was likely sitting on his bucket next to the still, growing crosser with each playing card he dealt. The final barrel of mash wasn't going to run itself, and it was about to go bad. Flynn sat up, rubbed his eyes, and searched for his keys. Then he saw Briar—on the morning of his own wedding—leaning against the Chevy's tailgate.

Briar stared off into the tree line, his white eye lilting back and forth. It looked like he'd forgotten how to move. Flynn touched Briar's shoulder, but he didn't stir. It reminded Flynn of how Briar had looked after lightning struck—his features frozen as sweat slid down his temples.

"Briar," Flynn whispered. "What is it?"

Briar turned. He looked feral and unchurched in the low light.

"Something happened to Ruby." His voice chafed the mountain's still air.

"Tell me." Flynn could barely manage the words. The last time he'd seen Ruby, she'd been striding down his hill in the dark.

"An outsider found her walking the mountain road alone after sundown."

"You know him?" Flynn asked.

Briar shook his head. "Ruby had never seen him before. Said he had a bloody earlobe, split in two."

Flynn crossed his arms to keep himself from shaking. "He put his hands on her?" he asked.

"He tried." Briar hesitated, then kept on. "Ran her off the road in his Silverado and clocked her with the driver's-side door. Somehow Ruby managed to get away into the woods and wait him out."

Flynn felt a pang deep in his chest, something akin to the meeting place between dread and relief. Briar shared that he'd found Ruby hunched outside his mama's cabin, quaking in the dirt, her dress torn up the back. Gently, Briar had walked her home and slipped her through her bedroom window so her daddy wouldn't see. Promised he'd meet her in a few hours at the end of the aisle when she walked down it in her white dress. Then he ran to find Flynn.

"The one thing I can't figure," Briar said, his eyes fastening to Flynn's, "is what she was doing out at night."

Flynn groaned, scratched the stubble on his jaw. "She came to see me. Wanted me to stand up with you today."

Briar whipped a pebble against the Chevy's tire. "You're a selfish son of a bitch, Flynn."

"Seems we're a good match, then." Flynn hopped out of the truck and turned his back to Briar.

"That's why you're gonna help me fix this," he said, grabbing Flynn's elbow. "Now."

Flynn didn't believe in the magic of Briar's touch, and he never would. But the pulse he felt from Briar's hand, its ardor and sincerity, caused Flynn to turn. The thought of Ruby alone in the woods, in danger, stormed in his mind. Part of him wanted to head back to the still, where Sherrod's temper was sure to be brewing as hot as his shine. Part of him ached to run after Ruby. All of him longed for a day when Ruby would run after him. He didn't know what else to do with such a violent undertow of emotion, so he agreed to help Briar one last time.

Together they choreographed their revenge against the stranger who had come after Ruby, and the dance had the haunted melancholy of a final duet. This was their scheme's brilliance as well as its defect—it would only appear to ease any pain, the same way whiskey pretends to keep a body warm on a cold night.

REFRAIN

The man with the torn earlobe was driving a white Silverado with two fishing poles hanging off the back, Ruby told Briar as he walked her home. She'd tried to pierce one of the Silverado's tires with her switchblade. It barely pricked the outer layer of rubber flesh before the outsider took it and threw the knife into the back of his truck. Briar pressed for an explanation of the bruise above her collarbone, but Ruby wouldn't give one.

"We'll search every fishing hole on the mountain until we find him," Briar said to Flynn, climbing into the passenger seat of Sherrod's truck.

The Chevy's engine turned over, and Flynn realized why Briar had come to him. Briar had readied himself for a hunt. Just as he was with his serpents, he'd swear that no mountain was too high or stream too fast to conquer for his spoils. Briar set his sights high but never had the means to see them through. He left it to Flynn to find the better way, the smart way.

"That could take hours," Flynn countered. "Let's start with the motel."

So Flynn and Briar drove to town as the sun came up, not a word between them. The Princess Saw-Whet was the only motel in Trap, and it sat next to Teddy's Tavern, right beneath a large wooden billboard of Princess Saw-Whet herself, her dark eyes a double eclipse that cut through the dawn.

The town streets were bare when Flynn drove in, a set of paltry streetlamps casting a soft glow onto the billboard princess's bare shoulders. Flynn could see an Impala and a Silverado stopped in front of the single-story motel. He parked across the road near the barbershop and waited while Briar prowled his way along the shadowed storefronts. The Silverado looked gray in the dimness.

Briar hopped into the bed of the truck, pawed around until he shoved something small and luminescent into his pocket. When he returned to Flynn's Chevy, he tossed the item into a cup holder by the gearshift. Flynn saw its sheen. It was Ruby's switchblade.

Flynn and Briar watched the row of motel rooms for signs of life. At half past six, a brawny silhouette left room 4B.

"Look at that," Briar whispered, as if the man could hear. "His ear is bandaged."

Flynn nodded, grave. "It's him."

The Silverado growled to life and pulled onto Trap's main road. Flynn trailed ten seconds behind as the truck left town, headed for the upper gorges, where water pooled from the highest streams into a deep fishing hole. Flynn knew the spot well. He and his daddy had used it for a season of shine a few years back, before it became popular for its trout. The Silverado exited the asphalt and skidded to a stop on a dirt road. The man stepped out, blew a tunnel of smoke before stamping his cigarette in the dust. He was nothing but a shadow on their mountain, a stain. Flynn cut the engine and hid his truck in the thatched grass. Then he and Briar waited.

Here was the scheme they'd hatched: Once the man disappeared down the towpath, Flynn and Briar would slash the Silverado's tires. Puncture his gas tank with the knife Flynn's daddy kept in the bed of his truck. Strand him twenty miles from town, with no way back but on foot.

That was the plan, at least.

Flynn slid beneath the tailpipe, stabbed the fuel tank, and watched as gas leaked to the ground. But when he emerged, Briar had disappeared.

Flynn didn't need to yell Briar's name to find him. He knew where he'd gone.

By the time Flynn reached the fishing hole, Briar had already entered the water. Blue-lipped and snake silent, he crept behind the man with the bandaged ear, who stood waist-deep in the creek. Before Flynn could stop him, Briar took the outsider by the neck and squeezed. The laces of the man's boots slapped against the water—*tsk, tsk*—as he tried to free himself. Flynn sprinted toward the creek, but he was too late. The passing water skinned the rocks, and even the crows didn't dare call out while Briar held fast until the body went limp beneath his grasp.

Flynn clung to the trunk of a sycamore, stunned. This was a Briar that Flynn did not know—and yet it was the kind of man Briar had always been. Only now did Flynn have the eyes to see.

X X X

Flynn couldn't remember the last time he'd cried. He didn't bother to wipe his face. His oldest friend had murdered someone, and Flynn hadn't stopped him. Barely eighteen, Flynn had thought they were waging the kind of boys' battle often fought by men: *You took something of mine, and now you'll pay.* A slashed tire, a half day's walk. Why wasn't that enough to quell Briar's rage? This kind of revenge would do nothing for Ruby. Flynn could see that now. She'd be filled with guilt if she ever learned what Briar had done. They'd found no mercy that day, no vengeance. What they'd done, they'd done for themselves.

"We're fucked, Briar," Flynn finally said as the two of them sat side by side on the bank beneath the sycamore. "And we're shits. The both of us."

"At least we're in it together, then."

"You killed that man out there. *You.*"

"An eye for an eye." Briar bounced his knee, shook his head until his face blotched. "Doesn't that make it fair?"

"It doesn't."

Briar grabbed a handful of stones and threw them into the waves. "You don't love Ruby. Not like I do."

"Shut your mouth," Flynn grunted.

Briar leaned back against the dirt. His skin was spotted and gray.

"She told me you kissed her down by the hardwoods." Briar laughed. "That wasn't nothing but pity."

Flynn flinched. Briar already seemed to have forgotten he'd just strangled a man. He still thought only of his own jealousy, prized his own impulses above all else.

"You're a coward, Briar. You see that?" Flynn pointed to the body. "That's what a coward does. Get up."

Briar shook his head. "I don't want to fight you, Flynn."

"We ain't gonna fight. We're gonna get rid of that body."

Briar glanced at the corpse wafting in the creek. "We can't just leave him?"

"Shiners use this water. If the law comes up here to poke around, we ain't gonna pay for your sins."

Briar wrung water from his sleeve. "So what do we do?"

"You killed him," Flynn spit. "You decide."

Briar nodded slowly. "The ravine." He pointed beyond the water. "The stream pools down there. It'll look like he slipped and drowned, if anyone ever finds him at all."

Flynn swallowed. Briar had gone cold—beyond even Ruby's ability to warm him.

"It'll work," Flynn said.

With not a little effort, they hefted the corpse and started to hike. It was a tough climb, even without a body to bear. The ground had gone soft in all the rain. Flynn bit the inside of his cheek to keep himself from crying out. They dropped the body, then they dropped it again.

"Shit," Briar said, wiping his brow. "Let's leave him."

"The farther we take him," Flynn panted, "the better off we'll be. You want Ruby to find out what you did?"

They continued on. An hour passed, then another. Flynn grew dizzy. He hadn't slept in two days. By the time they reached the ravine, Flynn worried he might spill over the edge.

"We have to toss him," Briar said.

Flynn shook his head. "That ain't right."

"We're far past being right."

"No shit." Flynn put his hands on his knees and breathed. "What I mean is, we need to make it look like he slipped. So we drop him, feet first."

Briar grimaced. "Those rocks are gonna tear him up good."

"I know."

They knelt and let the man go without ceremony, so exhausted were the two of them. Briar didn't look, but Flynn watched the corpse skid all the way down and plunge into the rapids, and then he stood.

"Well," Briar said. "It's done."

They headed away from the ravine, faster and lighter now, until they reached the thatched grass by the road and hopped into Flynn's truck. They took the short route toward the gas station, where Ruby was waiting to be wed.

Flynn pulled to a stop by the downed hardwoods. Briar fidgeted in his seat.

"Promise me," he said. "You won't turn me in."

Flynn had spent his life dodging men in squad cars—a very basic fact of his life that Briar couldn't recall.

"You did the deed, now it's yours to bear," Flynn said. "The law ain't gonna hear it from me." He paused. "Thing is, though, that body's gonna wash up somewhere, someday. And that man's kin is gonna come, so you best be on your guard."

Briar nodded, the closest estimation to gratitude he could muster. "And Ruby?" he whispered.

Flynn itched to tell Ruby what Briar had done, to prove he'd been the better man from the start. But Flynn also began to worry over what the truth would do. Until today he'd believed that Briar, the spiritual show-off, was a real danger to their mountain. Now he saw that without the guise of his religion Briar was far worse.

"It ain't my place." Flynn sighed. "Tell her yourself."

Briar nodded like he would. Flynn figured he wouldn't. But maybe the illusion of himself as a holy man was what Briar needed to keep his dark side restrained.

"I don't want to see you again," Flynn said.

Briar opened the truck's passenger door, nodded in accord, and did not look back as he went to meet his bride.

x x x

The afternoon of the wedding was coppery and jaundiced. They'd seen the last of the rain, and the leaves skittered, lifeless, across the fields in the wind. After leaving Briar at the gas station, Flynn headed to Sherrod's empty still site. The shine season had ended, a man was dead, and Flynn didn't want to think of Ruby in that wedding dress. He didn't want to think of Briar taking it off her. And yet he thought of nothing else.

He remained at the still site until dark. When he made it home, he spotted in the shaft of his headlights a wispy figure sitting on the ground against the dark side of the house, knees drawn to her chest. *Ruby*, he thought, and his body went weak.

He shook as he walked toward her. But when she turned her head and her profile caught the moonlight, he saw that it wasn't his Ruby but her only friend. Ivy waited for him in the night, still in her best dress and barefoot.

She was pretty, Flynn knew. She'd fastened her blond hair up with two pearl barrettes, and her delicate collarbones peeked out above the floral scoop of her neckline.

"Ivy," Flynn said by way of greeting.

"Flynn," she returned. "I got a letter for you."

Flynn steadied his hand as he lit a match, opened the letter, and began to read.

Dear Flynn—

I know it ain't right for me to write to you on my
wedding day, but I figure it's no less wrong than your
absence. Today I packed all my things from my daddy's
house, and they only numbered two: my King James
Bible and my daddy's empty shine jars. I took them to
remind me to stand by the choices I've made.

I got so close to stopping time with your lips on mine
and your shine in my mouth that it made me afraid of
what's coming. A wedding, a marriage, a baby, another.
I'm only known to the rest of the world through the men
I belong to. I'm Hasil Day's daughter, I'm Briar Bird's
girl. You think I can't understand what it feels like for a
man's heart to get split in two. But it's worse than that
for women.

This is how I save myself, Flynn. And don't tell me
you're sorry. All I get from men are apologies, and I
don't have any use for them.

Yours—
Ruby

Flynn pocketed the letter and snuffed the match. He turned to Ivy,
who looked ready to lasso the night. Flynn didn't want to hear about
the wedding. He didn't want to think about the body he'd left in the
rapids. He didn't want to be alone, either.

"Let's fish," he said.

Down at the creek, they did more drinking than fishing. Over the
summer Flynn had used a pulley to stretch a clothesline across the

deepest part of the current, half the line sunk underwater with fruit jars of moonshine clipped to it. They took turns sipping from a cold jar on a cold night.

"Christ on the cross," Ivy said. "That's strong."

Flynn laughed. "You don't drink often?"

"I ain't got much occasion to drink, but I got plenty of reasons."

Their twin poles perched between two rocks by their feet. One tugged against the swell. Neither of them rose to tend it.

"You gonna get married soon, too?" Flynn asked.

Ivy's green eyes were lifeless. "Next month."

"Here." Flynn unclipped a fresh jar. "Drink your fill."

Ivy held up the liquor but didn't drink it. Flynn could see her freckles through the glass. She stood and waded knee-deep into the rushing creek.

"Careful," Flynn called. "Your dress."

She glanced back at him. "I don't care about my dresses the way Ruby does."

"Go on, then."

Ivy sipped from the jar and didn't bristle. "Folks asked after you today."

"They can add two and two, I suppose."

Ivy nodded. "It was sad."

Flynn couldn't help himself. "What was?"

"All of it."

Ivy passed off the jar and bent to run her fingers against the drift.

"We stood in the gas-station bathroom while I put blush on her cheeks, and she started to cry. She ain't never cried like that, Flynn."

She broke for a moment and looked up at him. In that half second when Ivy bared herself, Flynn could see that Ruby's love for Briar had injured Ivy, just as it had him. The same arrow, two hearts.

"I started crying," Ivy continued. "And we couldn't stop."

Flynn clenched the jar and spit into the water. "Why'd she insist on marrying Briar?"

Ivy shook her head. "She just can't see that Briar will be no better."

She took the barrettes out of her hair and tossed them onto the ground.

"Don't you want to belong to someone?" Flynn asked.

"Belonging's the same as being owned."

Her eyes fired, even in the dark. Nearby, the water moiled. Flynn was coming to see something he'd already known deep down. From that night on, he was going to spend much of his life alone.

Flynn leaned into Ivy and closed his eyes. His lips found hers, one mouth sought the comfort of another. He searched for the taste of his whiskey on her tongue. She ran her fingers through his black hair and gently pulled. Flynn felt himself falling, being led. He reveled in her ferocity, her cynicism, her nerve.

He knew he ought to head back to the house.

Flynn undid the front of her dress, clasp by clasp. So many buttons, each of them a clue on her treasure map. Ivy held him close, and that night she was deep enough to harbor all of his hurt, so he fell into her again and again and again. The two of them said nothing in the waning moonlight, not even when the sun told them it was morning.

BRIDGE

In the weeks after Briar wed, rumors spread about what had befallen the missing driver of the white Silverado abandoned beside Trap's favorite fishing hole. A few folks had spotted Briar lurking around the Silverado the morning of his wedding, but no one had the guts to ask White Eye if he'd done something unholy. He was too revered to be questioned, but Flynn wasn't. Folks expected him to answer for Briar, to account for his sins or provide an alibi. Flynn only told them he wasn't Briar's keeper and nothing more.

Soon enough, people stopped asking.

Time passed. Ivy married and had a baby. So did Ruby. Flynn didn't see much of anyone in those days. In the summers Flynn worked. In the winters he drank. He'd moved out of his parents' house into a squat hunting cabin near the peak of Violet's Run, just beneath the razor-backs. The cabin hid behind a stand of pines, small and cozy with a stone chimney and a decent stream behind it. The house—a quiet member of his family for generations—was the home he'd dreamed of giving Ruby if she'd been his bride.

Flynn was determined to find a way to run shine in the winter to keep himself from wallowing. A few months after Ruby and Briar had married, he built a copper pot in the middle of his kitchen and experimented with brown sugar and wheat in his mash. To keep the bubbling wheat warm while it fermented, he fashioned a square crib out of wood, stuffed it with hay, and nestled his mash barrel inside it. His corn was no good in the cold, and none of it lasted long anyhow. He dreamed of summer days where the corn fields reached beyond his grasp, and he could almost taste the river of shine he'd make from it.

Things became something like good for a while. Flynn perfected his craft. He drank it. He went fishing on Sundays. He missed Ruby. That much he expected. But he also missed Briar—the snake hunts, the hollowed fighter jets and creek jaunts, even the arguments. Flynn had never known a fiercer companion, and he couldn't reconcile in his heart how to love someone while hating him, too. Flynn didn't know what they'd named their daughter. He'd only heard from his mother that they'd had a baby girl nine months after they wed. Hen also told him that Briar's mother had passed away in her sleep. Briar had no family left now.

Soon after the wedding ceremony, Briar whisked Ruby away to a dilapidated cabin deep in the marshes. As boys Flynn and Briar had hiked up to the marshes once to kick through the swamp, search for snakes, and dare each other to invade the abandoned house.

"Ain't nobody could live here," Flynn had said back then, in awe of its barrenness.

"I could," Briar had answered.

Sherrod had heard that Briar paid for the property with his mother's wedding ring—a fee so paltry because no one wanted such a spooked piece of land.

He didn't want to be noticed; he didn't want to be easy to find.

Folks on the mountain figured it had to do with his gift, his intimacy with God. Only Flynn knew the truth. Briar was afraid. He knew if the lawmen ever found him, he'd go to prison. Worse, he'd lose Ruby. So he limped his way into the deep mountain to save his own skin.

Had it been guilt, Briar would have turned himself in. Flynn guessed as much. Shame had a way of making a man abandon what he once held dear, while fear would make him cling to it. Briar, in all of his white-eyed glory, would never stop grabbing hold of his wife.

Without much company to speak of, Flynn might have become an immortal recluse—the kind from which ghost stories and legends are built—if he'd been able to cure himself of worry for his lost love. He wondered at it every night around the meager fire he used as a stove, a heater, and a furnace for his whiskey. If he could just *see* Ruby, he thought as he swizzled the mash with a two-by-four. It had clouded into a thick corn soup, and Flynn sipped it with his palm. Good and bitter, it was just about ready to run.

Flynn had wanted to give Ruby all the cash he had in his pockets, as if money could cure what ailed her. Besides, he had more money than he knew what to do with. It wasn't much, but he didn't need much, either. Mostly he survived on deer jerky and his mother's gingersnaps. Other than that, Flynn grew what he cooked, cooked what he drank, and drank more than he ate. He found no reason to spend his earnings on himself, and he didn't dare put it in the bank. So he kept it in a jar he'd painted black, then another, then another, then another, in a hole he'd dug beneath the porch of the hunting cabin.

He had no occasion to dig it up until the night of the raid. Three years after Briar married Ruby, Sherrod got arrested at a new still site he and Flynn had opened near the base of Logger's Nook on the east side of the hills. It was getting harder to find strong, untainted springs for the still now that the coal treatment plant had contaminated much of the mountain's water. The creek near Logger's Nook was one of the strongest streams left. The law busted through their camouflage saplings after dark, while Flynn was down the mountain delivering a case of moonshine to Teddy's Tavern. He'd left Sherrod alone at the still and planned to return at dawn. When he reached the site, he found trampled moss where a pack of men's boots had torn through the land. Even worse—that dulcet scent of cooking corn had vanished. The copper still had been shot up with holes. Sherrod's bucket lay tipped on its handle, and Patsy, their hound, sat panting beside it. Sherrod was nowhere to be found.

Flynn surrendered thirteen jars of cash the following day in order to bail his father out of jail. Things weren't looking good. A lifetime of tax evasion and bootlegging off the back of his boat appeared to be catching up with Sherrod. On the jagged road home, he said just one thing, over and over:

"I ain't going to jail."

He declared it loud, then soft, then loud again, like the call of a circling crow. But something else ransacked Flynn's mind as they left Trap's city limits for their cabin in the hills. How in the hell had they gotten caught?

"What happened, Daddy?" he asked.

Sherrod spit out the window. The violets along the roadside were just beginning to bloom. "I did something stupid."

"What?"

Sherrod leaned back and closed his eyes. "Sold a few buckets to a stranger out of my Chevy."

Flynn swerved around an elbow turn. They didn't do business with strangers. "Why?"

"He offered a hundred and fifty dollars a bucket, and I haven't been paid that in years, not since folks started choosing dope over whiskey." Sherrod sniffed.

"Why does that matter? It wouldn't have led him to the still."

Sherrod glowered. "I gave him the five buckets we agreed upon, and he asked if I had five more. I wouldn't have done it if all the springs around weren't spoken for already by that treatment plant and folks still paid us what we're worth." He shook his head. "That fool must have followed me back to the site."

Sherrod was sentenced to eighteen months in prison for possession of a firearm and repeated bootlegging, set to begin before the week's end. Flynn wished upon wish that he'd gotten caught instead. Eighteen months was pennies to him. Two seasons of shine and nothing more.

His mother kept to her rocker and cried when they returned home.

"Don't worry, Hen," Sherrod said.

"You'll die in there," she answered.

Hen said what Flynn didn't have the guts to. It would kill Sherrod to bow to another man's rules.

"It's my own fault," Sherrod said, heading for his Chevy. "Now, just leave me be."

Never had Flynn been so filled with dread. He decided to appeal to the magistrate first thing in the morning. *Take me*, he'd say. *I'll tell you where the stills are. I'll give you my money. Just take me.*

But Flynn never got the chance. The next morning he set out in search of his father's Chevy and found it next to his daddy's smallest still near the silo at the cow pasture, the one he reserved for his personal whiskey. Sherrod's body lay there in front of the stone furnace, crooked and outstretched, a jar in hand. Flynn took one look and knew exactly what his daddy had done. He'd drunk the first pass of liquor—full of methanol—undiluted and toxic. And here lay his father in a puddle of his own sick, dead. Sherrod had always told Flynn that whiskey wasn't worth a life, but he'd meant Flynn's life. He saw that now. Shine was Sherrod's life. All of it.

Sherrod was light enough for Flynn to carry him the whole way down the hill, past the cow pasture, and back to the house. He laid him out on the couch in his favorite overalls and comforted his wailing mother. Flynn cleaned the dirt from his daddy's fingernails. He combed his beard, used a soft cloth to wipe the mud and vomit from his face. Then he searched in his old room for the book of Robert Burns's poetry that Ruby had gifted him, and he placed it between his father's clasped hands.

Flynn buried his father in a downy grove atop a crest of sugar maples on the eastern edge of his property, a spot that presided over the rolling hills full of trees. Many folks from Trap buried their loved ones there. His mother offered a prayer, and together they covered the grave with fresh dirt and larkspurs. Flynn took Hen back to her cabin, waited with her until she fell asleep. He returned home well after midnight, only to find a lithe silhouette tilting in the rocking chair on his front porch.

It was Ruby, with a newborn nestled next to her in a laundry basket.

Flynn mopped the grime from his neck. He was almost afraid to speak, lest it break the spell of her rocking. So he lit a match, touched it to a candle he kept in the bed of his Tacoma.

"Ruby?" he called out into the dark. "You all right?"

She stood, hands on her hips. Sweat wept from her temples. Her cheeks were sunken, her hazel eyes fiercer than Flynn remembered them.

"Flynn," Ruby said. Her thicket of hair caught the breeze and danced at her waist. "I'm real sorry about your father."

"Thank you." He wanted to grab her, hold her, whisper to her, cry with her. But he remained still, holding the candle.

"And I'm real sorry it's been so long since we've seen you." She looked at the infant beside her, then up again. "Why ain't we seen you in three years, Flynn?"

The silence slayed. Flynn cleared his throat. With Ruby in his sights, he felt grieved, frightened. She looked ghostly and wrung out. Her dress was a gray color Flynn had never seen her wear, and the edges of her skirt were rimmed in dried blood.

The baby stirred, and Ruby bent to gently jostle it back to sleep.

"Ruby," Flynn tried again. "What are you doing here?"

She opened her mouth to answer, but nothing emerged.

"Come on, now." Flynn set the candle into a glass hurricane that hung from the eaves. "You can tell me."

"I need you to take the baby," she said. "Care for it. Raise it."

Flynn kept his voice soft. "Where's Briar?"

"Asleep."

"He doesn't know you're here?"

"Leave Briar to me," Ruby snapped, then kneaded her forehead. "Sorry. I ain't slept."

"Here." Flynn handed her the flask from his back pocket. "This will help."

Ruby tipped it up and drank. "So?" she asked. "Will you take him?"

A boy, Flynn thought. Briar had a son. Flynn buckled at the envy that swam inside him. He'd never felt the need for a family before, not while he'd believed that the woman he loved was content making a family with someone else. Now that he'd lost his daddy, Flynn's heart felt lost at sea. He could use a ballast, a son to hold fast to. But taking a child from Briar was underhanded and cruel—even if he didn't deserve Flynn's kindness.

"I don't know how to take care of a kid, Ruby," he said. "Let alone Briar's boy."

"You're lonely here, ain't you?"

"That ain't a good enough reason."

Ruby sighed, ragged. "You're the only person who will care for him better than I can—and I just can't. Wren is only two years old. Please, Flynn."

Wren. So that's what Ruby had named her daughter. Ruby's stare, dry and shredded, rubbed Flynn raw. He watched her and felt trammeled with grief. Ruby seemed—above all else—hungry. But this hadn't unsettled him. Ruby had always known hunger. What Flynn found in her face that hadn't been there before was fear.

"This ain't for Briar," Ruby said. "He won't care one way or the other, I promise you. This is for me."

Ruby was right, Flynn realized. Briar loved his wife and his God, but he cared only for himself. The day of the strangling had proved it. Flynn thought about that last afternoon he and Briar spent together, Flynn so Ruby-crazed that he couldn't see straight. And he guessed he'd been wondering these past few years if his love had faded into all his solitude. Into all his whiskey. It felt different—a thousand notches had worn into tongues and grooves, forming a labyrinth in his heart—but love still remained.

"All right," Flynn said. "I'll take him."

Ruby nodded, and the moment hung without beginning or end. Flynn wanted to get swallowed in it, to never return to a life where his father lay dead. He wanted time to reverse in on itself, to go back to the lightning storm so Flynn could board up Briar's windows. Then he'd have a shot at Ruby. And he'd still have Briar.

Ruby turned her shoulder to leave. Reason grabbed hold and told Flynn they might never be alone again.

"I have something for you," he said, pulling his wallet from his back pocket.

"Flynn," Ruby said. "I ain't in need of your charity."

He handed it to her anyway. "Open it."

She opened the wallet and drew in a breath. Her pearl-handled switchblade lay flat in the center of her palm. Flynn had kept it with him since that night at the Saw-Whet Motel when Briar found it in the bed of the Silverado. The knife had become a relic of what Flynn once hoped for—a shared life with his beloved—and an emblem of a tarnished youth, departed. Now that he had Ruby's boy, he no longer needed such a grave vestige of the past.

"Flynn," Ruby whispered. "Where did you get this?"

Flynn shook his head. "Don't worry."

Ruby's voice gave out. "What . . . what did you do?"

Flynn blew out the candle, swore to Ruby the story wasn't his to tell. Sometimes there's no redemption left, he told her. Sometimes there are only lost things, getting found.

CODA

After Ruby faded into the woods, the baby boy woke. Flynn had never been so unsure what to do, with a howling infant cradled in his elbow. He fed the baby a bottle of formula that Ruby had left, and he ate, and ate, and ate. The boy nodded off. Flynn still didn't know what to do, so he slipped the baby into a pillowcase and cushioned him in the crib of hay he'd built for his winter moonshine.

Flynn decided this baby was all right, as far as infants went. Coral cheeks, an old man's stare. Fingers and toes small enough to lose. Flynn reclined on his bed, kicked off his boots, and watched the boy breathe. He remembered what Sherrod had called him when he was young.

"Listen, Sonny," Sherrod had said on the day Flynn had first seen a copper still. "I'm gonna teach you how to shine."

Sonny, he thought. A good name given by a good father. That's what he would call Ruby's boy.

He looked at the empty black jars he'd opened to bail Sherrod out of jail, left in a crowd in the corner of his bedroom. There were four more stowed under his porch, each of them like a sinkhole in his chest. Why store money in jam jars while Ruby and her girl went hungry? He decided to keep two of the jars for Sonny and mail the rest to Ruby at Ivy's trailer, with no return address. If the cash appeared anonymously, Flynn hoped she'd take it. From that day onward, Flynn sent her half of everything he had.

As years passed, Flynn grew thankful for the company Sonny gave him. He hoped Sonny would one day become his partner—the same way Flynn had been Sherrod's—even as he feared that his beloved way of life was dying. By the time Flynn reached his Jesus year, just thirty-three and already feeling older than a grandpa, conditions had gotten tougher than ever for moonshiners. Farmers grew more reluctant to surrender their sweet corn, purchasing sugar in bulk set off alarms, and planes flew low to the tree line in search of camouflaged stills.

None of that bothered Flynn as much as the mountain's infatuation with opiates did. Heroin gave folks the kind of community they'd once found in church—one with a leader and some loyal followers, a shared resolve to outlast another long winter. Just like Flynn, everyone in the hills hoped to divine some way to feel less alone.

But Flynn would keep faith in his whiskey, even if no one else would. He did his best to stop himself from mulling over how Briar might have made a decent partner, if he'd never gotten struck by lightning.

If Briar had never done what he did.

Flynn determined not to cast himself down over it. He found his chronic sadness a comfort. His whiskey told a story; it sang out a sweet and bitter tune. He wholly devoted himself to it. Moonshine was Flynn's art, his wife, his mistress, his life. His heart never grew back the strength to fall in love with another woman, but it fell for his moonshine over and over again every spring.

Flynn loved his whiskey so much that he shied away from describing its flavor. And yet every customer asked him to do it. Flynn never flowered his words the way Briar did, but he'd learned a thing or two from his old friend's elocutions. Folks didn't want details as much as they wanted to be told a story. And Flynn packed a tale in every bottle—the same story, in fact. When prospective buyers got around to asking after the taste, Flynn told them about Ruby instead.

"It tastes like heartbreak at midnight," he'd say.

Or, "Like kissing your best friend's girl."

These stories, of course, were exactly what folks hadn't known they wanted to hear. Flynn loved Ruby through his shine because he'd lost her. Making whiskey was an ode to his lost love, and people bought it, three bottles full.

x x x

All that changed the night Ivy died. It had been thirteen years since Ruby left Sonny on Flynn's porch. When the call came—Ruby's voice choleric—Flynn knew that something terrible had happened. He feared for her girl. Whispers around the mountain swore that Wren had almost drowned by Briar's hand, and Flynn knew exactly what the hands of that preacher could do. He'd known for sixteen years, and he'd never said a word.

"It's Ivy," Ruby said into the phone. "She's dead."

Flynn felt like he'd been socked in the gut with a brick.

"I'll meet you at the trailer," he said before hanging up the line.

He left Sonny fast asleep on the couch. Flynn hoped he'd stay that way until morning. When Flynn pulled the Tacoma into the gravel lot in front of Ivy's trailer, he found a great fire burning in the front yard. Greedy, it grew, clawing at the curve in the roadway. Flynn jumped out and ran toward it. *Crazy Ricky*, he thought. *He's gonna burn that body.* The hair and flesh would stink all the way to Trap.

Flynn readied himself to muscle Ricky to the ground. But on the other side of the flames, it was Ruby who stood with her legs apart, throwing Ivy's things into the fire. Her dark eyes swallowed the light from the blaze.

"Where's Ricky?" Flynn shouted.

Ruby tossed in Ivy's wedding quilt. "I sent him away. He ain't got the stomach to burn Ivy's things."

Flynn tried to be gentle. "Why do they need to be burned, Ruby?"

Her head snapped toward him. "They're all infected. All."

He stepped toward her and felt the fire on his cheeks. "Does it need to burn right now?"

She knelt and took up what looked to be Ivy's wedding dress. "I ain't gonna let this sickness kill anyone else."

Flynn reached out for a set of winter coats, but Ruby blocked his arm. "Don't," she said. "You'll catch it."

"Tell me, Ruby," he said. "What happened?"

She looked at him, and the ash in the air caught her eyelashes. "Ivy got religion, Flynn."

X X X

Inside the trailer Ruby took to scrubbing the floor. She trained her hand on a small square in the kitchen and scoured it until the edge of the linoleum started to curl beneath her force.

"Ruby," Flynn said. "It's clean."

But Ruby couldn't hear him. She rubbed her hands raw, then threw the brush against the wall. Flynn went to the window and opened it. The trailer had a spiced smell of sick to it, like molded tonics and gingered molasses. If Flynn didn't know better, he'd have guessed Ricky was making his own absinthe in their bathtub. Flynn had considered making the high-priced liquor at one time to double his money, but he couldn't stand the stench of anise cooking in a pot.

Ruby sank to the floor and stared at the ceiling. "I could kill Briar," she said. "Sure as he killed Ivy."

The boy inside Flynn who'd loved and lost Ruby wanted to coax even the smallest detail out of her, but her grief deserved better. It deserved tender silence. He watched her until she looked over at him.

"You ain't gotta stay," she said.

Flynn eased himself into Ricky's chair. "Let's sit with her awhile."

Ruby started to shake her head, and she couldn't stop. "I can't do this," she said.

"Don't worry," Flynn whispered. "I'll take her out of the house. We'll bury her next to Sherrod at the cemetery on our land. You don't need to watch."

"You think that's what I don't have the stomach for?" Ruby grunted as she sat up. "I can't survive here without her, Flynn. I can't be Briar's lover. I can't be the preacher's wife. I can't mother what's left of our mountain. I can't."

Flynn clasped his hands to keep him from reaching out for her. "You don't have to."

She didn't hear. Instead her head fell to the side. "We should have left when we were seventeen, just like Ivy wanted to. I kept her here."

"Ivy knew you loved her."

"It wasn't enough." Ruby wiped the soot from her temple, then shot a glance toward the trailer's front door.

"Briar's coming," she said.

"No, he ain't."

She stood. "You think you know everything, don't you, Flynn?"

"I know Briar. And if he's got something to feel guilty about, he ain't gonna show his face."

"His guilt is years too late."

The night Ruby sat up with Ivy's body was the only night Flynn and Ruby ever spent together. He could see how anger had devoured the grief she felt. He'd witnessed it before—hell, he'd felt it before with his own daddy. It wasn't hard to believe that if you got mad enough, the world might spin backward and undo that which could not be undone.

"There never was a woman so foolish," Ruby finally said, sometime after midnight. The lamplight glowed soft like the rising sun on Easter morning.

"Who?" Flynn asked. "Ivy?"

Ruby shook her head. "Me. I figured I was saving myself from an illegitimate life by not marrying a shiner. And what am I now? Married to a swindler, just like my mother."

"Briar don't see himself that way," Flynn answered.

"Humans do what's right in their own eyes. That don't make it right."

"What did you expect?" Flynn rubbed his jaw. "Briar ain't changed since we were young."

"I thought God was speaking through him. That whole story he told about seeing our mountains cast in sapphires—I thought he was prophetic. He saw the riches I've always known were hidden deep in our land, the ones that have nothing to do with coal. I thought he'd bring them here, Flynn. Now I see it was only Briar's delusions the whole time." She fingered the strands of hair that had fallen from her braid.

"He always had such a mystery about him. I trusted it would end up pointing somewhere, and it only sent me in circles."

Flynn dared not defend Briar, even if he did find that most good intentions, God-centered or otherwise, ended up pointing nowhere in the end.

"Here's what scares me, Flynn. I feel God in here." She touched her heart. "I feel it no matter what Briar does. But what if Wren don't?"

"You're afraid for her soul? That she's gonna choose the wrong kind of life?"

"She never got to choose." Her eyes fell. "I wanted to save her from the life I lived with my father, and that's exactly what I gave her."

"You did the best you could."

Ruby laughed. "Did I? Keeping Wren in Briar's house is the worst thing I ever done. Do you know what he did to her, Flynn? He tried to *drown* her. And still I didn't leave him."

"Ruby," Flynn said. "You're grieving."

"Well." Ruby straightened. "Grief can make clear what was clouded."

Flynn knew it was true. It seemed that night, with a fire of Ivy's possessions smoldering right outside the window, Flynn might have been granted a second chance.

"Leave him, Ruby."

"I can't."

"Why?"

"I promised myself and God that I'd serve Briar until I died."

Flynn exhaled. He longed to tell Ruby that he'd seen her husband strangle a man. Briar hadn't earned Flynn's loyalty or his silence. Even so, Flynn had pledged to remain faithful to the moonshiner's way of life, and that meant keeping his word. If a shiner forfeited it, soon he'd have nothing left.

"Ruby," Flynn started. "You can end this."

She broke then, and Flynn lifted a tear from her cheek.

"How?" she asked.

"Turn him in for trying to drown your daughter."

"To the law?"

Flynn nodded. "They'll give you a safe place to stay," he said. "Or you can stay with us until you're on your feet."

This might have been the first time in her life that Ruby stopped fighting. "All right," she said. "All right."

Flynn's heart shattered a little from hope, if such a thing were possible. "I'll take you to the station myself."

"I'll have to bring Wren," Ruby said. "I can't leave her."

Flynn nodded. He'd need to add another room to the hunting cabin for them. "Of course."

Ruby lifted her eyes to his. "No one in Trap will look at you the same."

"They'll still like the taste of my whiskey, I suspect."

"Let me bury Ivy." Ruby smoothed her skirt. "And then we'll go."

He nodded. "If you can wait at the grave, I'll come for you."

"And I'll need a divorce," she started.

"You'll need money."

"I got money." She reddened. "The money you sent—it was you, wasn't it? I've been saving it."

Flynn nodded. Ruby had been wanting out for a long time.

X X X

Flynn didn't want to die from happiness. He wanted to live for it. He rushed home and woke Sonny from his slumber.

"Find a broom," he said. "And quick."

Just after dawn Flynn collected a pile of fresh lumber to expand the sun porch. It wouldn't make a perfect second bedroom, but with a door and a daybed it would do the trick. He'd put in a skylight next to the lookout perch, he thought. Wren ought to like that.

Sonny swept the same patch of flooring three times over before Flynn shuffled him into the bedroom. Then he gathered some fresh violets from the nearby hill, placed them in one of his shine bottles. He pulled a red ribbon out from the sewing basket his mama had kept in his cupboard and tied it around the vase. He smiled. And then he fluffed the pillows and spread some fresh fabric over his worn sofa. His mama would have been proud. Ruby would feel at home here, and right quick, too.

But all of that was not to be. By midmorning Flynn had completed the preparations for the burial, since it was fixing to rain. He'd called in a favor with the gravedigger, waited next to Sherrod's plot as Ivy's coffin was lowered into the ground. Then he returned home.

He wanted to let Ruby grieve her friend. He wanted her to come with him, to choose this life, to follow it through.

Flynn had long ago befriended the agony of waiting. He hadn't slept, and the late morning passed like molasses. He sat on the porch between the rough lumber he'd just posted. The sky bruised. He took a sip of shine, then a swig. He'd meant to shower himself, shave, and change the clothes he'd been wearing since the day before. He'd wanted to cut down the rusted ring of tin cans Sonny had strung along the ridge of his property. Flynn paced, then sat, then paced again. By noon he gave in. He ought to pick Ruby and Wren up before the downpour started, he reasoned. He pulled out his keys and headed for the Tacoma until he saw Dr. Ed walking toward him.

It was no good sign, a doctor walking. Flynn prayed for the first time since he was seventeen.

Don't be for Ruby, don't be for Ruby, don't be for Ruby.

But it was. When he heard the news, Flynn sent the doctor away. The sweet sounds of his mountain ceased, even as rain started to fall.

"Hey, Daddy." Sonny came up behind him. "Hey, Daddy, hey."

His boy wasn't much for words, but he was there, and Flynn couldn't bear to be alone. He placed a hand between Sonny's shoulder blades and leaned in. The world had fuzzed over. Sonny led him to a spigot, where Flynn splashed water on his face.

"Go fetch the quilts. And the ax and the snake pole," Flynn said. "We got a serpent to kill."

Flynn might have killed himself for all the swerving the Tacoma did as he drove toward the sugar maples. He couldn't see straight. Sonny tumbled about in the back. When he saw Wren fixed over her mother's limp body, a weary wrath overtook him. He wasn't sure how, but he knew Briar was at fault. The horizon roved like an ocean wave. He slid to a stop, and Sonny hopped out with the quilts.

Flynn watched Wren, who looked first like Ruby, then Briar, then back to Ruby again. All the hope he'd stored up drained out of him. A hem of lightning stitched the sky. He cracked open the driver's-side door and planted his boot on firm ground. He swayed and steadied, promising himself Ruby's would be the last body he'd ever bury on Violet's Run.

X X X

Ruby's girl was a problem. Flynn didn't know what to do with her. He could have let Wren stay in his hunting cabin, but Flynn had business to tend to, vengeful business, and Wren couldn't witness it. *Keep her, Flynn,* he could almost hear Ruby begging as he watched her girl seated at the end of his bed. *Keep her safe.*

It knifed his heart to send Wren to the Tacoma so he could drop her at Aunt Bette's. He might as well have been leaving his own child, so strongly he felt that Wren ought to have been his. But if Briar came hunting for Wren, he'd come to Flynn's first. Wren would be hidden at Aunt Bette's, closer to town. He took a last look at Ruby before leaving, ran his fingers over her collarbones, her knuckles, her feet. All of her here, and yet none of her his.

"Sonny," he whispered to his boy, who was stationed in the rocker nearby. "I know it don't seem like it, but Ms. Bird is family to us. And we don't leave family alone in death till they're buried. Am I right?"

"Right."

"Can you keep her good company till I get back?"

"She'll get the best company, Daddy."

Sonny pulled the rocker close to Ruby, and it was the kindest thing Flynn's boy had ever done. The night Flynn agreed to take Sonny as his own, he'd thought of it as a gift to Ruby—one she didn't need to repay. But for a long while now, Flynn saw the debt as his. Ruby had given him a family, a friend, and a future. Briar's boy had grown into a young man that Flynn cherished, just the way Sherrod had once cherished him.

In the Tacoma, Flynn drove like he and Wren were falling down the mountain. Fog from the rain filled every breath, and the stars hid behind the storm. Flynn left on his windshield wipers long after the rain had stopped.

"You should turn me in," Wren finally said.

Flynn took a right onto Aunt Bette's crooked road. Trap lay sleeping at the bottom of her hill. "What for?"

Wren leaned her head into the window. "Killing my mama."

"You ain't killed your mama," Flynn said. "A snake did."

"You don't understand. She took it from my hands. I didn't believe enough, and it killed her."

"Belief ain't got shit to do with it," he said.

"Yes it does." Wren shook her head. "You don't know my father."

Flynn paused. "I know him some."

He pulled to a stop by Aunt Bette's mailbox. A dim light glowed from inside. Wren didn't move.

"My daddy blames me," she said.

"No he don't."

"Well, God does, then."

"God don't blame people." Flynn cringed. He'd never been one for offering spiritual counsel.

"How can you be sure?" Wren asked.

She asked without malice or sass. She asked because she wanted to know.

Flynn exhaled. "Ain't that why Jesus returned?"

"He ain't returned yet."

Flynn threw up his hands. "Apologies."

Wren smiled, brief. "Maybe God don't blame me, but I played a role just the same."

She spoke it as if it had come right out of a young Ruby's mouth. Flynn barely had the strength to speak.

"Aunt Bette's gonna take real good care of you," he said. "Funeral will be in three days. Somebody'll be by to get you."

Wren stepped out and looked back through the open window.

"Are you going to find my father?" she asked.

Flynn didn't answer. He whipped out of the driveway and hung a left, headed north on the road out of town, in search of Briar Bird.

Dear Wren,

I have to tell you—

You've heard the old proverb: Land is passed from father to son, confessions passed from mother to daughter. The only confession I have for you is this— Ivy and I did what we had to in order to survive.

In a world of unkind men, we fought to be kind to each other.

III.

DEAD WOMAN'S CONFESSION

Years before Flynn and Briar snared a coachwhip in the belly of a rusted plane, Ivy and Ruby met in the churchyard. It was the white of winter, they were seven years old, and soon neither of them would remember it.

Ivy leaned against the downed trees at the bottom of the gas station's hill. Her feet were buried in snow, and her thin coat shimmered crow-black against the ice. Ruby hiked toward her as snow swarmed her knees.

Ivy had seen Ruby in church before, though they hadn't spoken. Their mothers weren't friends, nor were they friendly. Their fathers hoisted serpents and spoke in tongues. They danced to the chime of a tambourine while a crowd of women watched in awe. The two men were opposite in likeness—Ruby's father, Hasil, was gray-haired and slack-faced, while Ivy's father was purple-necked and swollen—but they had one thing in common. Sunday was the only day either of them felt like a king.

Outside the gas station, Ruby crept close enough to see that Ivy was sitting on a pile of gloves. A dozen of them. Her hands were dahlia-red in the snow.

"You're cold," Ruby said.

Those winters taught girls in dresses what death would be like, the iced amnesia of skin forgetting how to feel. Ruby didn't ask for a pair of gloves. Most mountain girls didn't yet know how to warm themselves, didn't find themselves to be worthy of much comfort.

Ivy didn't want the gloves for her hands, either.

"I stole these," she said. "From men's pockets outside the Saw-Whet."

Up the hill the preacher's voice shuddered through the mountain quiet.

"Why?" Ruby asked.

Ivy didn't answer. She had no reason, no need for one. She lined up the pile of mismatched gloves and tied them together, thumb to pinkie finger, like a wreath. Then she knotted it loosely around her neck, took out her daddy's lighter, and set the wreath on fire. A ring of orange shot around her throat.

Ivy fell back into the snow, and the flame went to smoke before swirling into the sky. Fire to ice, black to white, one girl to another. Ruby lay beside her, and together they watched their breath escape.

That day Ruby witnessed Ivy's burnt offering for a sin she had yet to commit. By the time Ivy burned at Ruby's fire pit twenty-six years later, they'd barely remember the girls they'd once been—Ruby, the intrepid wanderer, and Ivy, who had crowned herself in fire.

X X X

After that morning in the churchyard, Ruby and Ivy's friendship became a handprint they shared, twin life lines that began and ended as one. Old churchgoers like Hasil and Ivy's father, Noble, used to have a name for this sort of union: a covenant, the kind that King David had with Jonathan in the Book of Samuel. They spoke of it as if men had invented the mystery of friendship, as if it hadn't been the libation that sustained mountain women ever since water split rock to form the razorbacks above the hills.

There was no solemn vow between Ivy and Ruby, no promise, no pressing of bloodied palms together in the firelight. They didn't need the boastful promises of men. The things they did for each other, they did in secret.

It started with Ivy, on the eve of her seventeenth birthday.

Twenty miles north of the Saw-Whet, Ivy's A-framed cabin sat on a skein of dirt that fed off the mountain's lone road. Her mother had been raised in that house, and her Grandmother Harper, too. They had no indoor plumbing, and it was Ivy's job to shovel the shit. She spent most summer nights smoking her father's Pall Malls behind the woodshed, and on the evening before her birthday, Ruby joined her.

Ruby had never left home after dark before. Hasil was the sort of father who punished his six daughters for things they hadn't done—things that mostly had to do with the faults of men. He never hit his children. That was for unsaved hillbillies, he often said. Instead he told his girls lies about what would be true of them if they got caught with a boy after sundown, if they risked donning a dress cut above the knee. *Ain't nothing worse,* he liked to warn, *than a harlot leading a man to sin.* One lash of his tongue stung twice as much as the lash of any whip, he reasoned, and the scar it left behind couldn't be seen. Ruby tried to anticipate his corrections, doing her best to swerve away from them as if they were oncoming cars. Ivy, though—Ivy wanted to play chicken with her daddy and his puritan rules. *Punish me?* she baited him in her mind. *I'd like to see you try.*

But that night, in the swell of summer, Ruby helped her daddy get good and drunk before sneaking out to see her friend for her birthday. She'd witnessed her mother do the same, once a month for the past year, as a means of keeping herself from getting pregnant for the seventh time—a trick that hadn't worked. Inside the cabin Ruby's mother lay in bed in the dark, a cold cloth to her forehead and a spoiled bucket of vomit at her feet. Her nausea worsened with every new baby her body grew. Ruby slipped out the door, her shoes in one hand and her father's latest jar of whiskey in the other. She left Hasil's moonshine next to his favorite rocker on their porch, and then she waited in the weeds. Two hours after sundown, when he slogged up the hill after a day at the junkyard, he perked up at the sight of the jar and had himself a drink. Then another. After he slumped deep into the rocking chair and shut his eyes, Ruby flew to the mule path behind her house.

Ruby could make it to Ivy's cabin in twenty-five minutes, if she ran. Beneath her arm she carried a poplin dress she'd sewn for Ivy with a small raspberry rosette stitched at the hip. The women of Ruby's faith were called to wear long dresses, lest they tempt a man with their bodies. They wore gray and black, brown and tan. This was why Ruby had begun to sew as soon as she could hold a needle and thread: to be able to wear the colors of her mountain. Lilac and turquoise and peach and magenta—Ruby loved them all.

She'd gotten the fabric for Ivy's dress in her home economics class, and she'd reworked an old McCall's pattern into a style she'd seen Ivy eyeing in *Seventeen* magazine. The rest of her classmates had moved on to sewing pairs of oven mitts, while Ruby traded the pattern's waistline pleats for darts, hand-stitched seashell scallops along the skirt's hem. It had taken an entire semester of school to perfect.

Ruby knew that her friend would have no occasion to wear such a delicate dress. Still, she wanted Ivy to have something beautiful stowed in her closet. Ivy kept it for the rest of her life, never wore it again after her seventeenth birthday had ended. The dress would be among the first of Ivy's possessions that Ruby would burn on the night she died.

Ivy was waiting at the woodshed when Ruby arrived, the smoke from her cigarette like a mist settling over the firewood. The friends crouched in the stiltgrass, said nothing, so they wouldn't wake someone inside the house. When Ruby presented her gift, Ivy hugged her tight.

Then Ivy stripped in the moonlight. The dress slipped over her shoulders, and Ruby zipped up the back. Ivy twirled, laughed at herself. The skirt flashed in the shadows.

"I have something for you, too," Ivy whispered.

She handed Ruby a switchblade with a pearlescent handle, and Ruby fastened it to the belt loop on her skirt. The gift made her smile, made her blush. She'd never owned such a graceful weapon. Ivy had chosen the knife at last summer's flea market because it was sleek enough to hide, unique enough to be worthy of her friend.

Up the hill the dry growl of an engine turning over cut through the stillness. Together Ivy and Ruby watched Flynn Sherrod and his father steal away from their own cabin across the road to make whiskey after dark. As the headlights of Sherrod's Chevy threw golden daggers into the night, Ivy ached to slip into their truck and hide herself among their carboys of moonshine.

Getting drunk didn't bait her, but ruling the hills like a mountain man did. Ivy longed for the kind of escape a man like Sherrod would never need. She wanted to get wherever he headed with his son, to reach beyond the crater of rotted wood her father pissed in behind their cabin, which meant getting anywhere at all.

Ivy loathed her life on the mountain, even though it was the life she and Ruby shared. Guilt nagged at her for wanting something more than her friend could give. Ivy hated the lime her father spread in their outhouse to stanch the smell, the scabbed chicken in their coop that ate its own eggs, the pair of brothers she had who fought more than they slept. She wanted sidewalks, curbs, and strangers—each a wonder she'd have forsaken a treasure for, if she'd had one to give away.

x x x

Ruby stayed with Ivy until Noble returned home from a night at Teddy's. His truck eased into their gravel patch before he spilled out of it and headed for the house. The kitchen light flicked on, then off. The house settled, and Ivy exhaled. Ruby kissed her on the cheek, wished her happy birthday, and disappeared into the shadows.

Ivy crept through the cabin's back door and found Noble leaning against the cool of the woodstove in the dark, his feet spread-eagled on either side of it. He hoisted a cast-iron pan in the air and then he let it drop. It clattered against the floor. He'd done this before, waiting for her just inside the house without so much as a candle lit. Noble liked to startle his daughter as a teaching method, one meant to scare her straight—even when she'd done nothing wrong.

That night Ivy's daddy put his hands loosely around her neck. His thumbs grazed her chin as he kissed her mouth, lost his balance. He was whiskey-drunk and sloppy, and his tongue swam down her throat like a trout.

"Mountain men are all the same," he said, swiping the back of his hand across his mouth. "Sooner you learn that, the better."

Then he staggered and fell on his daughter. Ivy kicked and clawed at him until he passed out by the woodstove. Barely a breath left in her, she slithered her body out from under his. Noble, big as a bear, could not be moved. Ivy lit a match, tossed it in the stove, and waited for it to scorch. She imagined shoving her father's forehead against the belly of the piping iron until he woke up with a fist-size blister on his face. Ivy would make sure tonight was the last time Noble dared come near her.

Then she heard Ruby's voice calling her name.

"Ivy," Ruby said.

Ivy jolted at the brush of Ruby's hand on her shoulder. She must have returned after the cast-iron pan sent a clang into the woods, slipped through the porch's screen door without making a sound.

"What did you see?" Ivy asked.

"Enough."

Ivy looked away, caught the beads of sweat on her father's brow. She had no need to feel ashamed in her best friend's presence, but she did. Noble had punished his daughter for her beauty, her curiosity, her spirit. The things she loved most about herself, he meant to destroy. He had a good chance of succeeding if she didn't destroy him first.

"I think you got two choices." Ruby's voice was softer than the whisper of the creek in the distance. "*We* got two choices, really."

Ivy fingered the black arrowhead she kept on a chain around her neck. Its point scraped against the flesh of her thumb.

"We either kill him or we leave," Ruby said. "There ain't no in-between."

Ivy didn't hesitate. "We leave."

She couldn't bring herself to use the word "escape." They'd never said the word aloud to each other, the promise of it too holy to be real. But Ivy aimed to be known for the things she did rather than the things done to her.

"All right," Ruby said. "It'll take some time to plan, but we'll leave."

Ivy nodded, and Ruby swept out into the night. Then Ivy couldn't help herself: She pressed her foot into Noble's skull just enough for his cheek to rest against the hot stove, held it there until he quivered and fell back asleep.

Ivy spent the night watching her father from the kitchen corner. His freshly laundered long johns swayed like ghosts from their hangers by the open windows. She could suffocate him in five minutes with nothing but the tail of her skirt. She wanted to, if only to feel her own strength pulsing through her palms. But the thrill of it would be empty if he never knew what she'd done. That she'd won and he'd lost. Ivy wanted him to live until age turned him frail, knowing she'd left him behind.

When Noble stirred the next morning, Ivy's Grandmother Harper appeared and nudged his jaw with her foot.

"Women give this mountain its splendor," Harper said to Ivy. "And they get nothing in return."

Noble's mouth hung open. Above him a paltry collection of tiny spoons dangled in a wooden cabinet, a delicate, silvery hook for every state Ivy's mother had visited. They numbered three. Noble slammed the pocked flooring with his fist as he came to, and the spoons shook. Harper poured a pitcher of water on his head, then reached for his bottle of rotgut on the table. Took a swig.

"A temper is good," she said to Ivy as Noble's spit pooled on the floor. "But a plan is better."

Ivy's mother rushed in then, cradled her husband's head in her lap, and went about soothing his burn with a cloth and some salve. This was the true original sin, Ivy swore. A man always had a woman to clean up his mess. Ivy wished she could keep her temper. At least a temper would flare and die. What had replaced it was disquiet, everlasting.

Ivy promised herself that day she'd never clean up a man's mess. Instead she'd make a mess of her own.

Harper gestured toward the porch. "Come sit with me."

Ivy joined her grandmother in the pair of rockers that overlooked the swirls of gravel in their front yard. The two of them often sat together, just so, while Harper regaled Ivy with stories of their mountain. Now that Ivy had turned seventeen, her grandmother told her it was time she learned about the kind of cunning she'd need to survive.

No legal record of it existed, Harper began, but coal miners' wives had been forced to use sex as a shield since the 1930s, when mining companies had yet to purge the hills of ore, and coal barons thought they owned the right to all the land's riches—including the women. An Esau Agreement, Harper called it.

"The law around here denies it ever happened," she said from her rocking chair, twining a thread of waist-length, heathery hair around her finger. "Someone ought to know the price we paid."

Back then, if a miner fell ill or broke a limb and couldn't report to work, his wife was permitted to earn scrips to the company store in his stead. The agreement had the appearance of kindness, but the catch was deadly. A mining wife earned scrips for food and clothing by sleeping with her husband's boss—or bosses, in Harper's case. A woman who wore trousers and preferred three daily meals of tobacco rather than food, Harper had stepped into the agreement, wide-eyed and daring.

"None of those limp-dicked cowards could look me in the eye," she said. "Not one."

Often the agreement took place in the company store's dressing room while a woman tried on an item of clothing. Some of them were prepared, and some weren't. When Ivy asked why local police hadn't put a stop to it, Harper laughed.

"The law around here don't do shit for women," she said. "You know that."

The term "Esau Agreement" came from the Old Testament, Ivy's grandmother explained. Esau, Isaac's beloved firstborn, had returned from hunting so famished that he sold his birthright to his younger brother, Jacob, in exchange for a bowl of stew. Harper had sneered her lip at the name.

"Esau was so desperate it made him stupid," she said. "Just another man, prisoner to his own appetites."

Sooner or later, Ivy's grandmother warned, a woman would do what she must for the ones she loved, and she ought to find no shame in it.

After that night Ivy and Ruby plotted their escape each time they were alone. Once they saved enough cash, they'd dump their fathers' bottles of whiskey and disappear without a note. They'd catch a bus to Morgantown, where Ivy would learn to tend bar and Ruby would find a job keeping books. No one would gawk at them as strange statues of an even stranger faith, the way they did in Trap. The friends would work, they'd keep their own money. They'd forget about shitting outside in winter and bartering for penicillin in the cracked lot of the Saw-Whet. They'd buy themselves denim and rhinestones and drugstore perfume, all the wondrous things forbidden to them by the religion of their fathers. Ruby and Ivy vowed it would be the gift they'd give each other for high school graduation, and Ivy had even begun to pack her sweaters.

Then Briar Bird fought a lightning bolt and won.

X X X

The saddest truth about Ruby: She believed that miracles happened only to men.

Their whole mountain purred with the story of Briar's boldness. No one mentioned the mudslides that had leveled most of the houses on the eastern edge of the hills, or that Ivy's own father had disappeared since the night lightning struck. He'd been gone for almost three days, and no one at the mine had seen or heard from him. Noble had skipped town before, as men were sometimes prone to do. All that was nothing compared to Briar's miracle.

Ivy had never seen her friend so flushed or fainthearted.

She'd never thought much of Briar, the dreamy-eyed logger's son who'd rather charm a snake than a girl. His mama had been hotfooting around the mountain to spread a brewing redneck legend, the new gospel of a boy called White Eye.

Ivy pitied Briar for such a stupid tale. He'd forever be known as the boy who got hit by lightning, like the girls down in Trap were known for what farmers' sons did to them in horse stalls when school let out in June.

Ivy and Ruby had been told the same bedtime story by their mothers since they were young: Bold girls become loose girls, and loose girls get broken. Ivy could see no other future if they remained. Even church girls as innocent as Ruby ended up nursing four babies and a husband. If the measure of a man lay in the deeds he'd done, then women paid from their own empty pockets. Ruby had paid a fortune to her scamp of a father. What other way could Hasil Day starve his daughter that he hadn't already done? He drank all he earned, and he earned next to nothing. Ruby and her younger sisters had to hunt wild ginseng and sell it at the 4-H fair so they could keep potatoes and carrots in the cellar. Ruby also subjected herself to crimson welts from Old Lady Frye's chestnut cane because she earned an extra ten dollars a month by clearing dead chickens out of her coop. If she missed a feather or two, Frye's cane struck. Hasil had taken Ruby's health, her heart, and her pride, and all he'd do when she turned eighteen was surrender them to her husband—unless she and Ivy left, and left soon.

x x x

But now Ivy felt Ruby slipping away from her, even as they whispered to each other under the gas station's weeper on Sunday mornings. When Ruby got poison ivy after a night at the creek with Flynn—a fool's error that proved she'd lost her sense—Ivy went to Ruby's cabin to remind her friend of the promise she'd made to leave the mountain behind.

As she stepped through the front door, she bit back the laugh in her throat. It looked like Snow White had bustled through with her broom and left a shiny quart of apples perched on the table. Gone was the trash of Hasil's daily toils. No spindles of pilfered copper sat stacked in the fireplace. The spew of old tires in the backyard had been rolled into the woods. The hundreds of keys without locks that once littered the floor had been collected in a tin can. Today Hasil had cleaned up after himself, and it wasn't for Ivy's sake.

Briar, the storm wrangler, had come to visit. He was seated at Ruby's bedside, that tale of lightning girdling his blond head like a crown. Ivy watched them from the doorway.

Ruby had never looked ugly before. Poison ivy sores pitted her face, her lips chapped as a boar's hide. Even her mama couldn't look at her, but Briar drank her in. His blue eye slid into her while that white eye vaulted to the sky.

Goose bumps sailed across Ivy's arms, and she laughed at herself. Briar had been credited as the mountain's miracle worker, but Ivy had never wasted her time on stories of magic. Then Briar went about proving her wrong. He cupped his mama's mintweed lotion into his hands and spread it over Ruby's screaming skin. His palms swept across her like a swallow skimming the morning creek. Then he blew on her neck, a soft breath so gentle that Ruby moaned and opened her eyes. A chill scuttled across the room, even though the sun pressed in through the open window. And Ivy—despite herself—swore she felt a spike of ice hit the base of her spine. She shivered.

When Briar left, Ivy took his place at Ruby's side. Ruby turned toward her, her face aglow.

"Your daddy." Ruby's voice, a scratch. "I've been thinking. Maybe more than one miracle happened that night the lightning came. Maybe Noble's gone for good."

Ivy's stomach curdled. "And now we don't have to leave. Is that it?"

"I didn't say that."

"You didn't have to. I can see it all over you."

That unspoken word—"escape"—hung between them again, dangling like a dead fish on a hook. Ruby caught the despair in her friend's voice, sought to calm it.

"I've finally let go of the breath I've been holding all my life." She sighed, raptured. "I never knew."

"Never knew what?" Ivy asked.

"I never knew how much I've been longing to be touched by someone. *Felt*. Ain't you been hungry for that, too?"

Ivy couldn't answer. What Ruby spoke of seemed too precious to be real. She didn't know that the worst thing about a man wasn't his malice. It was his kindness, which he used in order to get what he wanted. Briar, Ivy knew, was about to take everything Ruby had—every last, good thing.

"It's better than leaving, Ivy," Ruby said. "It's peace."

Ivy released a laugh, dry and floundering.

"You don't have to tell me that sounds crazy." Ruby watched Briar follow the dirt path from her window. "I know it does. But I don't care."

Ivy hadn't laughed because she found it funny. She hadn't even laughed because it was sad. She laughed because for the first time since she'd grown, she was scared.

x x x

It didn't take long for Ruby and Briar's love story to settle in Ivy's chest like a summer sickness. She wilted as Briar's grandeur swelled alongside the August heat. In six weeks her best friend would be married, and Briar's engagement to Ruby marked the first of a hundred tiny losses. While Ruby dreamed of white dresses, Ivy fumed. Ruby's romantic heart had failed her, and Ivy determined she'd do something about it.

The day Briar proposed to Ruby, Ivy slipped to the Saw-Whet in the back of her daddy's truck. He'd returned after three days away, and no one demanded an explanation. Noble hightailed it down the mountain to waste the evening playing euchre at Teddy's Tavern, and Ivy hid herself beneath a tarp next to the pickax he used to chisel ore from strip mines.

She loved going to town. In the past the parking lot between the tavern and the motel had been a good friend to Ivy while she waited out her father's rounds of cards. It gave her a smattering of pocket change, a weekly crop of strangers for Ivy to fool into buying her a Popsicle at the Shop 'n Save while she filched extra cash from their wallets.

That day Ivy wanted to abandon the thought of Ruby as a young and troubled mountain wife. Instead she met the man who would turn her into one.

Ricky Reynolds found her on her hands and knees in the Saw-Whet's back lot, where the loggers liked to trade opioids in the ironweed. Sometimes they'd spill a dollar here, a nickel there. Ivy had her fingers on a quarter when a body sidled up behind her.

"Just how I like to see a woman," a voice said. "On her knees."

"Spoken like a boy," Ivy said as she stood to face him, "who ain't got what it takes to be a man."

Ricky tried to laugh, his body fragile like a tomcat's caught in a squall. He'd spoken words that belonged to someone else, a brute who had taught him that the best way to lasso a woman was to put her down. Long and lean, Ricky slouched as his dark hair fought against the wind. A cloud of smoke from a lit Marlboro plumed his head.

"What are you doing here?" Ivy asked.

"Scouting streams for fish," he answered.

"Why ain't you?"

"Just about to start, once I find my way." Ricky looked forlorn and aimless, and it gave Ivy a thrilling kind of pity for him.

She smiled. "I'll leave you to it, then," she said as she turned slowly toward the mountain. She knew how fine her profile looked in the late-afternoon sun.

"Come fishing with me." His hand grazed the nook of her wrist before he pulled it away. "To hunt for streams."

"Is that a command or a request?" she asked.

"Your choice." Ricky crossed his arms to hide the stains beneath his armpits.

"You ain't from around here." Ivy slid the quarter into her pocket and stepped toward him. "You don't know nothing about fishing holes."

"So show me."

Ivy relished this moment with every man she met. The tides between them would rear until he found himself at her mercy.

"Tell the truth," she said. "Fishing ain't really what you want to do with me, is it?"

"No, it ain't," he said, all red-faced and hopeful. Ivy knew then that she had him.

He took her to his motel room, and she commanded the clothes off his body. He lay flat on his back, palms upturned as if he had something to offer. Ivy hitched up her dress and rode him hard. It gave her no pleasure. She stared straight into his eyes as he dug deep, clutched her hips, and cried out. Her lip snarled as he came, and she didn't blink, not once. If there was one truth the men Ivy had been with knew, whether they'd spent one night together or a hundred, it was this: She would not be forgotten.

Ricky was scared, he was kept, he was fervent, he was spent. And something else—he was older than he should have been. Ivy hadn't turned eighteen yet. Ricky was twenty-four, and no lawman or daddy in their hills would stand for it if they knew. But Ivy was no victim. She pitied any foolish boy who thought he could run away with her heart.

"Marry me. Please," Ricky said as he panted.

"No," she said. She would not let him kiss her mouth.

It wasn't about love. It was about power. And Ivy had just gotten some.

X X X

The night before Ruby's wedding, Ivy floated townward in the back of her father's truck for the last time. Twilight had hit the woods, and not half a mile away Ruby stomped up the hill to insist that Flynn come to her wedding.

Don't bother, Ivy had told her earlier that afternoon. *He ain't gonna come.*

She rode toward Trap with her back arched against the truck's wheel well and her arrowhead necklace clutched to her chest. Made from black flint, the arrowhead had a mossy patina and hung from a gray chain.

A pretty little necklace for a pretty little thing, according to the squat logger who had sold it to her along the broad side of the Saw-Whet. Ivy relished the look of it hanging just above her breastbone, sharp and slight. Her father had laughed when he caught sight of it around her neck.

"That's nothing but a trinket. Who you think you'll hurt with that?" he asked as he heaved his steel-toed boots to the floor, and Ivy thought of only one word in response.

You.

With or without a weapon, Ivy knew to fend for herself. Mountain men had done her no favors. She had no need for a knight in a Carhartt jacket. Instead Ivy wanted a phantom.

She found one that sweltering night, cruising through the parking lot that split the Saw-Whet and Teddy's. His devil's silhouette cut into the dashboard of his truck. A green-eyed city boy with auburn hair, Lovett Quick had the kind of name Ivy dreamed of while she slept. Love her quick, love her hard.

Make no mistake—Ivy knew he was trouble. She'd seen Lovett seep out of room 4B after her father disappeared into Teddy's for his card game. Noble wouldn't stagger out until last call at two a.m., which gave Ivy hours to find some entertainment of her own.

Ivy licked her lips. Naive city boy was a male breed she had yet to try. A mountaineer would never dress like a cowboy, and this boy didn't know the difference. Lovett's brisk Stetson saluted, his new Wranglers stiffened, his checked flannel went soggy in the heat. Lovett had stumbled into Trap from elsewhere, the very place Ivy longed to go.

"Hey, girl," Lovett called to her from the side of his truck.

"The name's Ivy," she answered, resting her hands on her hips. "Ain't you got any manners?"

Lovett whistled, and Ivy pretended not to hear. She let him smile first, introduce himself. When he did, she strutted up to the Silverado's window, lifted the cigarette from Lovett's fingers, and took a slow drag.

Lovett Quick had eyelashes for days. He stroked the side of his door, and Ivy ran a finger against the truck's shiny white paint. She felt not one speck of dust. Here sat a man, she thought, who knew how to care for what he loved.

"Hey." She took another pull from the cigarette and slid it back into Lovett's hand. The Silverado throbbed in the heat. "You think you could give a girl a ride?"

A girl: what Ivy knew to become when asking for what she wanted.

"Depends," Lovett said. His voice sounded feathery and sick, like the dirge Harper liked to play on her fiddle.

"On?"

"Where you want to go."

Anywhere, she thought. *Anywhere but here.*

Ivy lusted after no man the way she lusted after a chance to escape. Ruby couldn't see the noose she was tying around both their necks. Ivy knew of only one remedy to cure such an illusion, and it was pain. That was another lesson her grandmother had taught her. *Suffering is the only friend you've got,* Harper had said. *Because it don't lie.*

Ivy knew then what she wanted from Lovett. She wanted him to find Ruby on that forsaken road that led to the razorbacks. She wanted him to slow down just enough so Ruby could see Ivy coming, standing brazen in the back of a quicksilver truck. She wanted Ruby to hear her laugh flying in the sky as she sped up the mountain and left her behind.

Ruby was about to make the worst decision of her life by marrying Briar, and Ivy wanted her to buckle beneath its burden. She wanted Ruby to taste, and envy, that Ivy was free.

"Drive past my friend who's walking the hidden mountain road," Ivy told Lovett. Ruby was bound to be whipping down the hill by now, reckless and untamed after talking to Flynn. "So she can see us riding high."

Lovett considered it.

His teeth clenched his cigarette. "She pretty?"

Ivy stared him down and did not answer.

He ashed the flame and sighed. "Long haul up there," he said, "and I don't know my way."

"I'll show you, if you can keep up."

Lovett laughed, tossed the cigarette to the asphalt. It flared orange before it choked.

"Get in the back," he said.

From the minute Ivy climbed into the back of Lovett Quick's Silverado, she knew she'd made a mistake. The moon hung like a scythe in the sky, the deadly kind of pretty that Ivy once loved best. *Pretty kills,* Harper liked to say. *Or pretty gets killed.*

× × ×

Ivy set Lovett on a secret path up the mountain toward the razorbacks. Those mountains, sprawling upward like stone geysers, spiked above the trees in the distance. Over them the night brimmed with fireflies. Outsiders had never been welcome this far north, but Ivy cared nothing for tradition. She'd pay any price to see it rust. Already the night felt rare as the sun fell away, the moon no wider than a blade.

Ivy thought it would feel fast and fatal to ride in the bed of a stranger's truck as the wind whipped her hair. Instead she felt a quiet panic nest in her throat. Her hills felt chilled now, distant. As Lovett fought the elbow turns and his truck pitched up the mountain, Ivy tried to settle into the cool steel of the truck's frame and watch the stars blur above her.

To her left Ivy spied what she couldn't have seen if Lovett had invited her to ride in the Silverado's passenger seat.

A tackle box.

Most mountain men carried tackle boxes in their trucks, but Lovett's was a museum. When Ivy lifted the lid, she found a different kind of ornament in each compartment. The first held mismatched earrings—pearls and gold hoops. The next housed twinkling bracelets. The third had platinum necklace pendants, an opal ring. Like someone trapping butterflies in jars, Lovett was out to collect pretty things.

In the back of Lovett's truck, Ivy clung to her necklace. She knew she was in trouble, and so was Ruby. For the first time in her life, Ivy wished she'd never dared to dream of what lay beyond her mountain.

X X X

The Silverado was still two miles off from Ruby's path when Ivy decided to act. As the truck slowed around a stiff turn, Ivy leaped over the side. Lovett screeched to a stop, and Ivy sprinted to the white ash trees at the edge of the woods. She heard Lovett jump out and slam the door. Then she skidded into the brush. Close behind her, Lovett wrapped his arms around Ivy's waist and jerked her toward his chest.

"It ain't got to be like this," he said.

But it did. His muscles heaved against her back, and Ivy prepared herself. The longer she could stall him, the better Ruby's chances of reaching home. Ivy tore her arrowhead from its chain and thrust it behind her. The arrowhead sank into Lovett's right earlobe, slicing it in two.

Blood spilled down his neck. Lovett howled, wrestled Ivy's arrowhead away. Tossed it into the trees. Then he took her by the wrists. Ivy wasn't a praying woman, but she prayed then. *Please, God. Let him leave me in the woods.*

The saddest mercy of Ivy's life: God listened. Lovett left her in the roadside ditch. The Silverado's engine rumbled. The sound withered away as the truck headed north. Ivy felt relief, she felt panic. She was safe, for the moment, but Ruby was not.

A few minutes later, a car approached. Ivy lay flat, prayed for a stranger who wouldn't see the fresh skid marks the Silverado had left behind. She once prided herself on her ability to conquer, but this she couldn't win. If Lovett had returned, there would be hell to pay tonight. If someone else found her, there would be hell to pay tomorrow once Noble discovered she'd been out after dark.

The motor hummed, then cut.

Lovett had come back for her—she could feel it. Ivy tried to scream, but no sound came out. She couldn't see the man who lifted her beneath the armpits and slid her out of the dirt. They reached an Impala, and the man threw Ivy into the passenger seat and sped down the mountain without his headlights. The spare moonlight caught his silhouette, frail and mussed.

Ricky's profile appeared. He cast a glance at her, then kept his eyes to the road. Once he caught the dull glow of Trap's city lights, Ivy started to shout.

"Turn back!" she yelled. "Ruby's up there."

But Ricky would not. He parked the car at the motel.

"I ain't no hero," he said.

Ivy slapped him. She'd never been so relieved to be rescued, and she'd never forgive him for it, either.

"You were following me," she said, her voice gone hoarse.

"You're lucky I was." Ricky tried to touch her cheek but then thought better of it.

"You have to go back."

"I'll call the police," he offered.

Ivy shook her head. It would take close to an hour for police cruisers to arrive from the county seat, and once they did, they'd notify Ruby's father. If Hasil Day knew that his daughter had left the house, he would humiliate her in front of the whole mountain.

While Ricky returned to his motel room, Ivy paced through the Saw-Whet's barren lot. Her father was still playing his rounds of euchre at Teddy's, and would be for another two hours. Never had Ivy been so ransacked with dread. She wanted to scream until she woke the town.

Eventually, Ivy knew, what rose up the mountain would fall back down again. Lovett would return to Trap, and then Lovett would leave. He had no reason to stay, and Ivy didn't care to watch him go. Revenge hadn't crossed her mind. For now Ivy longed only to reach Ruby's side. She wished she'd never left it. So she did what she had always done, the one thing she knew she could—she climbed into the bed of her father's truck and hid beneath the tarp. An hour and a half later, her father floundered out of the bar and fishtailed his truck up the mountain's crooked road.

When Noble slowed for a swift turn not five yardsticks from Ruby's dirt trail, Ivy held her breath, closed her eyes, and hefted herself once more into the ditch.

X X X

She raced to Ruby. Early yet, the day still held shades of blue. Overnight Ivy had grown into a kind of mountain woman she'd not yet seen, the kind with enough fast-hearted fury to outrun the morning. Stiltgrass swarmed her thighs as she paced her sprint. *Just a little farther now*, Ivy whispered to herself. *Just a little more.* Her body ached to see her friend.

The morning's ground clouds gathered thick enough to keep the sun from waking Ruby's father, but Ivy took no chances. She crept through

the moat of holly around the cabin's perimeter to reach Ruby's bedroom window in the back. She tapped on the glass, and Ruby's face
appeared, bracketed with blood. Flooded with relief, Ivy remembered
that it was Ruby's wedding day.

"How did you know?" Ruby could barely speak as she lifted the
windowpane. A bruise marred the skin just above her collarbones.

"Shh," Ivy said after she climbed inside, taking a cloth from the
nightstand and touching it to Ruby's face. "Your sisters will hear."

Ruby's bedroom was crammed with three bunk beds for seven sisters, and Ruby and Ivy had no space to speak. The pair squeezed into
the closet and sat knee to knee with their backs against the wall. Above
them Ruby's wedding dress hung from a steel pipe—six yards of white
muslin. On the back wall, she'd also taped up pictures she'd cut out of
Ivy's stash of *Seventeen* magazines—photos of dresses and crop tops,
plaited bracelets and headbands—all the things Ivy had admired and
Ruby hoped to make for her. An old quilt covered a cavity in the floor.

"Ivy," Ruby said in the dark. "A man found me."

She didn't need to say any more. Ruby and Ivy had heard this kind of
parable as a sober ushering into their girlhood, a story imparted to
them by their fathers. *A hard dick knows no conscience,* Hasil had
warned Ruby on her thirteenth birthday, in lieu of a gift.

"I never wanted a story like this." Ruby's voice cracked.

Ivy had no answer.

"You know what the worst part is?" Ruby rested her chin on the scab
of her knee. "My daddy was right. Nothing good happens to a girl after
midnight."

Ivy didn't ask what had happened. She didn't ask if Ruby was all
right. She asked only one question—how Ruby had gotten away.

The Silverado had run her off the road, and the driver threw open
the truck's door. It hit Ruby in the head before she fell into the ditch.

She stumbled, too dizzy to stand. The man left the truck and crouched over her. Ruby reached for her knife, and he sank his knee into the soft skin above her heart as he wrestled it away and tossed it into the truck bed. His earlobe was sliced in two.

Ruby didn't know how long it was before the headlights of an oncoming car lit up the pines in the distance. The man hid in the shadow of his truck, and Ruby ran.

She could have flagged down the car and asked for help. But Ruby knew the driver would take her home to her father, and she knew what he would have said:

Only one kind of girl is out this late at night.

It was an impossible choice—to die this one death or to die a thousand new ways every time her father looked at her. Ruby wouldn't give him the satisfaction.

The closet air hung heavy in the quiet. With this, Ruby resigned herself to silence. Ivy should have spoken then, told Ruby she'd led Lovett to her. She opened her mouth, but the words would not come out.

Before that night in the Silverado, Ivy believed that the truth wasn't hard to tell. It was harder to live a lie, and a lie was all that the women on her mountain knew—how to submit to their husbands and swallow their vomit and serve a second piece of pie on Sunday afternoons. She swore she'd never be among them, and neither would Ruby. But the world felt wicked now. Pressed in the closet with her friend, Ivy feared that this lie was all she had left.

She couldn't stop herself. "You don't have to marry him, Ruby."

"I do."

Ivy wanted to shake her. "Why?" she whispered. "There's nothing for us here. These men are all the same. We could leave all this. Escape."

Weary, Ruby laughed. On the other side of the bedroom door, a baby wailed. Ruby's mother stirred.

"You should go, Ivy." Ruby's hands lay at her sides.

Ivy shook her head. "Your mama won't mind if I spent the night."

"No. You should leave the mountain, I mean. Leave me behind."

The words, knives in Ivy's back.

Ruby leaned her head against the wall, shut her eyes. "I don't have the strength for it. I'm not sure I ever did."

"Listen to me," Ivy said. "Strength is in my love for you and your love for me. Staying here don't make you weak. All right?"

Ruby nodded. The floorboards creaked underneath the soft weight of Hasil pulling on his boots in the next room.

"If you want to stay," Ivy said, "then we'll stay."

Before Ruby could protest, Ivy crept across the room and lifted herself out of the window. Then she ran toward her house to bathe the night off her. Once her skin felt clean, if not her conscience, she'd catch a lift toward town, where she'd find her weak-hearted Ricky and agree to marry him. In this she'd join her friend.

Never again would Ivy abandon her.

x x x

Both Ruby and Ivy got married in autumn. They stuck to their men, spotted each other from across the gas-station meeting room, and sighed like ghosts. Ivy wondered how they'd gotten so old in only a month's time. The leaves had yet to fall from the trees, and still all Ivy could feel was winter in her chest.

Her every thought settled on Ruby. So much so that she couldn't see how well her lovesick husband doted on her. His jars of crocuses went unwatered, his pastel love notes went unread. Ricky even went along to church, though he didn't care much for it. Jesus, he said, could never give him the high that Percocet did.

Since their night in the Impala, Ivy had fallen for the hero Ricky was, even as she hated him for the hero he wasn't. The two feelings brawled within her. The only way Ivy could show her husband any affection at all was through barebacked, body-blinding sex. They made love anywhere but their bed—Ivy hoisted herself onto the galley kitchen counter of their trailer, Ricky thrust against the Impala's backseat, both of them crimped with parched stiltgrass in their backyard. Sex said what Ivy's mouth couldn't: *It will never be enough.*

Ruby's every move had an edge to it now. She scrubbed Briar's collared shirts twice as long as she needed to, raking her fingers over the washboard until they bled. She tore out entire seams on her skirts, only to restitch them, and the rainbow colors of her dresses began to fade. She started making soap, then making more. Ivy even ripped off her own buttons just to give Ruby's hands a fresh purpose. Ruby saw no one, went nowhere, except for Sundays. Every time Ivy caught sight of her vacant gaze looking toward the razorbacks, her own remorse threatened to drown her. Ruby flew to dark places in her mind, leaving Ivy to wonder when—or if—she'd return.

Ivy knew she ought to tell Ruby the truth about that night in the Silverado. But this truth would not set Ivy free. It would cost her. If she lost Ruby, Ivy told herself, she would die. She couldn't survive life on the mountain alone. The problem was, Ivy couldn't be sure her friend would survive what haunted her, either. When Ruby's hands lingered on frosted windowpanes or over a crackling fire long enough to forget all feeling, Ivy feared she was losing her Ruby, even still.

X X X

Three years passed slow, then quick, full of nothing days that never seemed to end. Ivy's Grandmother Harper died the day Ivy went into labor with her firstborn, and Ivy couldn't parse the ache of losing her from the agony of giving life. When the clinic's doctor had handed Bobby to her and offered congratulations, she'd wanted to laugh. Congratulate her on what? The life she was given to squander and ruin? She didn't feel joy. She felt only the purest sense that Bobby belonged to someone else. Even his name—*Bobby*—sounded like he could have come from anywhere. Some other woman, Ivy knew, could have taken much better care of him. She didn't know whether Bobby's rightful father was Flynn or Ricky, and she couldn't summon enough shame over it to risk breaking her husband's heart. All Ivy knew: She wasn't fit for motherhood, even though it was all she had.

Ruby hadn't felt this way. Having Wren buoyed her, a miracle Ivy thanked God for. Never had Ivy seen a more beautiful baby than Wren, who was rosy and light-eyed like her daddy.

Ruby wouldn't bear any more children after her first. She didn't like sex, another sadness Ivy blamed herself for. Ricky remained the only person who knew that Ivy had led Lovett up the mountain, and she shuddered in the face of such unwanted intimacy. He'd seen her at her worst, yet still he wanted her. Ivy had no reason to trust that depth of loyalty from a man. Either he was a fool or he was biding his time to use her secret against her, even though Ricky never would. He loved Ivy and pitied her, though not as much as he pitied himself.

She couldn't tell Ricky she didn't want their second child. He wouldn't understand. Ricky thought babies were all coos and snuggles, little blessings who magically learned to sleep through the night and piss in a toilet. Ivy knew the great pain of bringing a child into the world, and it had nothing to do with labor. It had to do with poverty of choice—either Ivy would give birth to a man or she'd have a daughter who'd grow up to serve one. *There ain't no in-between,* as Ruby had said to her once before, when they'd reckoned with abandoning their hills. Ivy knew she had nothing left in her heart to give. Motherhood gave her a lonely squall in her gut, and Ivy didn't dare bring her affliction to the one person who would help her bear it.

Turned out she didn't need to. Ruby could sense her friend's despair from a mile off, the same way bloodhounds knew to search for signs of buried life in the hillside after a heavy snowfall. Ivy, out of luck, was the very thing Ruby needed to revive herself.

It was her idea to give Flynn the baby, her plan to keep Ricky and Briar in the dark. Ivy had always been the conniver among them, but Ruby's love for her friend brought forth a primeval instinct. Ruby knew what Ivy needed, even when Ivy herself didn't.

"You don't have to keep it," was all Ruby said one morning as they stood side by side at the cliff. Together they stared into the lavender lowlands.

Behind them Wren and Bobby took turns counting paces toward the snake shed. They dared each other to see who could go the farthest in the fog. *Five steps, six steps, seven steps, eight.* A witchy consonance clung to the mist. Ivy could feel a change stirring, guided by Ruby's careful hand.

Only after it happened could Ivy see how well Ruby had fixed things for her, and for Flynn, too, by arranging the trade. It seemed simple enough. Ivy would birth the baby, then Ivy would give the baby away. Flynn would have someone to love—an absolution for Bobby, who Ivy alone knew might have been Flynn's rightful son. In this way Ruby unknowingly worked her own miracle, mending two hearts in one act. It reminded Ivy of how as girls she and Ruby had played tag beneath the gas station's willow tree, conspiring ways to outlast the boys who circled them. It felt easy then to escape those confines, just as it felt impossible now.

X X X

Ivy gave birth the night after Sherrod died. She started having contractions as the sun slipped beneath the Royal Empress trees. Wren had fallen asleep at the foot of Ruby's bed, and there would be no getting Briar out of the house after dark. Suspicion grew on him quicker than a serpent's strike. Their only option would be for Ruby to abscond with the infant in the middle of the night.

"This is going to be hard," Ruby said, grasping her friend's hand. "But don't fret. I helped my mama do this plenty. You can't make a sound."

Already in enough pain to silence her, Ivy nodded. "You best run out, soon as the baby cries," she whispered.

Ruby kissed her hand and hoped Briar would sleep soundly. The moon hovered as a fragment of itself. The foxes kept to their dens. Ruby counted these as mercies, just as she did Ivy's short labor. When it came time to push, Ivy stood, grasped the bedpost in Wren's tiny bedroom, and bore down.

"It's another boy," Ruby said as the baby eased out. He was pink and blue and red, a stark cowlick already swirling on top of his head.

"Do you want to see him?" Ruby asked after she'd finished her work cleaning both Ivy and the baby.

"No," Ivy said, collapsed on the mattress. "Just go."

Ruby swaddled the boy tight, and then she hiked to Flynn's to ask him to take the child as his own. While she was gone, Ivy waited, unable to sleep.

She could not have prepared herself for how much it would hurt to give a baby away. So set in the comfort that her second-born would live a better life as Flynn's son than as hers, she hadn't stopped to consider the blow. Ivy didn't regret it, but the loss flattened her. In the hours after the delivery, her body fought her mind. Her breasts burst with milk for a mouth she couldn't nurse, and her stomach contracted like it wanted to take back the baby it had let go. She'd go on to have three more boys before the day she died, and all of them she would keep.

Ivy slept, fitfully, then woke and found herself alone in Wren's room. When Ruby returned with her empty laundry basket, she told Briar in whispers that the baby had died. Ivy listened from the hallway. She cracked the door, and a triangle of light spread across her bare thighs. The lie on Ruby's lips was sweet, full of mercy. A melody, if ever Ivy had heard one.

Ivy tried to let herself breathe. Then Briar spoke.

"It's for the best," he said. He didn't bother to lower his voice. "You know she ain't fit."

The words might have brought Ivy to her knees, if she cared what Briar thought. She waited for Ruby's reply.

"Ain't fit for what?" Ruby asked. "Motherhood? Briar, no one is."

The truth was that Ruby, like Ivy, had nothing left to give. Emptied, the both of them—whether by what happened the night the Silverado went up the mountain or by life itself, Ivy couldn't figure. But she knew Ruby had marshaled what remained of her strength for her friend, and now it was gone.

x x x

Thirteen years passed before Ivy saw Sonny again. She didn't track the time in years. Instead she tracked it in life lines. Three more boys, born. A father, dead. Ivy didn't attend the funeral. She and Ruby kept to their daily sacraments—Ivy climbed Ruby's hill, implored her to leave the house. Returned home before dusk. The rhythm had a natural rise and fall, the breath both Ruby and Ivy drew as one.

The friends aged, but their friendship didn't. It took on a hot, static distance—not because Ruby and Ivy were distant from each other but because Ruby was distant from herself. Ivy couldn't understand how Briar didn't see it. Ivy ached to be so blind. She longed to find that kind of distance from herself, even as it seemed to shred Ruby to bits. The secret Ivy kept was a burdensome pet, one she needed to groom and feed. Every time she drove past the Saw-Whet's empty lot, Ivy looked for a white Silverado—even though she never saw one. She found herself hunting for noise, running from the quiet. Always Ruby's mournful voice followed her.

The day before she caught fire, Ivy fell sick. It started with a string of dizzy spells, each worse than the last. Next came a heat rash that swept across her chest and back. She vomited, steadied herself. Checked the calendar she kept in the drawer of her bedside table.

She counted the days—*thirty-three, thirty-four, thirty-five*. A familiar weight cradled near her navel, told her what she already thought she knew.

Ivy was pregnant.

She forgot about her promise to meet Ruby and Wren that morning— something Ivy had never done. Instead she left her boys with Ricky and sped down the mountain. At the Shop 'n Save, she stole a pregnancy test. The inside of her Pontiac sweltered as she sat in the backseat, waiting for the results.

Down the street she saw Flynn's Tacoma parked at Teddy's Tavern. Ivy watched him unload a few cases of moonshine and take them through Teddy's back door. Sonny stood in the truck bed, sweeping dust into the street. A fissure in Ivy's chest—her baby had grown into a strong young man. Flynn had done that. And, in a way, so had she.

She looked down at the test, tried to divine some truth from it. Was that a line she saw—the faintest pink horizon? She looked again and saw nothing, like her body was waiting to decide.

Ivy felt the truth then. She didn't want another baby. She also didn't want to give another baby away. Ivy opened the Pontiac's back door and fell out of it before vomiting on the grass. Then she looked up, blinked against the sheen of the sun. A soft shadow moved in. Ivy wiped the side of her mouth and blinked again. Her vision went from black to gray to light. Then she caught sight of Sonny Sherrod staring back at her.

"Ma'am," he said, touching her elbow. "You all right?"

He helped Ivy to her feet. A stark gravity stretched between them as Ivy got drawn into Sonny's orbit. She felt herself ever spinning, unable to stop.

"Ma'am," Sonny tried again. "Are you okay?"

She nodded, locked herself in her car. Drove homeward, Sonny a distant sun in her rearview mirror, as Ivy wished for some way to heal one wound without creating another.

x x x

Later that night Ivy penned the longest letter she'd ever written to her best friend. *My Confession,* she titled it on the envelope. She tucked it into the drawer of her bedside table and promised herself one day she'd find the strength to give it to Ruby.

Inside the letter Ivy revealed everything she hadn't had the courage to say when they were just seventeen and itching to leave the mountain behind. She admitted she'd led Lovett to Ruby that terrible night, and that she'd never wanted to risk losing Ruby by telling her the truth. Ivy never blamed Lovett like she blamed herself. She couldn't show herself any mercy. No one had ever offered her any.

I'm sorry, Ivy wrote at the end of the letter. *I'm so sorry.*

The next morning Ivy rose before dawn, feeling sicker than she ever had. She wheezed, felt a chill, and tried in vain to ease the rash on her body with beeswax salve and tallow. Even a thick curtain of ointment didn't quell the itch on her skin. She and her boys walked to Ruby's cabin in a haze, and when she saw Ruby's face hovering above the fire pit next to Briar's snake shed, she wanted so much to fall into the arms of her friend, to lay the lonely burden down, that she tripped over the hem of her dress and found the flame instead.

The words she'd wanted to offer rang in her head as the blaze spread around her and the razorbacks in the distance glowed like the sun.

We should have run that day Briar got struck, Ruby. We should have run and never looked back.

Dear Wren,

I have to tell you—

The only legend that ever really mattered was ours.

IV.

LEGEND'S END

STAY

They say Moses once lost himself on a holy mountain, much the same way my father did after lightning hit him. Moses lasted forty days and forty nights. My father stayed hidden for sixteen years, until his wife got bit. Then it took only three days for his life as a prophet to rot.

Once news of my mother's death hit the local papers, my father couldn't hide anymore. His wife now had a death certificate as well as a marriage certificate, both searchable by name, but that wasn't all. Briar Bird's faithful had turned on him. After years of silence, his secret keepers began to speak.

Stories of what had happened at Ivy's funeral leaked off the mountain like water through a sifter. FAMED SNAKE HANDLER MURDERS WIFE, one headline read. WOMAN SLAIN BY HUSBAND'S SERPENT, read another. I couldn't get enough of them. When my mother married White Eye, she gave her life for his legend. It turned her into a ghost. Ruby Day was nothing but a memory, even before she died. Seeing her name in print brought her to life in a way my father had never allowed. She'd always been flesh to me, but now she was ink and parchment—a weight any stranger could hold. It felt like finding her. It also felt like losing her again.

None of the articles mentioned a daughter. I'd been living as a ghost, too.

Not since the mining boom of the 1930s had our mountain captured the heart of the outside world. Young journalists and retired cops flew down Route 28 by the truckful—this time looking for something more seductive than sorry tales of overdoses. Theirs was a high that only damned heroes like my father could satisfy, but he was nowhere to be found. After his wife's death, Reverend Briar Bird finally started to draw the attention my mother once thought he should. He hadn't fooled me. It was simpler than onlookers had charmed it into being. Either he was hiding or he was dead. And for his sake, I hoped he was dead.

He couldn't survive without my mother. I didn't think I could, either. We'd lived our days side by side, sunrise to sunset. I promised Flynn I wouldn't return to the mountain, but my mother *was* my mountain. I couldn't leave her behind. She'd been my best friend, even though I wondered now if I'd ever known her. I'd been searching for the real Ruby Bird all my life. I hunted for her even still.

The county library—a shipping container crammed with water-stained paperbacks and three desktop computers—became my sanctuary. It used to be an hour's drive from my father's land. Now it took fifteen minutes to walk there from Aunt Bette's front door. For three days after my mother was buried, I camped at one of the computers and pored over the front page of every news outlet in the state. I'd never learned to type, and my fingers searched for the right keys.

R-U-B-Y D-A-Y B-I-R-D

My mother's life was sick with untold stories. A scatter of articles from the past fifteen years formed a list on the screen. I discovered things she'd never shared about who she'd been before she fell in love with my father. She'd graduated at the top of her high school class and tutored her schoolmates in math. She'd been a part of 4-H and the hiking club. She and Ivy had written in the school newspaper about their plans to leave town after they received their diplomas.

At first I couldn't recognize this young woman who became my mother. Then I remembered something I'd forgotten. I'd lost her once before she died.

I was eight years old, and spring had just come. We'd gone hunting for bloodroot around the barracks of an old strip mine. Henry had caught the croup. My mother aimed to cure it with tea made from the plant's red sap. The torn stems stained her hands crimson, and she went to the river to wash them.

I spun a circle in the sun, and suddenly I couldn't find her. All I saw were remains. A crooked fence of chicken wire, a crowd of empty mailboxes, and an abandoned auger left in the tall grass. No one had lived here in years. Even then we walked among the dead. I just couldn't see it until my mother had gone.

She found me quickly and dried my tears. Looked at me square with fists tucked at her hips.

If ever you can't find your way home, she said, *draw a map of the woods on your hand.*

She showed me how to follow the ridge of my ring finger to land on the dirt trail that led to our cabin. How to wade through the creek along the crease of my palm to find the clearing where Ivy's trailer stood. The razorbacks hovered farther north, at the tip of my middle fingernail. If I slid into the pit of my thumb, I'd hit the holler that fed into the only road that escaped the hills.

Your father might be lost here, my mother said to me. *But you don't have to be.*

Even then she was trying to tell me she wanted to leave.

After she died, I counted the hours that my father hadn't come for me. Rumors about him swarmed the parking lot of the Saw-Whet Motel, not more than fifty paces from the library. I turned my mother's switchblade over in my palm as I walked toward it, stunned I'd never noticed that my hands looked nothing like hers. Her fingers were able and sturdy. Mine were lean and red at the tips. I searched for a trace of her left in me. Ivy had always said I could have been my mother's twin if it hadn't been for my daddy's light eyes, but I couldn't see it anymore. All I saw when I looked in the mirror was my father staring back at me.

In less than a week, anyone would have sworn I'd washed away my mother's memory along with the first shower of scalding water I'd ever taken. The water was hot, endless. It smelled like rotten eggs. I wore Emma's denim skirt and a Dolly Parton T-shirt, and she cut my hair so short I could no longer braid it.

"It'll be easier for you," she said as she brushed shorn hair from my shoulders. "Once school starts next month. No one will know who you are."

My hair settled into a nest on the floor of Aunt Bette's kitchen. I didn't want long hair if my mother couldn't braid it. Emma handed me a compact mirror. The silver earrings she gave me, shaped like two birds with wings outstretched, shimmered in my reflection. I'd gotten what I'd wanted—to look like everyone else. But all I'd become was a series of blank spaces on Aunt Bette's paperwork. I had no family, no address. No stories of my own.

At the crosswalk by the Saw-Whet, I tucked my mother's knife into my pocket and watched the town stoplight blink red. Folks like me, ones with nowhere to be, got to talking. Some swore that my father had killed my mother. She'd never loved him, they said. Others figured that Ruby had died a long time ago. They talked about my parents like they knew them, because they did.

"Ruby lasted longer than any of us thought she would," one man said.

"Briar's been living on borrowed time," said another. "For that outsider he killed."

The first man sucked his teeth. "Ain't nothing but rumors."

I stopped at the curb. This was a story I'd never heard. The words sounded nothing like the legends of my father's life as a man of God— but the truth of them still hovered too close, the way a vulture circles a carcass. Even Moses was a murderer.

The onlookers in the parking lot were about my parents' age, but from a different time. They sat in lawn chairs, drank beer from tin cans. The women wore sunglasses and jeans. Bracelets that jangled. The men held cell phones in rough palms. My father's hands—those viperous hands—were the softest part of him. His religion kept him pinned to a past century, kept his fingernails clean.

My mother and I had passed these strangers many times on our grocery trips, and they'd stared at us. I thought it was because we looked odd. Now I wondered if they stared because they remembered who Ruby used to be—the tutor, the beauty, the wanderer. Not once did my mother look back at them. She rushed by every time, keeping her eyes hitched to the horizon.

The loggers who passed through town made bets about what had become of the snake handler's daughter. She was still everyone's beloved mystery, more lore than ligament or bone.

"She's here somewhere," they said, petting their chain saws in the backs of their Dodge Rams. "Waiting to take revenge on her daddy."

"Snake handler's daughter?" Caleb said, soft enough to turn their heads. "She's not here. She spent one night at Aunt Bette's and then left town."

"Headed to Kentucky," Emma added as she took a drag from her Virginia Slim. She and Caleb were my conduits to a world where I didn't fit. "And she ain't coming back."

It was the kindest thing they could have done for me, letting the legend live so I could let it die. I looked up at the billboard of Princess Saw-Whet. Her muted eyes had been shot out by a hunting rifle. This was the spot where Ivy and Ricky had first met, she once told me. It had sounded romantic then. Now, with the princess's hollowed-out eyes, it sounded like a horror story.

My father remained the mountain's favorite outlaw, my mother his sacrifice. I hated my part in the myth. I was nameless, faceless. A pause in my father's tale of glory. Briar Bird was not a man, a father, or a husband. He was a story, and nothing else.

I didn't want to be a story. I wanted to live.

X X X

In the days after my mother's burial, living felt like dying. It wasn't enough to say I missed her. Her absence shredded me. I left pieces of myself everywhere I went—the porch steps, the bathtub drain, the dust on the side of the road.

My father had kept me on the mountain for so long because the mountain he could rule. Men he couldn't. When I returned to the library on the morning of my fourth day at Aunt Bette's, I heard Ivy's fading whisper in my ear as I read her obituary. *Men don't play nice,* she used to tell me. *And they don't play fair.*

On the computer screen, an etching of Ivy's young face stared back at me. A few short sentences followed. Birth, death. Wife, mother. Nothing about her that a hospital record wouldn't reveal. I recognized the photo. It was half of the picture I'd found in my mother's Bible, she and Ivy sitting beneath a weeper. When I'd found it, the pair looked locked together. With my mother cropped out, Ivy gazed off toward the unseen. She looked torn and unfinished without my mother—just like my father, and just like me.

I used to think Ivy's warnings about men were meant to save me from what lay beyond our mountain if I ever left. Now I suspected she wanted to protect me from a more intimate threat. Ivy knew that my father had never played fair. On the day I was baptized, he'd clamped his ill, holy hands on my throat and pretended to save my soul. The world inverted as the sky met my feet, and then I started to fight back.

For only a second, before instinct won, I remembered this—

I thought my father had the right.

He had the ear of God. He had the gift, the power. He had it all, and he could do whatever he wanted with me. I was disposable. So was Ivy. That was the battle my mother fought in her final hours, and it had killed her.

When I was a girl, my father taught me that men were bred to hunt, like Samson hunted for jackals in the Book of Judges. Women, like Delilah, only enjoyed the spoils. My father never thought one day I would be the one to hunt for him.

Everyone in our hills underestimated the snake handler's daughter, my father most of all. The outsiders who came to our mountain, hungry for a piece of my father's wicked majesty, did not deserve to steal any reckoning with Briar Bird. It rightfully belonged to me.

x x x

I decided to start my search at the Texaco. The old gas station had been my father's castle, his kingdom come. But I would wait for nightfall. I could walk the hills in my sleep. My father wouldn't be able to see me coming for him.

I planned to leave for the Texaco at midnight. Caleb and Emma waited with me in Aunt Bette's backyard. Like the rest of Trap, it was overgrown and apocalyptic. A rusted trampoline rattled in the wind. They tried to convince me to stay as the distant bluffs towered overhead. Once the sun fell, Caleb lit a fire and the highlands danced in the wake of the flames.

"Don't go," Emma said. "Nothing good will be waiting for you up there."

"You're free now," Caleb echoed. "There's no use in going back."

I knew they were right.

"He doesn't get to disappear," I said. "Not this time."

"Then we're coming with you," Caleb said.

"I've got a riddle for you." Emma lit a Virginia Slim and held it up. "What did serpents eat before the fall of man?"

No one gave an answer. There wasn't one. I wanted to ask my father the same question, to watch him squirm.

"Tell us about him," Emma said, the edge of her cigarette burning like a tiny star. "Your dad. We only knew him as the snake handler."

Briar Bird—my villain, my hero. I could spin the tale of Briar's blighted eye, the lightning bolt, the hands that had cooled Ivy's burn without ever touching her. I could let the myth continue to comfort and deceive.

"You want to know why life up there was magic?" I asked.

Emma nodded.

"Then I'll tell you about my mother."

I told them about the scent of her soap, the lullaby of her voice, the workmanship of her hands. I told them about Ivy, the way she'd been swindled by her own miracle and my father's hand in it. The clouds cleared as night set in, and the August heat held. Emma drifted to sleep. As the campfire mellowed, Caleb and I sat together in the smoke. We sat side by side after the fire had gone out, this night on the outskirts of town not unlike the one we spent hiding in my father's snake shed in the woods.

He exhaled. "I don't like this. It's not safe."

I leaned into him. "He won't know we're coming."

"That's what scares me."

He looked away. We hadn't touched each other since the night Ivy died.

"Hey." I knelt in front of him.

The whites of his eyes cut into the night.

"Stay," he whispered.

I could almost hear what he hadn't said—no one who followed my father up the mountain had survived it. Caleb let his hands linger on my waist. I felt his fingers crest the small of my back, and the muscles beneath his shirt rippled as he tensed. He pressed in until our foreheads met, and then he backed away.

"I can't stay," I said.

Above us the sky was shuttered with fir trees and scarlet oaks. I didn't wonder if my father was gazing up at the same stars, and I didn't wonder if my mother was looking down from them. What did it matter? They'd both still left me alone.

X X X

The old Texaco station loomed larger in the dark than it did in daylight. The country shadows were impenetrable, the mountain's nights black against the restless flicker of neon lights in Trap. There was a life-and-death romance to these hills, the kind that slit hearts wide open. The kind that had nothing left to lose.

The gas station sat halfway between town and my parents' cabin, tucked into a holler behind a stand of uprooted hardwoods. Caleb, Emma, and I had crept into Aunt Bette's van and drove with the windows down as we wound around the mountain. Only one other pair of headlights passed us. Mostly the night kept quiet. When we pulled off the main drag toward an old towpath, we found the Texaco hidden at a fork in the creek. Emma put the van in park and waited behind the wheel.

Outside the van the air smelled like moss. I slid around the side of the station with Caleb close behind. The boughs of the weeper at the bottom of the hill stretched wide, and they groaned in the wind. Next to the gas meters, my father had stowed a hidden box with a latch. I lifted it and reached in to find a ring with three keys on it.

I fitted the key into the back door's lock, it unhinged, and we entered my father's palace.

The truth: My father's church was the ugliest room I'd ever stood in. The half-light would cast even my mother's face in a garish glow, a reminder that from dust we came and to dust we would return. The fan above hung like a bat. The room had no spirit in it, but I couldn't associate the Holy Spirit with anything except this sorry place, with a sweat and a buzz and a fever—and a longing, most of all.

The room still stank like gasoline. And it was empty.

I held up Emma's lighter and spread it across the room. Folding chairs formed disheveled rows, and an old music stand served as a pulpit. Two old Coke bottles crowded the pulpit's feet. They'd been filled and refilled so many times the outsides had gone slick. A container of oil, a vial of strychnine. One to anoint and one to poison.

I knelt down and took both vessels in my hands. These, like me, my father had left behind.

"The first thing my father taught me," I said, "is that a snake is not a snake. It's an agile tapestry, a piece of the wild you can hold in your hand. It's opening a lock without a key, it's speaking in another tongue. It's the skin beneath your nails and the dreams you forget at night."

Caleb listened.

"Folks like to yell here." I lifted the bottles. "It's a noise you fall into, one so deep you can't hear it anymore."

I cleaned the outsides of the old Cokes with the hem of my shirt.

"What are those?" Caleb asked.

"One is holy oil and one is strychnine," I said. "The holy oil will bless you, and the strychnine will suffocate you from the inside out. It's hard to tell the difference."

He smiled. "All you need is a match."

Caleb removed a matchbook from his back pocket and lit one. It glowed like gold. He took the first bottle and dropped it in, and together we watched the flame drown.

Then he lifted the second bottle out of my hand and unscrewed the lid. He dipped his finger inside and drew a cross in the hollow of my collarbones.

"This isn't for play," I said.

"I'm not playing." He kissed the cross he'd made.

I'd never felt the miracle of a tongue on my skin. It glittered and flashed as he worked his way up my neck and found my mouth. I could barely breathe, he was so gentle. His lips still had a trace of oil, and I drank it. I wouldn't leave a drop of it behind. All my life I'd been aching to be touched. I wanted the risk it promised—the kind Briar Bird would never understand.

When I went to the bathroom to wash the oil from my hands, the faucet shuddered. I knelt to fiddle with the pipe. Next to the wall, I found a note Ivy and my mother had left behind.

Sixteen years ago Ivy had etched these words beneath the sink:

Ruby and Ivy were here.
October, 1999

For a moment they were with me again. Ivy bringing fire, my mother bringing wind. Together forming a voice out of the silence that confined them.

I asked Caleb for his pencil and etched the markings onto a paper towel. Then I hid it in my pocket as we made the slow drive north toward the short life my mother had lived.

"Ivy's," I said. "We have to go to Ivy's."

Ruby or Briar—I couldn't tell who I was hunting anymore.

HUNTER

It was three o'clock in the morning by the time Emma pulled the van off the road in front of Ivy's old trailer. My mountain had never looked so dark. Since the last thunderstorm, on the day Ivy was buried, a crater had formed in the trailer's roof. Rainwater spilled out. The sound of it shushed like a whisper. Their lot, ripe with stiltgrass and weed trees, looked smaller than it ever had when Ivy lived there. The largest swath of it had been scorched by a burn pile. Ivy's old belongings—her quilts, dresses, and linens—lay before us in ashes.

The trailer's front door busted open with one kick. Caleb reached for the kitchen light, and it flickered before going out. Emma sparked her

Zippo. Light fanned across the trailer's tiny entrance and into the galley kitchen. Her frown quivered in the glare.

"That smell," she said.

"Ivy was ill," I said. "This house ain't been cleared out. Cover your mouths."

I lifted the collar of my shirt toward my nose, but Emma shook her head.

"This sickness isn't airborne," she said.

She picked up one of the water jugs on the floor, uncapped it to sip the water, then spit it into the sink.

"This water is poisoned," she said as she wiped her mouth with her sleeve. "Did she get this water from town?"

Emma opened the kitchen window, and a breeze swept through.

"Yes," I answered. "From the spigot by the Saw-Whet. They haven't had running water for months."

"Didn't you hear about that chemical spill at the coal treatment plant back in June?" Emma asked. "Most of the folks down in the foothills got sick."

I remembered the day Ivy had burned. I'd been standing in the same spot, looking for a glimmer of afternoon sun and some food for Ivy's boys when the story flashed on Ricky's television. I was too shaken by Ivy's fall to notice.

"Same thing happened to my mother a while back when our house got condemned," Emma said. "Crude MCHM got into our water supply. We were all sick from it."

"Sick how?" I asked.

"Rashes, vomiting, nausea. Delirium sometimes. My brothers had blurry vision and wheezing."

Emma had described each of Ivy's symptoms without fault. Ricky and the boys had gone sluggish these past few months, and Job's cough had worsened since the spring. Even so, Ivy was the sickest among them. Her sons often drank milk instead of water, and Ricky drank whiskey more than anything else.

My mother, father, and I were convinced Ivy's illness had been caused by her catching fire, that somehow my father's mysterious God had been at the root of it. He wasn't. A chemical poison was. I realized something else. Ivy hadn't spoken in tongues at the Sunday service after the burning, either. She'd only been light-headed and mumbling. She must have thought my father was the only one who could help her because he'd cooled her burns after she fell into the flames. All the signs of a rational explanation had been present, and we hadn't seen them.

"How did you treat it?" Caleb asked.

Emma shrugged. "We got the hell out and stopped drinking the water."

I rested against the back of Ricky's recliner in the same spot he'd used to keep his carboys of moonshine. Many times my mother and I had entered the trailer over the past summer and recoiled at the smell. Ivy had been living in it.

In her bedroom I threw open the drawer of her bedside table and sifted through the contents in the moonlit dark. Old letters from her Grandmother Harper, a dull knife. A calendar. Not one item of Ivy's own that might speak for her.

My mother couldn't speak for Ivy anymore, either. No one had believed her when she insisted that Ivy needed to see a doctor, not even my father. She died before her instincts were proved true. I felt it for a moment—the desolation my mother must have sustained when Ivy stopped believing her, too.

The drawer slid from my hands onto the floor. The papers scattered across the rug. Caleb held up the lighter in the center of the room, the beam a feeble beacon in the middle of the night.

Emma lifted a tub of salve from Ivy's nightstand and screwed off the lid. Inside, it had been licked clean.

"Tallow and beeswax," she said. "This is what my mother used for days before she heard about the bad water on the radio. Even five jars wouldn't cool the itch. Ivy was in pain." She replaced the lid. "Enough pain to drive her crazy. She just couldn't see it."

Emma was right. Even Dr. Ed couldn't have diagnosed Ivy's illness without knowing that her water supply had come from the town's contaminated pipes.

I knelt to right the spilled drawer. A letter skirted the edge of the bed. By the gleam of the lighter, I could see two words written on the envelope's face in Ivy's handwriting: *My Confession.*

I opened the letter. In it she shared all the things my mother had never told me about the night an outsider rode into town in a white Silverado and the private path Ivy set him on because she knew that her friend would be walking it after dusk. Ivy had only wanted to make Ruby jealous, the letter said. She'd never meant to scare her. Then my mother got married and hid herself away in the highlands, and the two of them never left the mountain like they'd dreamed. For sixteen years Ivy had blamed herself for what a man had done.

Near the end of the confession, Ivy wrote that her only anchor in a sea of contrition was her choice to give her second child to Flynn Sherrod. It was a selfless act she hoped would atone for the rest of her regrets.

I read that sentence, and then I read it again. I'd always thought Ivy had four boys, but she'd had five. Her dead baby had lived. I saw it then, the likeness between Sonny and Ivy—pale hair and freckles, green eyes deeply set. She only felt shame, Ivy said, because Flynn had believed that the baby was Ruby's.

I placed the letter back inside its envelope, convinced Emma and

Caleb to return to Aunt Bette's before she woke and found her van had gone missing. The next leg of my journey I could travel alone, on foot.

As I hiked northward, I recalled Flynn's waterfall of kindness toward me. *A man's folly,* Ivy had used to say, *lies in what he thinks he knows.* When Flynn buried Ruby Day, he thought he'd buried his boy's mother, that I was his sister.

He'd also asked me to stay off the mountain, but he'd never told me why.

x x x

It took over an hour to hike to Flynn's hunting hideout. When I reached the top of Violet's Run, the house stood empty and unlocked. While waiting for Flynn to return, I fell asleep next to the same bed where my mother's body had lain.

I dreamed of her—the sensation of her fingers braiding strands of my hair, the echo of her laughter when Ivy poked fun, the way she wiped her hands on her apron when she was fixing to give my father a piece of her mind. I wanted so much for her to speak to me.

I woke just before dawn. The half-moon glowed from the window, and I rose to look through it. In the distance a meager light shone through a flock of sugar maples, and I left the quiet house in search of it.

As I climbed the slope, the violets cooled my feet. I passed my mother's and Ivy's graves, the mounds of dirt like two shut eyes. I'd never see Ivy blazing up our hill again, and I'd never hold my mother's hand as we dipped under the creek water and disappeared. These women had raised me. They taught me how to survive our mountain but not how to live without them. I would have to learn that on my own.

By the time I reached Flynn's still, I could feel the heat. Up high on the mountain, near the peak of Violet's Run, I found the firelight I'd spied from Flynn's bedroom window. In the dark of night, the smoke kissed the mist and the world smelled like candy.

I crept to the edge of a square hole and looked down. Inside it Flynn had dug a deep pit and fitted a copper still within. Next to my feet lay a rolled layer of sod that he must have used to cover the still during daylight.

I watched Flynn work. He'd tucked two barrels in the corner next to a stock of empty glass jars. Water flowed in from the far stream. Flynn dripped in sweat, shirtless. He touched the thin copper tube that connected the barrels, and he winced from the heat.

He looked up when the moonlight hit him and gave me a sad grin.

"Ain't the prettiest setup I ever built," he said. "But it's the smartest."

He wiped the sting from his eyes.

"Where's Sonny?" I asked.

"Sleeping." Flynn pointed to his truck in the shadows. "Why ain't you at the home?"

"I need you to hear the truth," I said.

Flynn waited.

"You were kind to me because you thought Sonny was my brother, but he ain't." I watched his eyes fall to the flames beneath the still. "He's Ivy's boy."

Flynn rubbed his brow. His face was sun-beaten, his hair still as black as midnight in the mines. "That ain't why I was kind to you," he said.

I sat on the edge of the pit and let my feet hang.

"Won't be long now." Flynn nodded toward the twine stuck into the end of the still's spout. "Gonna start to sing here real soon." He readied a glass jug beneath the rod and waited.

The shine started to pour, and he took the first glass and threw it into a bucket.

"Why are you pouring it out?" I asked.

"That's the foreshot." Flynn wiped his hands on his pants. "It'll kill you."

My father had similar jars, his filled with strychnine, like the ones Caleb and I had seen at the gas station. Two men, two different brands of poison. One purged, the other swallowed, one noxious portion at a time.

Flynn filled a pint jelly jar with whiskey, capped it, and shook it until it fizzed. "Got a good bead," he said, relaxing. "That'll do."

I watched him fill and cap the rest of the jars—fill and cap, fill and cap. I climbed down into the bunker and handed him the jugs. His hands worked magic. Not a drop fell to the ground. When the stream waned, he cut the fire, leaned against the wall, and closed his eyes.

The still sighed, the copper creaked. He watched that copper pot like he'd watched the boy he'd raised, with a father's care.

I counted twenty jars while Flynn's head lolled against his shoulder, and for the first time since my mother's death I felt at peace. I took a glass and held it up to the firelight. The bottom third was painted white, just like the jars my mother collected in her kitchen.

"Flynn," I said, eyeing him through the liquor he'd made. "How did you know my mother?"

He exhaled. "I would have been the best man at your parents' wedding," he said. "If I hadn't fallen in love with the bride."

Flynn lifted the jar from my hand and unscrewed the lid. He took a sip and then offered it to me.

"Here," he said, and I took the glass and brought it to my lips. "This is how we share our secrets."

X X X

Flynn told me that even now he had never loved another woman like Ruby Day. It was a tragic and terminal love, and still every morning when the sun rose, he chose it.

He looked at me as he spoke, maybe remembering how my mother's hair used to turn a thick braid across her shoulder the way mine did before Emma cut it. I took another sip, and Flynn did, too. He told me of the night he and my mother spent in the creek, not a hundred yards away from where her father slept, their feet racing and their hearts racing even faster. Then he told me of the sickness that swept over him, that it was the best night of his life, even still.

I pictured my mother there in the summer dark, her skirt flowing against the current. Her eyes blazing like shooting stars.

"And she still married my father," I said.

Flynn sucked his teeth. "I ain't gonna defend your daddy. But there's one thing he understood. He knew that faith—in God, in this West Virginia ground, in each other—only becomes real by putting something on the line." He paused. "I just wish it hadn't been his own life. Or Ruby's."

I took a fresh jar of liquor and shook it in my hands, watching it froth. The coming sun painted the sky orange, and the still had cooled. Flynn let the empty jar fall to the floor.

He told me that after Ivy died, my mother had planned to leave my father. I thought back to the money spread out across the kitchen table, the muted phone calls, the foreign prick in my mother's tongue. That was why she sent Ivy's boys away. She hadn't only been preparing for Ivy's funeral. She'd been readying our escape.

"She must have loved you," I said.

Flynn ground his boot against a patch of leftover cornmeal on the floor. "I ain't a praying man, but that's my daily plea. Even though I know it don't matter anymore."

"My daddy was ruined by his own grief," I said. "That's why he ran."

Flynn shook his head. "Ain't grief that makes a man run," he said. "It's fear."

"Fear?" I said.

"Briar might have handled snakes," Flynn answered. "But he wasn't a brave man."

And then he told me the truth about my father.

x x x

After Flynn left my mother's corpse with his boy and delivered me to Aunt Bette's, he spun out of her gravel road and tore into the dark. His eyes blurred with rage. He knew where Briar would go to mope, a private place that would call him back to his own glory. He'd retreat to that fork in the river where old Arledge had nested his hollow F-86 Sabre plane. Briar had snatched his first snake there, with Flynn by his side— a memory more precious to him than a thousand strikes of lightning.

The river ran strong from the rain. He hoisted his daddy's Marlin .35 above his head, a single bullet locked in a capsule strung around his neck. When he reached the fork, he ran his free hand around the nose of the plane, across its boiled rivets. Then he heard a groan.

"Briar," Flynn called out. "Show yourself."

Briar let himself down, and the pair stood chest to chest while the water spit rivulets around them.

"What are you doing here, Flynn?" Briar asked. "We ain't got Ruby to fight over no more."

Flynn remembered what Ruby had called herself—the bartered calf. He'd fought her on it, but she was right.

"You got two choices, Briar. You can confess or you can hide," Flynn said. "I ain't gonna tell you which."

"Ain't much of a choice," Briar said.

"Either way, you can't see your daughter again." The Marlin glistened in the river's spray.

"You must think I'm a fool," Briar said. "I know that gun ain't loaded."

Flynn tore the chain from his collar and ripped the 200-grain bullet out of its capsule. He loaded it into the chamber, then cocked the gun and pressed it to the artery pulsing in Briar's neck.

"Do it," Briar whispered. "Do it."

Flynn drove the Marlin's nose deeper until Briar buckled and sank to his knees. Flynn kicked him square in the chest and forced him under before yanking him up by the hair. Briar screamed, and Flynn screamed until he relented and collapsed against the bank.

"If I have to live without Ruby," Flynn said, panting, "then so do you."

Briar fell beside him and wiped a strain of blood from his temple.

"Confess or hide." Flynn's voice hitched. "Pick."

"Confess? I didn't kill Ruby, if that's what you think."

"You strangled a man sixteen years ago."

"And you had no part in it, Flynn?" Briar asked. "Can you swear it?"

Flynn knew Briar was playing him, pressing on his tender seams. And yet he also saw that his old friend had no light left inside him, now that Ruby was gone. If Briar went to jail, he'd take Flynn down with him. Briar was too much of a coward to sit alone with his sin—and maybe that was the rightful cost for Flynn's silence. But Flynn couldn't bear to leave Sonny without a father. He would not let his boy pay the price for what Briar had done.

"You know I can't." Flynn's voice trembled at the words.

"Then I guess you better leave," Briar said, rising to his feet. "And I guess it's best that we not meet again."

Flynn nodded and watched his friend walk away from him into the dark. That was the last time Flynn saw him.

"My father killed a man," I said now, the jar between Flynn and me half empty.

This was the reason my father had never let me attend school or talk to strangers. He was afraid of getting caught. The revelation didn't shock me like it should have. The burden felt too familiar, the same rot that had spread its stench across my mountain ever since the night of the storm.

REVENANT

Every Sunday in my father's old church, just before the serpents bared their slit tongues and the tambourines started to shiver, the old women used to gather in the gravel lot and tell stories. They talked of husbands dead and children gone, they talked of being young and in love, and no one listened. They were too old to matter anymore, folks figured, so the women told their stories to one another. I'd always thought Ivy and my mother would one day be among them.

Theirs was a tale worth telling. If I told my mother's stories, it wouldn't make her return to me. They weren't magic like my father's, but they were real. They still had the power to draw a wayward heart home in this lifetime, if not in the next.

Heaven ain't so far off, my mother used to whisper when we would look over our violet meadows as the colors burst against the sky. I could not imagine a life or an afterlife without her.

Three weeks after she died, I visited my mother's grave. September had come, and just as my mother had dreamed for me, I started attending school. It wasn't what I'd hoped for. I was behind in every subject except for English. Typing felt impossible, and my classmates looked at me like I was strange. But the school had a library full of books for me to read, and Emma and Caleb guided me through the hallways until I could manage it by myself. The best part: I had my own work to do. I didn't have to steal it from a boy.

After Flynn told me what my father had done, he offered me a place to stay. I paid my debt to him as well as I could—even though he'd never asked it of me—by helping post a roof over the porch for my bedroom and scrubbing still parts. But it was the debt I owed my mother that had kept me away from her grave. She had given me life, and I still felt I had taken hers.

As she had done the day my mother was buried, Emma kept me company when I visited my mother's burial ground. Emma brought her guitar, and the two of us walked the mourners' trail on Violet's Run as she played "The Lord Is My Shepherd." Her voice rang deep and raspy, and my mother's tambourine chimed against my hip.

A bouquet of white ladies' tresses had been laid on my mother's plot as well as Ivy's. Flynn had tied a burlap ribbon around each of them and brushed away the dead leaves. I envied him. He knew how to sit with his own sorrow, how to court it into talking back.

It's an art, the way women punish themselves. I kept myself from my mother's grave after she died because I feared I was just as much at fault for her death as my father. Ivy had spent years blaming herself for the sins an outsider committed. And my mother never let herself trust her own heart. At the end of her life, she wondered if there might have been another way. She didn't want me to wait as long as she did to find it.

Wren, she'd written, *I have to tell you—*

Seated at her grave, I didn't say good-bye. I ran my fists through the dirt and told her that the pain of missing her cut me fresh every morning. I promised I'd remain to bear witness to her stories and to tell my own, which I'd start to do in autumn while standing in the back of Flynn's pickup truck. I promised her if any outsiders asked me about the snake handler and his wife, I would tell them the truth.

The sky went goldenrod, and I thought of my mother in a thousand afternoons, a woman whose face always seemed to find the sun. I touched my lips to the ground, and I said, *Amen, and amen, until we meet again.* And then I left her in peace.

By the time I reached Flynn's cabin, dusk had edged in. On the hill Flynn messed around in his graveyard bunker. He'd gone to pack up his still supplies for the season while Sonny set up Flynn's first computer in the cabin so we could complete our schoolwork without having to leave home. Sonny had just started sixth grade, and I'd need his help to survive my sophomore technology seminar. Summer had ended, and Flynn wouldn't run shine again until the spring crop of corn grew past my waist. I rose to my feet and hiked to the bunker, held out my hands as he lifted the still's cap out into the open. He set it in the shade of a sugar maple and smiled at me.

"This ain't so easy on my own," he said.

"I can help," I said, taking up the copper worm. "I'm stronger than I look."

Flynn nodded, then sat down against the maple and gave me a five-card-draw stare.

"What was the first miracle Jesus performed?" he asked.

His question didn't throw me. My father had quizzed me just the same in the marshes for most of my youth.

"Turning water into wine," I answered.

"That's it," Flynn said. "See that stream there?" He pointed beyond the hill to the peak of Violet's Run. "That fresh water turned to whiskey by my hand. Don't need no snakes, no poison. It's a miracle all on its own, every time."

"There's a few more steps in that miracle for you than there was for Jesus, I think."

"A few." He laughed.

"Flynn," I said, running my finger along the soldered edge of the still's cap. "Why did you never leave the mountain?"

"Some good people got to stay." He grinned. "Besides, there's always shine to run."

I sat beside him beneath the shade. "I want you to teach me," I said.

He thought on it, softly rocking back and forth to the music of the wind.

"Moonshining is a way of life," Flynn said. "And not because it makes you an outlaw. It asks you to stare down your fears and remember all you've lost. Once the nights get lonely—and they will—you'll wonder if you've lost your way. But take heart and don't turn back. Shiners don't wait out the dark. They rise in it."

Flynn sat up and turned toward me. "I have one condition. You'll take a wage for your work, and you'll save it for school. Some good people may need to stay on this mountain, but that don't mean you have to."

I extended my hand, and we shook on it. Flynn unearthed a fresh jar of whiskey from his bucket of tools. He spun off the lid and took a drink.

"To a partnership," he said, and handed it to me.

"To a partnership."

I brought the whiskey to my lips. It tasted like my mother's laughter, the sound of her calling my name, the warmth of her skin in the creek on a hot summer day.

"If only my daddy could see me now." I wiped my mouth. "If we knew where he was."

Flynn clicked his tongue, and his face went blank. "I never said I didn't know where he was."

My head whipped toward him. "You do?"

He nodded. "He's squatting in his mama's house up in Logger's Nook on the other side of the mountain. Been hiding there ever since the last night I saw him, I'd wager."

My father had taken me to his mama's cabin just once when I was a girl to show me the lightning's scorch marks on the floor. I'd been easily impressed then. After I helped Flynn load the Tacoma with the rest of the still parts, I headed to bed early. The next morning I rose before the sun and slipped out of the house. I headed for the highlands with a creek map of Sherrod's in my hand. It would take till midday to make the hike to Logger's Nook, and I'd need to return to Flynn's cabin by dark so he wouldn't worry.

x x x

My father saw me coming. He stood on the porch, waiting. At first I figured Flynn must have called to warn him, but it wasn't hard to see that my father had nothing here, not even a phone line. He saw no one. The cabin cleaved to a bare skeleton of a structure, one of the walls almost blown out from a fallen tree limb. A fruitless rhododendron bush larger than the house itself camouflaged its presence.

An old sadness washed over me. For the past month, my father and I had dedicated ourselves as distant accomplices in my mother's death. It was the closest we'd ever been. He looked tired as I neared the house. Thin, but not gaunt. Pale, but not squalid.

"Well," he said as I forged the rhododendron's branches. "Well."

One thief doesn't greet another.

"You're a hard man to find," I said. "But that's how you like it."

"I get by on my own," he answered. "With God's help."

When I didn't respond, he broke the silence. "How did you find me?" he asked.

"Flynn."

My father's smile sagged, and his white eye settled on mine before shooting to the sky. He held fast to his hurt like it was a locket at his throat. As I climbed the porch steps, I heard the habitual hiss from my childhood sneak out of the pine boxes stacked by the door.

"You still have your serpents."

"I never needed an audience." He rocked back on his heels and puffed out what was left of his chest.

The space lingered between us long enough for me to remember what it had felt like to want to be his heir. I didn't ask if he blamed me for my mother's death, and I didn't ask if he regretted what he'd done to Ivy. There was only one question I needed him to answer.

"Why did you try to drown me?" I asked.

He sighed.

"I always wondered if you were my child or another man's," he said. He must have meant the outsider from Ivy's letter, the one who drove a white Silverado. "That day my doubt got the better of me."

It was the closest he'd ever come to an apology.

"But I look like you," I said. "Don't you see it?"

He looked into my eyes but somehow couldn't see his daughter.

"Are they still there?" I asked. "The lightning's marks on the floor-boards?"

He nodded.

"Show me."

I followed him inside the house, where the interior wilted, dank and ridden with must. A mattress lay on the floor next to a shallow pot. My father had been living in a cave of shadows, and when I pulled back the window's curtain and light flooded in, the house couldn't even muster the illusion of his blessed origins. There was no ghost, there was no spirit. White Eye, the mountain magician, had been left empty, just as he'd been born.

"Watch your step," he said as he led me around the tree limb toward the loft's ladder.

We went up into the flimsy attic, stocked with the old pillowcases and homemade snake poles of my father's youthful exploits.

"There," he said, pointing.

I followed his finger and saw two black tracks striking out from the window. His mother had never replaced the glass, and a sour wind shot through the hole. The beam that had knocked him unconscious still lay crosswise on the floor.

"Still don't remember the lightning," he said. "But I've spent my life chasing the feeling it gave me."

I stepped toward the open window and peered through it. Fragments of clouded glass clung to the splits in the porch roof below me. They looked like they'd been lodged there since the night of the storm. I glanced back at my father, then again at the glass, as a question insisted itself on me. If lightning had burst into the cabin through the window, as my father's legend swore it did, would most of the broken glass remain on the roof? A better question was whether a bolt of lightning would ever come through a windowpane at all.

I knelt to touch the scorched flooring and started to imagine a new origin story about that night, one perhaps more akin to the truth. The darkened marks could have been forged with charcoal, a sharp knife, and a lighter. Maybe my father did it. Or they might have been the scratchings of a mother desperate to tell her fatherless son a hopeful tale, rather than the truth of what had happened to his eye after he'd been knocked unconscious. Many trusted accounts of old mountain healings had been witnessed by women from my grandmother's generation. She might have wished for her child to have a legend of his own.

I thought back to the last time I saw Ivy, the real Ivy, before she fell on the fire pit. She and her three boys had crested our hill, and Ivy glistened with sweat beneath the sun—or at least I thought she had. Emma had shown me the empty jar of salve that Ivy had coated herself with to treat the rash from the poisoned water. But it wasn't sweat that made her skin glow. It was the beeswax and tallow.

The salve must have kept most of her skin from burning until my mother dampened the flames. My father hadn't healed Ivy. His own myth convinced him and the rest of us that he had. Briar Bird believed in nothing as much he believed in himself. He had staked his life on what he called a miracle, and so had his faithful. It cost my mother her life, just as it had cost Ivy hers.

My father stood over me in the loft, watching those floor markings like the anchor they were for his soul. I could have disputed his power to heal—but I didn't. I couldn't prove the lies of his past, and neither could he.

"Tell me about the serpents," I said.

His good eye glinted. "What do you want to know?"

I thought of what I'd left behind to come here. Emma tickling the strings of her guitar, Caleb worrying the pages of his sketchbook. Flynn and Sonny bedding down for the coming winter.

"I want to know what snakes ate before the fall of man," I said.

He thought, and his stare measured me. Then he laughed.

"Damned if I know," he said. "What does it matter?"

"It matters because you're just a man," I said.

He led me back to the porch, and as he spoke, he held his favorite yellow timber rattler in his hands. Its elliptical eyes glossed like marbles. I waited to see venom drip from its fangs, for it to pull its head back and sink itself into my father's loving arm. But it didn't. This serpent, this odd thing, became a movable sculpture in his hands, one he'd fashioned into a passage toward the mind of God.

"God is glorious in the thunder," my father said as he watched a cloud scud overhead.

"I spy," I said, and he smiled.

We used to play this game in the ginger fields when I was a girl. *I spy,* we'd say, and take turns reimagining the world that held us. He'd never spy ordinary things like trees, wildflowers, old barns. *I spy a trumpet,* he'd say, or *a priestess in a red, royal robe.* As a child I could have played that game for days. Just once I wanted to see the world the way he did.

Grasping that snake, my father talked to me the way he used to. He told me of speaking without words, of the unknowable things of the Spirit, of Christ's sacrifice and resurrection. As I listened, I was reminded of my favorite proverb: *Words kill, words give life; they're either poison or fruit—you choose.* My father had made his choice, and it was time for me to do the same.

On that September afternoon, my father talked on, and a new premonition swept over me. This was my father's life, and it also would be his death. One day I would come here and find his body, swollen and hard, double dash marks left by angry fangs. And it would be his time, and he would go willingly, embracing the mystery even as it turned on him.

x x x

On my way back down the mountain, I stopped at the fork in the trail that led to the creek where I'd once waited to be baptized, the same place my mother and Ivy used to swim when they were young. I hiked toward the bank and saw that Caleb had beaten me there. He was flat on his back at the overhang where we'd first met, his breath curling upward into the cool air. A catbird whistled a low, sweet holler, and Caleb whistled in response.

"Seems like we had the same idea," I said as the catbird returned his call.

He glanced over his shoulder, sat up, and wiped the dirt from his knees.

"Sit with me," he said.

I sat next to him, and together we gazed out over the trembling water. The sky was graying, and the trees shook. I looked at Caleb, his stare already chasing mine. His eyes were hungry and cautious, bold and constant. Coal grumbled a thousand yards away, and miners freed it, shard by shard, and ferried it to a hundred far-off places we would never go.

Ruby Day understood what every minute of her life would become from the moment Briar Bird walked into it. Her death had stripped me of all I had and left the birth of something new in its place—something that thrummed at my mother's core and pulsed strong inside me. A mountain woman's heart.

"Didn't you ever want to escape?" I asked. "And leave this world for a better one?"

Caleb shook his head. "Only one world."

I loved him then, because together we would dare to live this mountain life—the slick autumns and the fields of violets and the rivers of whiskey and the relentless moonscapes left behind after the coal companies had their way—we would dare to live this life even as it slipped away from us.

Caleb held me close, and together we turned our backs on the water. A fox crouched nearby and pierced the cold with her wild-eyed heat. I studied her until she turned and fled, the sheen of her coat catching the light of stars hung in a country sky. At the end of the night, Caleb and I would walk hand in hand back to Flynn's hunting cabin, back to Aunt Bette's, back to Emma and Sonny, back to what we would someday think of as home. Some might say we were destined to repeat the mistakes of our mothers and fathers, but I didn't believe it. We'd have our own mistakes to make. We'd fight with each other, and we'd fight for each other, too. We'd tell the truth about our mountain's ghost stories. We'd give our children their own stories to tell. We would take part in this West Virginia earth and let it take part in us.

And once the winter faded and the rains came and the corn grew high and strong—we would cull it and grind it, soak it and shine it. We'd let the heat of the fire refine us and the cold of the creek wash us clean. And like the hills that watch us get born and die and be born again, we would rise.

ACKNOWLEDGMENTS

I am deeply grateful for my agent, Meredith Kaffel Simonoff, who continues to point me toward my best work and my best self. Her foresight, wit, tenacity, and integrity are unmatched. Danya Kukafka loved *Shiner* with all her might, and so much of that love is in the heartbeat of these pages. Sarah McGrath took this story to a new level I didn't know I could reach. Getting to work with her has been this writer's dream come true.

Alison Fairbrother, May-Zhee Lim, and Delia Taylor at Penguin Random House all worked tirelessly on my behalf. Thanks also to Maureen Sugden, Andrea Monagle, Lucia Raatma, and Anna Jardine. I couldn't be more excited to be a member of the incredible Riverhead family. Thank you for embracing me with open arms. Heartfelt thanks also to Linda Kaplan, everyone at DeFiore and Company, and Sonatine.

I worked many mornings at the Franklin Township Library, and I'm indebted to its wonderful staff. The Foxfire series and *Salvation on Sand Mountain* by Dennis Covington were instrumental in the early days of my writing, and my friends at Black Draft Distillery patiently answered all my questions while also holding my baby. Their moonshine is the best I've had, and visiting their operation is the happiest way to spend an afternoon.

ACKNOWLEDGMENTS

This story wouldn't have become a book without the love and support of my incredible community. Paula Beisser and Haile Bell loved and cared for my children so I could work. They are both treasured members of our family. I'm also thankful for the stellar writers I'm lucky to call good friends: Samantha K. Smith knows me better than I know myself, Jessie Male always makes me laugh, and Krystal Sital brightens any room she enters. Anica Mrose Rissi is the best lunch date, a source of wisdom, and a generous spirit.

Hannah, Kathy, and Amanda are three faithful friends from home I cannot live without. Thank you for continually modeling love, forgiveness, and a great sense of humor. My late mentor and friend Louise DeSalvo left her heart and her fingerprints all throughout the pages of this book and in my life. Thank you to her family for loving me the way she did.

My parents talked through all the details of this story with me, from cigarette brands to outhouses. Thank you for believing in me, always. And to the rest of my family—the Burnses, the Allans, the Kandathils, and the Mammens—thank you for your unwavering support and for reminding me of home.

My husband, Mat, and our kids, Sammy and Sana, kept me great company while I wrote this book. I love getting to spend my life with the three of you.